AN HONOURABLE MAN

AN HONOURABLE MAN

GILLIAN SLOVO

ISIS
LARGE PRINT
Oxford

First published in Great Britain 2012
by
Virago Press
An imprint of Little, Brown Book Group

Published in Large Print 2012 by ISIS Publishing Ltd.,
7 Centremead, Osney Mead, Oxford OX2 0ES
by arrangement with
Little, Brown Book Group
An Hachette UK Company

British Library Cataloguing in Publication Data
Slovo, Gillian, 1952–
    An honourable man.
    1. Stead, W. T. (William Thomas), 1849–1912
    - - Fiction.
    2. Gordon, Charles George, 1833–1885 - - Fiction.
    3. London (England) - - History - - 1800–1950
    - - Fiction.
    4. Sudan - - History - - 1881–1899 - - Fiction.
    5. Historical fiction.
    6. Large type books.
    I. Title
    823.9'2–dc23

ISBN 978–0–7531–9016–6 (hb)
ISBN 978–0–7531–9017–3 (pb)

Printed and bound in Great Britain by
T. J. International Ltd., Padstow, Cornwall

To Robyn for the drugs.
To Cassie for the dog.
And to both for their unfailing generosity.

We cannot send a regiment to Khartoum, but we can send a man who on more than one occasion has proved himself more valuable in similar circumstances than an entire army. Why not send Chinese Gordon with full powers to Khartoum, to assume absolute control of the territory, to treat with the Mahdi, to relieve the garrisons, and do what can be done to save what can be saved from the wreck in the Soudan?

W. T. STEAD

Pall Mall Gazette, 8 Jan., 1884

PART ONE

CHAPTER
ONE

John would have preferred to say goodbye at home. It was Mary who had insisted on accompanying him to Waterloo station, the better to fix his departure in her mind. Now she couldn't help seeing how John, dressed, as ever, in sober black, let his gaze stray across the platform to those other men, whose red uniforms, hanging swords and cheerful camaraderie labelled them part of the rump of the Sudan expedition.

She looked at those bluff officers who, intermittently swallowed in steam from the train, were exchanging handshakes and cheerful words. Their pretty wives in pretty hats, women accustomed to letting their men go, stood at their sides and smiled as she could not. Perhaps John is right, she thought. Perhaps doctors' wives, especially those who questioned their husbands' decision to go to war, are not supposed to come to the station.

She pulled nervously at her gloves and smoothed a hand down her plain, blue serge coat. How out of place I am, she thought, as she heard, above the din of the station, two of the officers promising each other that their late departure would not stop them joining Wolseley's expedition in time to go into battle.

"How admirable to speak so easily of war," John said.

"They're soldiers." Mary knew she must sound petulant, but that did not stop her emphasizing the point. "It's their job."

When John did not reply, she looked down at her tightly buttoned boots and tried to swallow her resentment. If he thought he needed to go to the Sudan, he must be right. She was, anyway, too prone to foolish questions, sudden laughter and strange tears. Perhaps that was why he was leaving her.

A porter trundled past, his wooden trolley piled with leather trunks, cases of Veuve Clicquot balanced perilously on top.

"Look at him." John indicated an officer who, in striding by, had all but shoved them aside. He was curling the ends of his moustache with one hand, while with the other he urged on the porter. "He has provisions a-plenty, and not a care in the world. Wolseley knows what he's about, as do his staff. There's no need to worry."

"Of course there is. You are going to war."

"I am," he conceded impatiently, "but not to the front. I am to run the rear hospital. As you know." He looked at her, sharply at first, but her glistening brown eyes and the furrowing of her pale brow tempered his irritation. How selfish I am, he thought, even as he knew that, faced with an identical call to action, he would make an identical decision.

"Will you promise me that you will stay back from the fighting?"

4

Such a long journey ahead of him. From Waterloo to Portsmouth, from Portsmouth by steamer to Alexandria, and then on to Cairo where one of Mr Thomas Cook's boats would carry him up the Nile to Aswan in southern Egypt. And that was only the beginning. At Aswan he would be met by one of General Wolseley's especially adapted boats, which would transport him and his equipment to Wadi Halfa in the Sudan and on again to Korti, where Wolseley had set up his forward base. It would be, by all accounts, a difficult journey. Novice as he was, he must preserve his energy.

Why could Mary not understand this? And why was she making such a great meal of their parting?

"Promise me?" she said again.

The irritation that had steeled his shoulders drained away, and in its place came compassion, with guilt, both of which extracted from him a "Yes". He said it softly but not so softly that she would not be able to hear, "I promise."

A warning blast of steam and the shouted "All aboard," of a railwayman relieved him of having to continue the conversation.

"Well." His eyes darted towards the train into which the soldiers were clambering. His mind raced. "Well . . ." Carriage doors began to slam.

She wanted more than anything to throw her arms around him, to plead with him not to go — and, yes, she could almost see herself doing it to restrain him.

"Keep well." He touched her hand gently.

She felt his touch like a scald even through her glove. She stepped away.

This, it seemed, was what he was waiting for. "I'll write as soon as I can." He turned and was almost running. So quickly did he go that one of the officers must have remarked on it. She couldn't hear what was said, but by the way the back of John's neck reddened, she knew it must have been a joke that hadn't sat well with him. Now he slowed his pace and walked, without looking back, up the steps and into the train, as if this was something to which he was accustomed.

She knew him too well to believe in the display of confidence. And yet, she thought, if I really do know him, how is it that I cannot understand why he is doing this?

She looked up into the high span of the railway shed. She could see the rising steam from John's train and, above it, the triangulated iron girders of the roof interspersed with glass. A miracle of construction, she thought, just as Wolseley's expedition to rescue General Gordon was considered a miracle of modern warfare. Perhaps that was why John, who was always anxious to be at the forefront of new developments, had been so determined to join in.

A loud whistle caused her to drop her head in time for the lowering of the flag.

The crowd was on the move, shouting and waving alongside the accelerating train, leaving her where she was. She was too far away to see past the backs of waving onlookers to where John must be. Dread constricted her throat. She had missed the moment of his departure.

She thought of running, but it was too late. Besides, John would not like to see her running. As the train wheels turned, and the huge hulk of iron and steel chugged down the tracks, she let her tears fall.

As his companions waved wildly at the platform, bellowing over each other's din, John stood at the window craning to see Mary. Through a gap in the cheering crowd, he eventually spotted her. There she stood. Alone, tiny and dark.

Why had she insisted on coming to the station, he wondered, only at the last to stand back? It hurt him that their parting had been so remote and that, even now, she was holding herself aloof from the other wives, with their gaily waving handkerchiefs. It was as if she were declaring herself not to be one of them and, in doing so, saying that he could never be at one with their husbands.

At that moment a blond officer, a cigarette dangling from his lip, clapped John on the back — "Here you are, Doctor" — and handed him an empty glass. The train juddered and champagne frothed out, some of it making it into the glass.

The train was gathering speed and Mary was out of sight — yet his last vision of her stayed with him so strangely that, for a moment, he found himself wondering whether that prim, navy-blue Mary might have been an apparition. Except he knew she had been real. There she had remained, apparently quiet and unmoved, though a few strands of her raven hair that had escaped her chignon and fallen across her face gave her the appearance of restraining something quite . . . untamed.

"Death to the Mahdi," an officer called.

"Death to the Mahdi," they echoed, raising their glasses. "Forward to Khartoum."

John turned away from the window and made his way into one of the compartments, which was already smoky and hot. There, he threw the champagne down his throat. "To Khartoum."

Mary weaved her way through the mass of impatient travellers. Past pedlars she went, past railwaymen blasting whistles, and newspaper vendors yelling their headlines. The hubbub rose high into the railway shed. For a moment she imagined herself rising, as light as air, into that great expanse, there to hover just below the roof and look down on the ant-like throng below. How odd it would all seem. How puny.

She thought about John on the first step of a journey to a country he did not know, in the service of an army that was likewise alien to him. She wondered whether his anxiety would be threaded with the strange excitement she was feeling.

She walked this way and that, through a maze of platforms and ticket offices, past hoardings advertising soap and jelly until, at last, she recognized a wooden archway. It was the one they had come through on their way in for, as she emerged, she was met by the same frenetic chaos they had witnessed earlier.

Men banged picks and shovels into the ground as others pushed barrows up planks, unloading earth, mud and dust into wagons that soon trundled away. Their drivers bellowed warnings to publicans who, balancing jugs on yokes around their necks, were supplying the navvies with beer, all in the vast building site that John had told her would become the Grand Metropole Hotel. How small she felt, and lonely, until at last she found the driver who had brought them to the station. She fell gratefully into the hansom cab and he whipped his horse forwards.

The journey from Waterloo was slow. She knew that the crowds, the horse-drawn omnibuses and carts seemingly intent on collision, the din of hawkers and costermongers, the uneven cobbles, the digging of drainage ditches and underground stations were just all part of London's expansion of which John was always complaining, but she felt buffeted by the clamour. She held tightly to the leather strap at the window, staring out, seeing but not seeing. Had the driver deliberately sought out the roughest roads?

It should therefore have been a relief to roll to a stop in the quiet Barnsbury street, which, with its sedate white three-storeyed houses, invited her back into its familiarity. But Mary did not feel relieved. She felt ill at ease.

She stepped down from the cab and pushed coins — too many, she was sure — into the driver's dirty hands. He drove off so abruptly that she had to jump aside.

A neat pathway led through the ordered front garden to a gleaming black front door.

She still thought often of the house in Oxfordshire, with its grassy surroundings, as home. There, as a girl, she had loved to roam. This house in Barnsbury, the first of her married life, held no such fond memories. It was her home only because she and John had made it so. And now he had gone and, despite his promise, she feared he was not coming back.

She lifted a gloved hand to the brass lion's head knocker, but before she had touched it, the door swung open. "Oh, there you are, ma'am." Betty, the maid, gave a frightened little curtsy. "I was beginning to wonder."

Annoyed that Betty should consider her incapable of finding her way from Waterloo, she brushed off the girl's clumsy attempts to help and hung up her own coat.

"Will you be wanting tea?" Despite a voracious appetite, Betty looked permanently underfed and now, as always, she licked her lips at the idea of food.

"Is it not tea time?" Mary opened the door to the drawing room. "Why is it so cold?"

"I laid the fire, ma'am, but I didn't light it. I thought —"

"That I would not need a fire now that Dr Clarke is away?"

"No, ma'am." Betty's thin bottom lip trembled. "But — but —"

"But what?"

"You have your tea in the library."

This was correct. And even if it hadn't been, she should not take out her misery on the maid. "I will let it pass this time, Betty," she said, "but with my husband away, you will take your orders from me."

"Very good, ma'am."

10

"Tea?"

Betty turned and fled.

The sight of that thin, skittering back destroyed the vague consciousness of her own power that had buoyed Mary up. Now she looked around the drawing room, with its plump chairs and covered side tables, its polished mirrors and silk brocade. It seemed empty.

Of life.

Of her husband.

How would she manage now that he had gone?

The day dragged interminably. She took up her needlepoint, but her stitches were so haphazard that she made herself unpick them. Fresh air, she decided. She walked out into the small garden, but it was so bleak and cold that she soon went back inside. She took up *The Trumpet Major* but, with John away to war, it had become distasteful. She put it down, unread.

She wandered through the drawing room and the library, grasping objects and turning them, as if inspecting them for dust. Eventually she made herself pick up the book again, but it provided such little interest or meaning that she was grateful when the light faded. She stood up and went to the canary's cage. John had bought the little bird to keep her company, but when she put a finger through the bars to stroke it, it hopped out of reach. She told herself it would get used to her. She was sure it would. She refused Betty's offer to light the lamps, and sat, unthinking, in the dark.

She wasn't hungry, but when Betty served asparagus soup, boiled beef and stewed apple, she ate a little. Then she was consumed by lethargy. Why should she be so tired? She had done no more than go to Waterloo, far less than she would accomplish in a normal day.

Her life, her old life that had now come to an end, had been structured by John's needs. By making sure he had breakfasted; remembering which of his patients would collect medicine from his dispensary, then writing down what she should charge; inspecting his wardrobe for necessary repairs; planning the hearty pies that would tempt him to eat; making shopping lists and telling Betty where to purchase the items; writing up the accounts; and, above all, preparing herself for his return from work.

The last, it now seemed to her, had consumed most of her day. How would she fill her time now?

The sensation that had overcome her in the station, which she had partly recognized as excitement, returned as dread. Her heart was thumping. Was she ill — and, if so, who would care for her?

She jumped up and, in her agitation, knocked a tall vase off a side table. It bounced against the skirting board and broke. Shards of glass spiked around its twisting silver-plated frame to lie glinting on the rug.

She was bending to pick up the pieces when Betty's "Let me, ma'am" made her jump. The maid took from her a piece of glass, which Mary hadn't been conscious of holding.

She realized she was crying.

"What is it, ma'am?"

"The vase was a wedding present. It meant a great deal to me . . ."

She woke up with a start.

Someone had been shouting.

She pulled herself up in bed, and propped herself against the pillows. The room was quiet, and so was the rest of the house. The shouting voice could only have been hers.

It was not the first time that her own shouting had awakened her. But in the past John had been there to calm her. He would gently rub her hands and feet, and should she be really overcome, he would go down to his dispensary and fetch her a small dose of laudanum. Now she lay in the emptiness of their cold bed and, even though her teeth were chattering, she was too hot. She pushed off the covers and, without lighting the lamp, made her way barefoot across the floor to the window.

It was very dark outside, and when she touched the window she felt ice on the pane. She remembered the cold touch of John's parting and realized her face was wet: she must have been weeping in her sleep.

Why? She could not remember. Which, again, was not unusual. How often had he asked her why she was crying? And how often had she tried to find words to explain what she herself did not understand?

Was this why he had left?

She turned away from the pitch of night that was pressing in on her. She could, she knew, go downstairs and see if there was fire enough still to warm some milk. It might help her sleep. Or, she thought, I could . . .

No. She would not, could not, allow in that thought. Not with John away.

She made herself go back to bed, pulled up the cover so that it was almost at her chin, and calmed herself by thinking of her husband.

The sound of gunfire catapulted John to his feet so fast that he hit his head against the wall. No time to attend to that. He stood stock still and tried to work out what was going on. His heart was banging — it seemed to have produced a visible tremor in his chest — and although he had only been reading, he was panting as if he had been running. He forced himself into calm and stood listening.

All he could hear was the relentless grinding of the ship's screw propeller. They were in open sea, not yet at Port Said. His first thought — an attack — must have been wrong.

His embarrassment at his panic — he was glad no one had witnessed it — he set aside. There *had* been gunfire, but why? Taking care not to knock over the stool that stood beside the two narrow bunks, he peered through the clouded porthole.

Sea was all he saw, no longer as grey as it had been on their departure from England, but still empty water. If he wanted to know what was going on, he must leave his cabin and investigate.

He pushed open the little wooden door and looked out into the dark corridor that ran past a line of similar

14

cabins. Nothing. And, apart from the ceaseless noise of the screw, no other sound.

Had he dreamed the gunfire?

It came again: a volley that was the unmistakable discharge of many guns. Something was happening on deck but, in the absence of running feet and urgent cries, it could not be an attack. Mortified by the fear that had flooded him again, he grabbed the oilskin hanging from a hook at the back of the door and left his cabin.

With both arms out, he swayed along the corridor, then hauled himself up the iron ladder and on to the deck. Spray hit him as he emerged. He looked to the prow as the huge old steamship rolled through the waves. Nothing to see there. He looked back to the stern. Men crowded at the rails facing out to sea. Most appeared to be loading guns, but others were carrying a strange assortment of objects, including shapes made of straw, old boxes and empty bottles.

"Give them room," someone shouted, and the gunners stepped back.

The packmen lined the rail. When a sergeant shouted, "Get ready," they whirled both arms and, to the slow count of "One, two, three," flung their projectiles high, then stepped smartly out of the way. The gunners unleashed their fire at the surface of the sea so that bottles jumped, boxes were holed and straw dissolved. One salvo, and the first line stepped back to be replaced by a second, the last shots aimed, as far as John could see, at waves and foam.

Thick clouds of white smoke filled the air. John held his nose against the acrid stench of gunpowder.

The packmen were readying themselves to fetch more targets but the sergeant yelled, "That's all for today." The military order dissolved and the men, alone or in small groups, strolled away.

They were dressed in the grey serge of their newly created desert uniforms, so that the only way to distinguish one man from another was to read the red cloth patches on which had been sewn their corps' initials. Strange, John thought, how each unit stuck together, but that was the ethos and camaraderie of the army: those who fought together bonded together. Something else to learn.

In Portsmouth he had felt himself to be very much the odd man out. After five days at sea, he was more acclimatized and beginning to deepen his acquaintance with the officers, the first step, he hoped, to friendship. As if in proof of this, a young major, whose 5L label proclaimed him one of the Lancers, now peeled off from his fellows to throw in John's direction, "Quite an exhibition of firepower — and of the men's ingenuity. They have ammunition a-plenty but no targets. Care for a snifter, Doctor?"

"Why not?" Seasickness and timidity had kept John too long in his own company. Now as he strolled beside the major and another officer who had joined them, he realized that his isolation had been partly self-imposed. "Physician, heal thyself," he muttered under his breath.

"Talking to yourself," the friendly officer said. "First sign of madness."

16

The second chipped in, "Wouldn't be surprised if Gordon hadn't started talking to himself, poor bugger, trapped in Khartoum by the Mahdi and with only savages for company."

"They say he can't last much longer," John observed.

"That's complete rot." The first officer laughed. "Gordon's as valiant and able a soldier as ever was. He'll hold out until we get there. Don't you agree, Thompson?"

A sage nod. "If anybody can hold Khartoum, Gordon can." Then he frowned. "Even so, it can't be much fun. Rumour runs that they're nearly out of supplies."

TO THE EDITOR OF *THE TIMES*

Sir, — Mr William Stead, the editor of the *Pall Mall Gazette*, has latterly used these columns to accuse our Prime Minister, Mr Gladstone, of failing to rescue General Gordon. I trust I may take the liberty of alerting your readers to a misapprehension that may exist in their minds after reading the barrage of Mr Stead's accusations.

Mr Stead has implied that Mr Gladstone's hesitation in sending out an army to rescue General Gordon results from some particular lack of sympathy. This is simply not the case. May I remind your readers that, earlier this year, Parliament voted in support of Mr Gladstone's caution on the matter. Even so, Mr Gladstone must feel, as keenly as any decent man would, General Gordon's plight. It is, however, beholden on Mr Gladstone as Her Majesty's Prime Minister to take every advice before risking our troops in the rescue of a single man. And this is a man, I might add, whose questionable decisions, and indeed, whose questionable sanity, has helped fashion the very calamity which all fear might now befall him.

I am, Sir, your obedient servant.

A. BARTHOLOMEW
Chairman, Huddersfield
Anti-Slavery Society

I Dec.

CHAPTER
TWO

In Khartoum the trumpet boys, hand-picked from the gang of urchins who haunted the governor general's palace in search of food, were at their stations at each corner of the palace roof. Out of pity, General Gordon always chose the puniest boys, and this group were so small they had to stand on boxes to see over the parapet. They were a dirty lot, their uniforms unwashed — one stank like a badger — and layers of red sand glittered on their dark faces as if they had been rolling in the desert. Still, they were brave. Even when they were being shelled, they stuck to their posts, and blew their trumpets at the general's lightest nod. *We are strong*, they would blow, in code, *we are strong*, as the general had trained them.

He stood at the edge of the roof, looking out at the river, lifeblood of the city, whose banks were lined by dusty palm groves that stretched to Moghram Point, where the dark waters of the Blue Nile washed over the emerald of the White. When he lifted his gaze past the river, and past the green dhura fields of Tuti Island, to the mudflats of the northern shore where they faded into desert, the blue of his eyes almost matched the blazing blue of the midday sky. He did not seem to feel the heat. He would stand in full sun for hours, waiting for Wolseley's regiments to gallop across the shimmering land to his rescue.

Not, Will thought, that they would be here very soon. Instead of dispatching a small force through the desert, as he should have done, Wolseley had insisted that the huge army should drag its boats over the intractable Nile cataracts, thus delaying their arrival. "Just the sort of mistake a general would make," Will muttered to himself.

Will was the general's unofficial batman. His job was to go where General Gordon went and do what the general asked him to do. Now he turned away from Gordon to look past Khartoum's clustered mud houses to the adjoining town of Omdurman and, beyond, to the biggest concentration of enemy, the place where, it was rumoured, the Mahdi had set up camp. With the forest of black, green and red banners hourly increasing, it was growing faster than the others, while rising trails of dust told of many more men on their way.

"Not long until dusk," the general muttered.

Not long until they overwhelm us, Will thought. He lifted up his eyes to the rosy bruise that was spreading under the flat blue horizon. Soon night would fall, bringing relief from the relentless heat. He smiled with weak relief.

The ripple of a disturbance travelled across the roof. Will's spine tingled but he resisted the instinct to duck. There had been none of the whistling that heralded an incoming shell. Something different then. He looked at the trumpet boys, who usually knew what was going on.

They were jumping up and down, pointing to the west. He looked back in that direction and realized that what he had taken for sunset was the beginning of a sandstorm, which had already grown and was moving so fast that it would soon blot out the sky.

During his year in Khartoum, Will had experienced many such storms. He knew how dangerous they could be. "General," he called. "General." He ran across the roof to tug Gordon's shirt sleeve.

"Yes?" The general's glare showed that he hated to be touched. "What is it?"

"A *haboob*, sir."

"Impossible."

"It is, General. A sandstorm coming."

"Nonsense."

"Look." Will pointed. "It's close."

"Can't be. Not the season."

The storm was now a towering monster, hot rolling waves of sand enveloping houses and bending the highest palms. It was as if the sea, in all its breathtaking immensity, had risen up and dried to red. The air was thick with it, enough to choke the fittest man. Nothing could stop the onward march of this highest, darkest doom, which, if they did not go in, would engulf them.

Knowing that the trumpet boys were too scared to move without an order, Will racked his brains for a way to shake the general from his trance. In desperation, he called: "Charley!"

Eyes blazing, the general whirled round. "How dare you!"

"Look." Will used both hands to keep the general facing west. "*Look*."

Even crazy old Charles Gordon, general in the British Army and governor general to Khartoum, could not miss the red mountain of sand that had blotted out the horizon. Huge, tidal surges of it coming fast. Thickly layered grit and clay rearing out of the desert. A wall of whirling particles towered over the native city with its clusters of crudely fashioned dwellings. It would soon slam into Khartoum with enough force to split roofs and flatten homes.

"Off the roof!" the general roared. "Now!"

Will kicked shut the door just as the sandstorm hit. They could hear it raging outside where the sky would have darkened into premature night, creating misery in the enemy camp.

A brisk nod from the general sent the trumpet boys skittering down the stairs, while the two last Englishmen in Khartoum — one uniformed, squat and square, with hair that was rapidly turning white, the other a mousy, scrappy fellow in tattered half-trousers and a dirty shirt — continued just to stand. They were covered from head to toe with red dust, thick crusted on eyelids, in nostrils and other places that Will might, in different company, have mentioned. He swallowed, ingesting grit as a way of clearing his throat. He could hear the general's wheezing.

"A cigarette."

22

"In a moment, General." Will couldn't stop coughing.

"A cigarette," the general insisted. "Bring it to my quarters."

The palace with its long colonnades, verandas and many windows, most of which no longer contained glass, was cooler by far than most of Khartoum, yet no sooner had Will wiped his forehead than his pimpled skin was again slick with sweat. Along the wide landing he went, his footsteps pattering on the stone floor with something that sounded like their echo. He shot back a fearful glance. No one in sight. He walked faster.

The U-shaped red-brick building that was the governor general's palace had once been the bustling hub of Khartoum, the nerve centre of all Sudan. Then guards, soldiers, clerks, scribes, slaves, interpreters, officials, petitioners and hangers-on of all kinds would compete for the governor general's attention. Now there were only ghosts to haunt the rooms that Will passed. He stopped and peered into one.

With its velvet divans, tables, chairs and lamp, the room still contained the personal possessions of the Englishmen who had passed through it. First of these had been Colonel Hicks, who had been cruelly cut down with his troops. After Hicks's demise, Frank Power, the *Times* correspondent who, by an amazing stroke of luck, had escaped the Hicks massacre, had settled in this room. He hadn't had the heart to touch Hicks's belongings, so the colonel's gloves, papers and guns lay everywhere. Power's luck had not held out. He had ended up dying with Stewart and now his collection of Sudanese spears, swords, arrows, war horns, leopard and lion skins, as well as the golden bangles he had bought for the family he was doomed never again to see, bore witness to his death.

"Hello," Will whispered. "Hello?"

No answer.

There never was.

No one knew the details of the overwhelming of Power and Stewart — whether they'd been grounded and sunk on a cataract, betrayed by one of their own or lured into a trap — but what was clear, because the enemy had sent proof, was that they were dead.

"Poor Stewart," the general kept saying. "Poor Stewart."

Will tiptoed to the large mahogany desk on which Power had written his articles. There, in pride of place, were Power's most prized possessions: a war horn made from an elephant's tusk that had been hollowed out until it was eggshell thin, and beside it, on a separate stand, a large, flat drum.

Will lowered his dusty hands over the drum, closer and closer, skating across the surface without touching it. Grains of sand fell on to it. He resisted the impulse to brush them off: he'd made the mistake just once of tapping the drum — the ferocious roar that had resulted had sent the palace into such a panic and the general into such a rage that he had vowed never to do it again. But still: "I want to," he whispered. "I just want to."

He dropped his hands and backed out of the room. His ghosts now propitiated — he always made sure to visit them — he moved off down the corridor. Soon he was at what had once been Stewart's room. Poor Stewart, having not been long in Khartoum, had had little chance to collect much in the way of possessions. His room was easier on the nerves.

Will didn't often smile these days but he was smiling now. Or, at least, his desiccated lips parted over crooked teeth as he opened the door and gave a whistled tweet. "Frankie!" he called, although there was no need: the brown and yellow tufted ball of fluff that was his adopted dog was already hurtling towards him. Will bent down and Frankie jumped into his arms, his tongue lapping ecstatically at Will's face.

"That's right, boy." Will laughed. "You give me a good clean-up — get rid of the sand."

The dog's moist square snout sniffed at Will's shirt, then his pockets.

"Here you are, boy." Will pulled out a piece of *dhura* bread. "It's not much, but you can have it." He watched the dog snuffle up the morsel. "Good boy." He stroked the wiry back, and was rewarded with the rapid motion of a tail that seemed capable of turning a full 360 degrees, before the dog lurched up to lick his nose.

"Such a welcome and all for the taste of sand." Will couldn't help laughing. "Wait till we get to Gravesend. You'll have real English bread then, and a proper beef bone." Frankie licked his face again. "You won't believe the glory of the beef back home," he went on. "Them cows are thick and plump from eating grass, not sand like the poor beasts here — yes," the dog had worked out there was no more food and was struggling in Will's arms, "you can get down." Will put Frankie on the floor, where he stood panting as Will patted his wiry head.

"I know you want me to stay, but I've got to go before the general starts yelling." He took care to block the dog from the door. "You're a good boy but the general can't abide the sight of you. And you mustn't go out on your own. They don't like dogs here. One of them might even catch and eat you. Not that I blame them, hungry as they are, but we can't have you eaten, can we?" With one last ruffle of the spiky hair between Frankie's ears, Will slipped out of the room.

Despite the lack of food, the palace kitchen was the meeting place for soldiers, administrators, merchants and servants, who came together to exchange all manner of rumour and intelligence and now, with the sand still whipping up outside, they were all crammed in together. Bodies jostled, some in tatty uniforms, others dressed like the finest gentlemen in bright, silver-edged flowing robes, several in cast-off flannel shirts and a few naked, save for silver bangles and loincloths. Every single one appeared to be talking simultaneously — or they were until Will made his entrance.

From hubbub to instant quiet — in case, Will thought, he had brought the general with him. Drawing up his scrawny body, he pushed his way through.

They knew well enough that he had no power and, anyway, could not understand what they said. When they saw he was alone, they went back to their talk.

Sudanese conversation was usually conducted in a low bass hum. This was different. It was higher in pitch and much wilder, with gesticulations to accompany it. Something had upset them.

Will grabbed a passing trumpet boy, the one with a smattering of English. "What's going on?"

"The *haboob*," the boy said, referring to the sandstorm.

"This *haboob*? After all the others?"

"This *haboob* out of time."

It took a moment for Will to grasp that the boy was trying to tell him it was the wrong time of year for a sandstorm. Which explained their agitation. The people of Khartoum were a superstitious lot. They read omens into everything. Not, in Will's opinion, that you needed a fortune-teller to know their future: you had only to look to the perimeters of the city where the Mahdi's men were camped.

"Me go?"

Will nodded, sand dropping from his mouse-brown hair into his eyes. He blinked. "A basin."

He wasn't the general and he didn't have the general's manner. Nobody moved.

He fetched the basin for himself, poured water into it from a jug, then plunged in his head. He came out spluttering to find the water stained red with sand. He swilled it out, then rinsed the basin. He took a key from his pocket and unlocked the general's special cupboard, standing on tiptoe, cursing his lack of height and swaying until he managed to hook out cigarettes from the highest shelf. He could have asked for help, but something in the atmosphere made him wary, a kind of growing sulky sullenness.

He said loudly: "Wolseley's on his way."

Although they didn't speak much English this phrase had been so oft repeated by the general that they understood it. Someone sniggered. The rest just stared. In his careless walk out of the kitchen, Will tried to show he didn't care.

TO THE EDITOR OF THE TIMES

Sir, — I write in opposition to the calumny put out by your correspondent, Mr Bartholomew. He has traduced the reputation of the most honourable of Englishmen by repeating the assertion of an intemperate Member of Parliament, who shall remain nameless (and who, in my humble opinion, should have remained voiceless), that General Gordon might be mad.

I will not demean General Gordon by defending his judgement. It is sufficient merely to point out that this is a man who, affectionately known as Chinese Gordon, is the lone European to have been awarded the yellow robe by the Chinese Emperor for his part in putting down a terrible rebellion. General Gordon was also the first person to whom the Cabinet turned when they understood that they owed a duty of care to the Egyptian troops in Khartoum.

Mr Bartholomew has also cast aspersions on my attempts to secure General Gordon's rescue.

I am not ashamed, Sir, to call myself a patriot and neither do I flinch from defending the position of Her Majesty the Queen as Empress of India.

Should Gordon fall, the false prophet who calls himself the Mahdi will soon have charge of the whole of the Soudan. If this rebellion then spreads northwards into Egypt it will threaten the Suez Canal. The consequences would be felt throughout Her Majesty's Empire, something which no patriotic Englishman can desire.

Mr Bartholomew has made reference to the Parliamentary vote won by Mr Gladstone in February of this year.

It is indeed true that Mr Gladstone won the motion of censure against him. Your readers should know, however, that Mr Gladstone won by the narrowest of margins and only after members of his own Party, though they might disapprove of his failure to act, hesitated to bring down his Government. I surely cannot be alone among your readers in thinking that Mr Gladstone's eventual, and late, agreement to permit the dispatch of the Wolseley rescue expedition is an indication of the wrong-headedness of his original stand.

For eleven months General Gordon has resisted the Mahdi scourge. Now he is in mortal danger. Patriots, among whom I am honoured to be counted, have alerted the Public Platform.

Should the Mahdi overrun Khartoum, and should General Gordon meet an unthinkable fate, judgement will be passed on Mr Gladstone. I do not, as Mr Bartholomew implies, count myself above other people, but it would be a false modesty for me to deny that my voice sometimes prevails. I can assure your readers that, in the sad eventuality of General Gordon's demise, I will use that voice to the best of my abilities.

I am, sir, yours respectfully,

W. T. STEAD.
Editor

Pall Mall Gazette, 5 Dec.

TO THE EDITOR OF THE TIMES

Sir, — Mr Stead has seen fit to censure me for questioning General Gordon's judgement. Mr Stead may also have left your readers with the impression that my criticisms of General Gordon expose a lack of patriotism on my part. It behooves me, therefore, to defend myself.

I will not demean myself by exchanging jingoistic sentiments with Mr Stead. I will, however, if I may, cite as evidence of General Gordon's questionable sanity an extract from Mr Stead's own writings.

In his rousing article, published in his *Gazette*, Mr Stead, whose memory we are told is second to none, quoted the General as saying: "I consider Khartoum as safe as Kensington Park."

If Khartoum is as safe as Kensington Park, can we now expect a camel regiment to be dispatched from barracks to save our good citizens from the dangers of Queen Anne's banqueting house?

I subscribe myself again, sir, your obedient servant,

A. BARTHOLOMEW
Chairman, Huddersfield
8 Dec.   Anti-Slavery Society

CHAPTER
THREE

Mary pushed *The Times* off her lap and jumped up, and as she did, the pleats and flounces at the hem of her skirt unfolded in an affectation of softness at odds with the boned bodice. She felt . . . she felt unbearably constrained, her plain tight sleeves adding so to the rigidity of the outfit that, were she to fling out her arms as she wanted to, the whole would split asunder. She couldn't bear it. She would — she must — change into something simpler. She took a determined step forward.

The heel of her velvet slipper pierced the newspaper. She bent to retrieve it, but all she managed to do was rip it.

John, who liked his newspapers clean, pressed and neatly folded, would hate to see one torn. But John wasn't there. If she were to go further, and pull this copy apart, he would still not be there.

No sooner had the thought occurred than she snatched up the broadsheet, and shred it, picking up the tatters, and further renting them. Such a frenzy of unthinking demolition that when eventually she came to, it was to find herself standing in a sea of torn newsprint.

She sank to her knees, put her head into her hands, as if in prayer, and remained there for a while: a tight-laced maroon figure adrift in her own destruction.

She was like this increasingly, and had been since John had gone — except in the moment between waking and knowing herself to be wide awake. Then she would stretch out a hand towards the misty rays of winter light passing through the curtains and would feel as though she could almost touch the possibility that not only could she manage without John but that she could also enjoy managing.

And then she would properly awake and think: I am alone. Completely alone.

It might have been different, if she had had family, but since her parents' deaths and her marriage, she had seen little of the others, all of whom lived far from London. She had friends, of course — or, at least, she and John shared acquaintances, some of whom had left cards. She had not, however, considered herself sufficiently well attired to receive them. That was why she was dressed so formally now: she had had enough of Betty's sidelong looks: pity from that bedraggled child was more than she could bear. Should visitors arrive, she could welcome them in. And she would. In the meantime, though, she would calm herself with a very small dose of laudanum from the bottle John had left for her.

She got up, and went out, closing the door on the mess she had made. She would clear it up later, when she felt better.

John's steamer puffed into the jetty at General Wolseley's base camp in Korti ahead of the other boats that, crammed with troops, were waiting to disembark.

In the monotony of his journey he had had plenty of time to dwell on its difficulties: the swampish black flies that cleaved to moist skin by day and, by night, the mosquitoes, with stings like bayonets; the endless galloping of rats overhead and forward of his cabin; the tedium of being dragged slowly past the cataracts; and the suffocating heat that was replaced at night by bone-chilling cold.

Now he realized that his hardship must have been as nothing compared to what the ordinary Tommy, crammed into a whaling boat with only a canvas roof as protection from the elements, had suffered. The men had sat patiently and, despite the stifling midday temperature, he had not heard one grumbled remark, not even when his steamer had slipped past the queue into the jetty.

"Dr Clarke?" A young red-headed soldier, having identified John by his civilian clothes and his doctor's bag, offered him a helping hand. "This way, if you please." Hefting John's bag on to his shoulder, he set off up the riverbank.

John found the going harder than he had expected. Soon he had to stop to catch his breath. He looked towards the river, where the men were now leaving their boats. Sweating under their desert costume of grey serge jumpers, cord breeches and white pith helmets, they hoisted heavy packs on to their backs and, in a series of single files, began to trudge up the bank. They marched in synchronicity, seemingly without effort, heads down, streaming past John who caught whiffs of their stale breath, sweat-hardened, unwashed clothes and feet festering in socks unchanged throughout their long journey. He could almost see the lice jumping off them. He listened to the slither of their boots on the sand, the huff of their breath and the occasional clink of a tin cup against a pack. Despite the stench, their proximity filled him with pleasure. There was something if not heroic, then apt about being in the midst of such men and knowing he had come to help. He had made the right decision.

An ear-splitting sound rent the air: the bellowing of scores of camels being urged to their feet on the whalers, their protests all but drowning the curses of the soldiers and the guttural throat-clicking of the men on shore, who were pulling at their halters to coax them out. Like ungainly ships, humped instead of masted, the camels stood up, stepped over the rim of the boat and were led up the bank. Such a surprising sight. John was mesmerized as they made their way, swaying, towards him.

"Watch yourself, sir." John's guide used his hard, muscled body to push John out of their way. He stumbled and would have fallen if the soldier had not grabbed him. "Sorry, sir, but you don't want a kicking from one of them devils."

"Quite." John was discomfited by the sound of his voice, high-pitched with alarm.

"You'll get used to them," the soldier said.

They waited until the caravan had passed, then joined the files of silent soldiers sweating their way up to the point where the land levelled.

Still gasping — the heat was intolerable — John took off his jacket, wishing he could strip off his shirt too, and looked around.

About a thousand yards from the Nile, he could see the village of Korti. It was small — more hamlet than village — with low, crooked red-mud houses grouped together in areas of swept sand, and surrounded by either mud or reed walls. Although the houses were not much to look at, the labour of their occupants was visible in the groves of palms, the yellow-tipped mimosa trees, and the broad swatches of tall green corn that lined both banks of the river. Korti must once, John thought, have been a slow, peaceful place, the image of a settlement on the edge of the desert that his childhood Bible had portrayed. Now, set some yards from the riverside stretch of green, and encroaching into the desert, a huge modern sprawl had come to disrupt this ancient continuity. It was a makeshift city of small tents laid out in straight lines. There were open spaces for cooking, and others that appeared to be reserved for sleeping under the stars. And surprisingly: John sniffed the air. Could that be freshly baked bread? Following the direction of his nose back towards the river, he saw soldiers labouring over what seemed to be vast ovens.

"The bakery, sir," his guide explained, wiping his freckled face with a grubby handkerchief. "Four ovens, each turning out six hundred loaves a day. And next to them, that's the cattle depot. When we leave this blasted place, if we ever do, we'll be riding alongside our rations. We'll go this way, shall we, sir?"

They walked in through the centre of the tented city. With the flaps up, John could see bedrolls neatly folded and possessions neatly stacked. No one inside because the men, occupying every available piece of shade, were sitting under trees or propped-up canvas, strumming instruments, sewing, exchanging yarns or sleeping, mouths open, bodies sprawled. They were similarly dressed, save for a small group in white tunics and trousers.

"Blue jackets," John's guide explained. "Royal Navy, sir. What they're doing in the desert is as good a question as I ever did hear. But if we ever do take on the enemy, I reckon we'll be thankful for their Gardner guns."

As they pushed further through the camp John began to understand that the canvas-covered vastness bore a close resemblance to any other city. On the outskirts, there were the slums, where the non-British support troops from Aden and further east had camped. Next came the crowded, albeit clean, dwellings of the mass of ordinary soldiers. Finally, as their path bent right and curved back towards the river, the alleyways widened, the trees were more numerous and the tents larger, with floor planks, chairs, tables and real beds. Each was edged with a makeshift picket fence, which provided its occupant with at least the illusion of a private outdoor resting area.

In one of these John glimpsed an officer removing his uniform. He was about to step into a lined dug-out hollow into which water had been poured for bathing. Seeing John, the officer barked an order to his attendant, who held up a blanket to screen his nakedness.

"Blooming idiot." John's guide snorted. "As if anybody gives a damn about his maggoty body — s'cuse my language, sir." A moment later, he added, over his shoulder, "We'll try the hospital." He led John towards the river and into the first of a series of large canvas marquees that, erected on oval tube poles, stood on a shaded site overlooking the Nile.

John was surprised. "It's larger than I'd thought."

"Each section holds eighteen to twenty men. That, over there, is the operating theatre."

John's terrain. Once he had ensconced himself in it, he would feel truly at home with these fellows.

"If you'd follow me, sir, I'll hand you over to your ADC. Now where the bloody hell . . .?"

From behind the hospital marquee someone called, "Break step! Break step!"

"So that's where the bastard's got to." The guide and John marched to the back of the hospital.

Not many paces from the luxuriance of the watered land, sand scattered with black boulders and stunted mimosas stretched as far as the eye could see, on and on until the parched land blended into distant pink-tipped, black-rimmed hillocks. It was this wilderness, John knew, that a camel regiment would have to penetrate. He was torn by contradiction: relief that, because of his promise to Mary, he would not be going with them, and regret that he would be excluded from such a marvellous adventure.

"There he is." The guide pointed at a huddle of bodies whose plain trousers and open-necked shirts proclaimed them to be civilians. They parted to release from their midst a scar-faced, squat soldier. "Tom will be your ADC, sir."

The sunlight was so bright that all John had was an impression of pock-marked skin as the man began pairing his men, matching them in height.

"What a shambles," John's companion muttered. "Can't get a native to do a soldier's job."

"Pick up," the other soldier shouted.

Each pair fetched a stretcher from a heap, and stood holding them, one man in front and the other behind.

"When I give the order, you will march in a forward direction. With a steady step. Slowly, like this . . ." The soldier placed his foot gently on the sand, hardly raising it at all as he slid the other forward. "Smoothly." His body remained erect, and each step was the same length as the previous one. "Slide. If you spring, you jolt the wounded. Move smoothly. You are not doing this for your comfort. You will be carrying an injured man."

He turned to face his men. "At my command. And remember, break step. Man in front, left foot forward. Man at the back, right foot. Break step. Go." The stretcher-bearers moved forward but in utter disarray, those at the back pushing so hard that the men in front were shoved forwards, the empty stretchers bucketing up, down and sideways, and in one case slipping out of its bearers' hands. "No!" their instructor yelled. "Stop, for mercy's sake!" He clapped his hands. The laughing bearers stopped, discarding their stretchers and collapsing on to the ground.

"Bastards! Buggers! Idiots!"

The litany could clearly have been extended for some considerable time, but John's now red-faced guide called out, "Tom! Your new surgeon's here."

The man wheeled round. Now John could see him clearly: he saw a weather-beaten face, cratered at the cheeks and the broad forehead, with deep-set dark brown eyes. A face full of experience, a lived-in face, John thought, as the man lifted one rough hand to his head and saluted. "Major Clarke," reminding John abruptly that he had the honorary rank for the duration of the campaign. "I'm Sergeant Jennings. Tom Jennings. Your ADC while we're at camp. Sorry I wasn't there to meet you." He turned back to the stretcher-bearers. "Dismissed," and then, almost immediately: "No. Put the stretchers away. Neat, like, and don't go until you have." He readdressed himself to John. "We don't have enough bearers so I'm training this lot. Bloody waste of time, if you ask me."

"Not that anybody does," John's guide chipped in.

"Not that anybody does," Tom agreed. "Mark my words, first sign of gunfire and they'll be off. Still," this to John, "not for you to worry about. You'll be staying at base, won't you?" Without waiting for a reply he said, "Let me take you to the colonel."

"I wouldn't, Tom. He's in one of his . . ." John's guide paused.

A look passed between the two, and then Tom Jennings said, "Let's settle you in your quarters, major. Afterwards, I'll show you round the hospital."

Although the brown canvas flaps of the hospital marquee were tied back, there was no breeze. Sweat pouring off his brow, John followed his ADC along the rows of beds.

"Each day brings more men who can't abide the tropical heat," Tom said. "One death so far." He pushed through a canvas curtain that divided one section of the marquee from the next. "This is our enteric ward."

"Bacillus typhosus," John muttered, looking at the line of prone men, limbs limp, complexions jaundiced, skin covered with telltale raised red spots.

"If you say so. Nothing we can do for the poor devils but keep them comfortable and coax them into drinking. That's where your native helper comes in. He may not know how to heft a stretcher but he makes a good nurse. Some of the sickest even prefer them — say they make them feel more at ease."

John looked to where an Arab was squatting by a bed, trying to spoon liquid into a patient's mouth. He was, indeed, very gentle. When the patient turned away his head, the man cradled it in one hand and drew it back, to nudge his lips open again with the spoon.

"May I?"

The Arab shifted to let John in.

The patient's brow was clammy cold and rubbery, his skin blue-tinged, his pulse low and thready. He was in the late stages of the disease, his eyes sunken, slipping into death.

"He's one of our surgeons," Tom said. "He was to have carried on with his regiment — part of the Camel Corps. The colonel's doing his best to keep him alive but if you ask me . . ." Tom was clearly accustomed to working in a hospital because now his voice dropped ". . . he won't be with us much longer." He looked down, kindness on his blotched face.

John straightened and Tom clicked his fingers. An orderly brought a basin of water in which John rinsed his hands.

"Aside from the enterics," Tom said, "you have your dysenteries and your diarrhoeas — especially among the foreigners, them not being too wary with their sanitation — and also your general fevers. They're in that section over there. Then there's your eye problems. Conjunctivitis and one bad case. Poor bugger's gone blind. Which, apart from injuries cause by camel kicks and bites — a few broken limbs — and accidental bullet wounds, is about the sum of it. Oh . . . and there's a whaler tethered mid-river to a sandbank where we've had to quarantine a regiment because one man caught smallpox from a 'lady' he met in Cairo. The operating theatre is over yonder. The colonel must still be finishing there, so we'll leave it —"

"What did I tell you? You slow-witted whipper-snapper! You clay-brained puttock! You stuffed baboon! What did I tell you?" The roar issued from the part of

42

the marquee at which Tom Jennings had been pointing. The quality of the insults might have made John laugh, if not for the tone, full of menace, in which they were delivered.

"As I was saying," Tom went on drily, "Colonel Watson is just finishing. We'll come back in an hour."

Too late. The curtain separating the theatre from the rest of the marquee billowed and was roughly shoved aside to let out two men. The first, a weaselly private, wasn't so much running as flying. He was followed by a huge apron-swathed colonel, whose arms were bloodied to the elbow. "This man is useless." His voice was loud enough to shake the canvas. "Find me another and look sharp about it. And you," to the evicted man who was scurrying from the tent as fast as his scrawny legs could carry him, "if you ever so much as look in my direction, you'll feel the sharp end of my scalpel." With one dig of a substantial elbow, the colonel shoved away an orderly, who had hurried to him with a basin, and wiped his hands on his apron, fresh smears of blood now overlying the old. "Who's this?" He was looking at John.

"Major Clarke, sir," Tom said, and, as the colonel's bushy eyebrows closed in on each other in a ferocious frown, "the new surgeon, sir."

"Ah, yes. The civilian chappie. Took your time, didn't you? But welcome anyway." The colonel was upon John and thrust out a massive, bloodied hand that John had no option but to take. He felt the calloused force of the other man's grip.

"How's our doctor?" The colonel had moved his gaze in the direction of the enteric ward.

"Not good." Tom shrugged.

"As anticipated. One last thing to try. It won't be pleasant but needs must. Fetch me our biggest needle and my dissecting scalpel."

He barked, "Follow me," to John, then marched to the sick doctor's bed, where he bent over him to shout into his ear, "Now, now, Major. This won't do," and it seemed to John that the colonel was almost deliberately comparing his own ruddy good health with the patient's hollow cheeks and ghastly yellow-blue hue. "If you won't drink, we'll have to hydrate you."

Ignoring his patient, who was moving his head feebly from side to side, the colonel clapped his hands impatiently. An orderly rushed over. "Hurry up, Private." He took the scalpel from the orderly's outstretched palm.

The patient's lips moved. John leaned closer, straining to hear.

"I don't want . . ." the man whispered. "I don't want . . ."

"What's that?"

"I don't want him to . . ."

"Out of my way, lad." This from the colonel.

John began, "I don't think —"

The colonel cut him off: "You're in the army, Major. You're not here to think."

Definitely old school, John thought, like others he'd come across, whose arrogance had made some of his own training such a misery. But John was no longer a

44

student. He said loudly, "You can't ride roughshod over his will."

The colonel's head jerked back, almost as if he had been hit. His eyebrows had joined together in one thunderous line. "I beg your pardon?"

"He does not want the treatment you propose."

"What a patient wants and what is good for him are two entirely different things." The colonel's smile was devoid of warmth. "You must know that."

"Of course. And normally I'd agree. But this man is one of us. He's a doctor. He knows how painful the dissection will be. He must also know that, even if the treatment helps temporarily, within seventy-two hours he'll likely sink again."

"Have you a better idea?"

"Perhaps a Pravaz syringe. A sharp needle with a pointed trocar makes dissection unnecessary. Fluid could then be introduced slowly, bypassing the intestines. They say this gives the patient a greater chance of survival."

"Oh, they do, do they?" The colonel was glowering "And where in the desert do they say I am to locate a pointed trocar? Of course." He rubbed his hands in mock-delight. "You're a modern medical man. You brought one with you?"

"No." John shook his head. "I didn't know it would be needed."

"God save us from the theoreticians," the colonel growled. "Now if you wouldn't mind stepping out of my way, I will do my best to save this man."

"He doesn't want the treatment."

"It is not his choice to make."

"He's a doctor."

"He *was* a doctor, laddie, when he was hale. Now he's ill, he is a patient and *I* am his doctor. And, as it happens, I am also your superior officer. I will treat my patient as I see fit. Out of my way, sir." The colonel lowered his head — then lifted it. He was smiling — or, at least, his fleshy lips were twisted into what John imagined was a smile. "On second thoughts," he said, "you will perform the dissection. A test of your competence. I wouldn't wish to leave my hospital in the charge of a bungler."

No. John would not do what he did not believe in. That was not his way.

"Unless you are not up to it?"

TO THE EDITOR OF THE TIMES

Sir, — I cannot leave unchallenged the doubt your correspondent has cast on General Gordon's sanity.

May I remind your readers that a full eleven months have elapsed since Gordon left these shores. While he was still alive, the unfortunate Colonel Stewart, who travelled with Gordon, wrote of the fulsome welcome afforded the general in Khartoum. This is a further indication of the high regard in which the general is held by the people of the Soudan. It is this that had made the city safe for the general — as it has proved to be throughout his year's duration.

If anybody could have evacuated Khartoum, General Gordon would have been that man. He reported fully on the difficulties he encountered. It is Mr Gladstone's failure to act which is at fault.

Although your correspondent clearly harbours ill will towards General Gordon, the Public Platform does not. Should the worst unfold, I, for one, will ensure that Mr Gladstone bears the full consequences of Public dismay.

Your faithful servant,

15 Dec.   W. T. STEAD

CHAPTER
FOUR

Eleven o'clock, and the sun was already hot enough to scorch the moisture from men's eyes and sear their throats.

"Here, boy." Will pulled at the rope that was his dog's leash. "Here, Frankie." The dog lapped up the last of some water, then looked up and growled. "Sssh." Will laid his hand across the dog's snout. "You don't want to annoy the general."

The general, with the red stripe running down the trousers of his workaday uniform, was standing towards the edge of the terrace and looking through the long telescope, fashioned by Chevalier's in Paris. As he slowly panned it to the west, the image that filled the glass must have been drearily familiar.

First, the greenish-brown river running to the point where the Blue and White Niles converged. A hop across: the village of Omdurman with its sludge-brown houses bunched around a fort. It was held by Egyptians who, now that they had been cut off from Khartoum, spent most of their time asleep. The focus of the general's inspection, though, lay just beyond Omdurman: the place where men and animals, wives, camp-followers and slaves lived under a forest of waving green and white banners adorned by texts from the Koran. Even without a glass, it was clear how much the camp had grown recently.

The general shoved away the telescope so roughly that it swung full circle. "There's no saving Omdurman," he said. "I'll send a messenger to consent to their surrender."

Will got to his feet.

"The loss of life won't be too considerable." The general was talking not to but at Will. "The Mussulmans among them will slip into the Mahdi's army. The rest will be spared if they convert — and, most men preferring apostasy to death, they will convert." The general glared at Will. "He who denies me on earth," he said, "I will deny in heaven."

Despite the heat, something icy cold seemed to pass down Will's spine. He pulled his dog under his shirt.

The general had begun to pace. "Faith is not like a coat." He waved his arms for emphasis. "You cannot take one off and put on another. If you are a Christian, you must be like Him who from His birth to His death was utterly miserable." And then, in the lightning change of mood and subject that was increasingly characteristic, the general fixed his blue eyes on Will. "Get rid of the dog. It's time to see the steamers off."

As Will walked down one side of the matching flight of curving stone stairs that ran from the general's quarters to the arid paved courtyard, he could feel the general's breath on his neck.

To distract himself, he thought back to his first sighting of these stairs. How majestic they had seemed and how miraculous that they were there for his use. No longer. These days he couldn't go down, especially in the general's company, without fear churning within him. It didn't matter what he told himself, the fear would swell until it constricted his breath and wound itself around his innards as if to smother him. There was nothing he could do to slough it off so he was always thankful when he reached the bottom.

Outside, it was so dazzlingly bright that at first he could see only a fluttering line of thin, dark wraiths. He blinked, and the shapes solidified and turned into four chained convicts who, guarded by soldiers with fixed bayonets, were shuffling past. They were carrying a stretcher on which lay a dead boy; a thin arm hung out from beneath the shroud. There was no sign of blood, either leaking or dried, which meant that the boy must have died of natural causes. Or of starvation. Which was the same thing in Khartoum.

Will watched them go.

"To be buried as a dog," the general said. "Part of the glory of war. Come, Will."

Will was glad the general hadn't added, "Chop, chop," as he often did. That, with the sight of a corpse so fresh, and the fear still coursing through him, would have made him want to chop the general down.

He followed the general through gardens that had once been luxuriant. No longer. The meticulously raked ground was now untended sand and stones, and the plants had shrivelled, not because there was insufficient water but because no one had had the energy to water them. Even the high walls that had separated the palace from the Roman Catholic mission had been destroyed, and its banana, lemon and fig trees looted of fruit, their branches chopped up for fuel. Only the ripening purple grapes on the trellis of the palace had been spared, fear of the general's reprisals being stronger than hunger. But the palms that lined the river and must have been there since time immemorial were wilting, and because any bird that risked a fly past soon found itself catapulted out, the sky was empty of life. The crowd that always gathered when the general appeared was also much changed: serious and watchful now in a way they had never previously been.

The general didn't seem to register the changes. He had put on his ceremonial uniform and now, a peacock in braided white, topped by a scarlet *tarboosh*, he carved a path through a crowd of women who had come to ask for more grain. They were of all sorts — slaves, whose filched petticoats doubled as skirts, Dinkas with armfuls of jingling bracelets, women adorned by ostrich feathers that did nothing to hide their nakedness, all now pressing their case on a general who didn't deign to register their presence, although he paused to mutter something to his interpreter, who repeated the lie that hundreds of *ardebs* of grain would be released to see them through the siege, which pronouncement the general used to make good his escape.

At last the soldiers formed a line to hold the women at bay, and the general's further progress should have

51

been unimpeded, but before he reached the landing-stage, there came another interruption. A man, barefooted, in white cotton trousers and a frayed white shirt, slipped through the soldiers and moved towards the general. One soldier, bayonet drawn, advanced on the man, but the general's impatient hand signal and his angry words — "If he'd been an assassin, you'd already be too late" — stopped him in his tracks.

Will recognized the intruder. He was the hospital apothecary and spoke some English. "Ahmed." He darted forward.

The Arab whispered in the general's ear, and handed him a piece of paper, then melted back into the crowd.

The general looked down at the note. His expression darkened. He crumpled it into a ball. A mutter passed through the assembled throng. "I deny this false imputation." He had turned scarlet to match his *tarboosh*. "The rescue expedition is not coming to rescue me." He raised his arms high. "It is coming to rescue *you*. It is coming to save our national honour."

The crowd, most of whom would not have understand a word, were still. The general slapped his swagger stick against his thigh. The sound ricocheted. As one, the crowd stepped back. "I came here to relieve Khartoum," the general said, "and that is also why Wolseley is coming. I brought relief expedition number one. He brings relief expedition number two." The general glared at the crowd, who, despite the language barrier, knew that something was expected of them so when one of their number began to clap the others joined in. The first soft pattering gained in strength until the whole crowd was applauding vigorously.

"Humph." The general flung away the crumpled paper and marched off, a mad Pied Piper followed by his retinue.

When the general and his attendants had gone, Will picked up the piece of paper Gordon had discarded. He smoothed it open.

It was a scrap of paper torn from a newspaper dated 30 August 1884, almost six months ago.

Lord Northbrook and Lord Wolseley went to Osborne yesterday to see the Queen, after which Lord Wolseley returned to London. He will depart by mail train this morning. Lord Northbrook will go from Osborne to visit Lord Granville at Walmer Castle, and will join Lord Wolseley at Dover tomorrow on the first leg of the journey to the Soudan. Lord Wolseley is to lead the Gordon Relief Expedition.

That explained the general's fit of temper: he would never countenance talk of a mission to rescue *him*. He, or so he kept saying, was not important. All that mattered, and this he also drummed endlessly into Will, was that British honour be salvaged by the relieving of the Egyptian garrisons.

Such nonsense. The Egyptian regulars and tax collectors were as great a bunch of villains as ever roamed the earth: no one, not even their own kind, would think of rescuing them. As for the others, some were slaves, who did as they were told, others merchants, who would rather not pay the Mahdi's taxes, a few Christians, who wanted to keep the faith, and the rest were ordinary people who, like ordinary people everywhere, tried their best to keep out of harm's way. In other words, not one of them was important enough to rescue. Except General Gordon.

"And we can thank our lucky stars that someone thinks he's worth relieving," Will told the air. He tucked away the paper and hurried after the general.

The general's last remaining steamers — all but one — were lined up at the landing-stage. Freshly painted, they gleamed in the sunshine. There'd been no way to prettify their funnels, or their protective iron cladding, and the general had ordered that the bullet holes, the mark of earlier expeditions, be left unbeaten. In this he had been right: the scars of battles survived gave the steamers a dignity that set the crowd cheering as Gordon boarded the *Bordeen*.

The general's steamers, other than the one he would keep in Khartoum, were being sent past the sixth cataract to Metemma, there to await the rescue expedition. The *Bordeen* was different. She would take the general's journal all the way to Korti where Wolseley had set up his base.

The general walked slowly along the line of the *Bordeen's* Egyptian escorts. Despite his ferocious scowl, as he passed each one, they couldn't help breaking into smiles. For good reason. Once they reached Korti, they would not be coming back. The general had made this clear. Apart from the captain and the engineers, he did not want to see these men again.

The captain was small and stout, his skin shining wetly in the glare. It was his responsibility to get the men safely away. His foot tapped impatiently as he glanced over his shoulder at the opposite bank in fear that this ceremonial, on which the general had insisted, would alert the enemy and set them to shelling before the *Bordeen* had the chance to work up steam. But, like everybody else, he was in awe of the general. At Gordon's approach he raised his right hand, as if in salute, but then, changing his mind, thrust it out to receive the general's journal. Once he had it, he could cast off.

The general's hand also shot out. He was going to hand over the journal — or the gesture suggested that was his intention. But when the captain tried to take it, the general failed to let it go. The captain was not a big man. The general, at five feet five inches, was smaller. Still, there was no doubt, with both men's hands on the book, which one of them would win this foolish tug of war.

Seeing the two, the European and the Egyptian, the general and his captain, locked together in this peculiar manner, the crowd's hum turned to chatter.

The general let go, so abruptly that the surprised captain almost overbalanced. But he was accustomed to being tilted this way and that and quickly regained his equilibrium. Hastily stowing away the journal, he issued instructions to his crew.

The engines were stoked, the guns on the north side of the shore readied and, as soon as the general had left the *Bordeen*, the other steamers were sent to distract the enemy with fire. The *Bordeen's* funnel snorted steam, her wheels churned and her stout body began to plough through the water.

The enemy fired, their shells thudding into the water safely out of touching distance of the *Bordeen*.

"My valiant steamer," the general said. "My valiant steamer."

Will was close enough to see how tightly clenched his fists were and how a vein in his neck was throbbing as they waited, side by side, until the general's valiant steamer, followed by the others that were to wait for Wolseley's troops, rounded the bend of the river and was gone.

Now the full force of their predicament seemed to settle over the people of Khartoum. The crowd deflated, despair floating in with the dust.

"She will get there and she will return," the general said.

Dark muttering replaced the earlier cheers. It couldn't have been clearer if the buglers had sounded out *We are lost, we are lost.*

"She will come back," the general shouted, "bearing British reinforcements."

Khartoum was lost and the general was the only one who didn't seem to know it.

The general strode back to the palace, where he ordered the sentries to bar the way to strangers. Then, to Will, he said, "Come along."

With his boy running to keep up, the general marched to the lee of a side wing where he was in no danger of being overlooked. There, waiting for him, in accordance with his instructions, was a man burned black by the sun. He had a long, gaunt face, pointed at the chin, and was dressed in a white jellaba. He held in one hand the winding white wrap that was to cover his knotted hair. He had the look of a thorough rogue — Khartoum was overrun by Mahdi spies — but it might equally have been fear and hunger that lent him his shifty appearance.

Certainly the general saw nothing wrong in him. "This courageous man," he said, "has volunteered to travel the desert route to Korti. He is to take my personal message to Wolseley. While the *Bordeen* has to travel down the bend of the Nile, and negotiate two cataracts, he will go straight across the Bayuda desert. He'll get to Korti long before she does." The general held out a scrap of paper to Will. "Give it to him."

Will was about to hand over the note when the general said, "Read it."

It was no bigger than a postage stamp. On one side, to prove its authenticity, was the general's Arabic seal. Will turned it over. On the other — he could hardly believe it — had been written three words: *Khartoum all right*, the date, *14-12-84*, and the name *C. B. Gordon*, in the general's hand.

"'Khartoum all right'!" Shock caused Will to repeat the words.

"Give it to him."

"But, General —"

"Give it to him. Now!"

The messenger grabbed the paper and thrust it into one of the wild twists of hair over which he wound his long white headdress.

"Good luck." The general came forward and gave the man a cigarette, then turned on his heels. "Come, Will."

Come, Will, come, Will. That was all Will ever heard. With the sun burning through his flimsy shirt to his scrawny chest, he did not come.

Registering the absence of his follower's pattering feet, the general turned. He looked at the boy, whose chin, though juddering, was determined and whose hazel eyes flashed defiance. "Will?"

"I'll come in a moment, General."

A short flash of surprise at this insubordination from someone who never usually answered back, but all the general said was "Suit yourself", before he walked away.

In his eagerness to be free of the siege, the messenger was already halfway to the gates. Will pushed through a crowd that would not yield to him. They knew he was there, but would not move.

It hadn't been like this when he and the general (along with poor Stewart) had first got to Khartoum. The same crowd had been there, but much fatter. In the bustling bazaar beys and pashas had passed through on donkeys, while slaves had strolled the booths, bargaining for fruit, fish, meat and firewood and a man had been as likely to come upon a dromedary or a serpent-charmer, as a cow waiting for slaughter. As for their welcome, there'd been bands playing, soldiers saluting, crowds waving and officials jostling with each to be the first to bow before, and kiss, the general, all culminating in a celebration, the like of whose jubilation Will had never seen. Now all that was left was a crowd whose breath stank from hunger and whose faces expressed their resentment of the general.

"Wait." Will's breath was coming hard.

The messenger was almost running.

"Wait." With one last effort, Will lunged forward, forcing the man to stop. He beckoned to a guard. "I need an interpreter. Savvy? Someone who speaks English." Then, seeing the guard's hesitation, he shouted, "Chop chop, man, chop chop," and the guard reacted to the familiar phrase as if it had issued from the mouth of the Great One himself.

When the interpreter joined them, Will drew himself up haughtily and, in the manner of the general, said, "Translate what I have to say to this messenger." He told the messenger that he must say to the first British officer he encountered that the game in Khartoum was almost up. "Understand? You tell them we are nearly overrun." He was careful to use his general's speech patterns, padding what he said with facts and figures about the lack of food and fighting troops, and the size of the enemy encampment. How accurately his words were translated and how many the messenger took in, he could not know. The man nodded and smiled, but Will knew that nods and smiles didn't hold the same meaning as they did at home.

Anxious to be gone, the messenger shifted from foot to foot. When Will dismissed him, he was off and through the gates.

There went their only hope.

It wasn't much of a hope. First: the messenger had to find the British Army. Next, he had to remember enough of what he'd been told to repeat it, and if he did that, they had to believe a native who didn't speak the lingo and whose words were in direct contradiction of a note written in the general's hand. Finally, in the unlikely event that they believed him, they still had to reach Khartoum in time.

Will turned away from the man's retreating back.

Which was when he saw the general. He must have followed Will and had been standing close enough to hear Will's instructions to the messenger. Will looked at the general. The general looked back. Will had contravened his authority, and all Gordon could do was look at him?

A shadow crossed over him. He shivered. Not one shadow but many, moving fast, flitting across the dusty ground.

"Hawks," the general said.

Looking up, Will saw a flock of birds flying over the plain blue sky so that the white glare of a midday sun cast their shadows on the ground. They were moving so fast that no sooner had he glimpsed them than they were gone.

"They are destined to pick out my eyes," the general said, "for I fear I was not the best of sons." He smiled, broad and wide, as if he were not standing in the dustbowl of his ambition, waiting helplessly to have his head cut off. "Don't look so down in the mouth, Will," he said. "Our situation could be worse. According to Herodotus, Psammetichus besieged Ashdod for twenty-nine years."

Such words the general used — they defeated Will. He thought of what he had read in the journal that was even now steaming with the *Bordeen* away from Khartoum. "Now MARK THIS" — these were almost the general's last written words — "if the Expeditionary Force, and I ask for no more than 200 men, does not come in 10 days, the town may fall." After that he had added, "I have done my best for the honour of our country" and "Goodbye", and his name: "C. G. Gordon."

The same C. G. Gordon who had talked of a siege that had lasted twenty-nine years.

TO THE EDITOR OF THE TIMES

Sir, — Mr Stead threatens to rally the Public to depose Mr Gladstone should General Gordon fall.

Leaving aside a growing concern that Mr Stead's hat may no longer fit his head, I would remind your readers that Mr Gladstone's reluctance to send a force to the Soudan was based on a legitimate anxiety that an invasion would set in train a war of conquest against a people struggling to be free. And yes, as Mr Gladstone told the House, the Soudanese are a people rightfully struggling to be free.

Even General Gordon has conceded that Egyptian rule in the Soudan was heinous. Yet by keeping the Chosen Mahdi from the gates of Khartoum, he now supports the Egyptian bashi-bazouks who, under the guise of tax collection, have laid waste to that unfortunate country.

I bear no ill will towards the general. If he can be rescued without harm to others then we should rescue him. What we must not do is count the fate of one man more highly than the fate of an entire nation, and only because that one man happens to have been born an Englishman.

I remain, sir, yours obediently,

16 Dec.   A. BARTHOLOMEW

CHAPTER
FIVE

Mary was on her way downstairs when she heard a hansom draw up outside the house. Idle curiosity caused her to pause at the hall window and look out.

The cab was directly outside her gate. Although she didn't recognize the man helping out his female companion, the woman was an acquaintance. Mrs Ferguson, Mary thought. That busybody. What can have brought her here?

The man glanced up, and the biting glare of grey eyes seemed to run through her like a chill. She drew quickly out of sight. Then she remembered her resolution.

"Betty!" she called, her heart thumping. "Betty! There are visitors at the door."

"Gordon will be saved." Although he was not a particularly large man, there was something so energetic about Mr Stead that he seemed about to burst out of the armchair into which he had reluctantly sunk. His voice, booming from behind a thick brown beard, was as full of confidence as his words. "This I can guarantee."

Mary nodded, as if she was agreeing, although in fact she was trying to work out why the renowned journalist William Stead, whose recent correspondence in *The Times* had so puzzled her, would visit her.

"But tell me, Mrs Clarke," she heard, "what news of your husband?"

"It is more than two weeks, Mr Stead, since I last received a letter from John." Was it because she had grown unaccustomed to company that she felt so wrong-footed? Or was it that the rising of Mrs Ferguson's feathery eyebrows seemed to confirm her own embarrassment at John's silence?

"An understandable delay. It would have been quite a dash for him to catch up with General Wolseley's relief expedition in Korti."

"A dash?" She frowned and corrected him: "John has been gone a full three months."

When William Stead smiled, the hard red line of his tight lips lifted clear of his beard. "We live in a small, populous island, Mrs Clarke, with the most advanced forms of transport. The Sudan — it means the black country — is a vast region, stretching south of Egypt all the way to the equator. It is through hundreds of miles of this inhospitable territory that your husband must journey before he can join Wolseley."

"And there are those dreadful cataracts." Mrs Ferguson's thin voice always scratched at the upper register. "From the etchings in the *Illustrated London News*, they do appear formidable."

"Indeed they are. Some sections of the Nile are so treacherous that boats must be dragged by native rope from the shore."

Mary swallowed.

"If not for General Wolseley's foresight in engaging experienced Canadian *voyageurs*, I doubt our forces would have got even as far as they have."

She was thirsty, as her visitors must be.

"Your husband . . ." she heard.

Her fingernails, she noted, were nicely pearled.

". . . would no doubt have written as soon as he reached Wolseley's base in Korti. Taking into account the difficulties of the mail, by the time his letter reaches you, he will already have moved on with his battalion."

"Oh, no." There was a small hand bell on a nearby table. "John is not a military surgeon. He will not be assigned a battalion." She picked up the bell and flicked her wrist twice, causing it to sound sharply. "He is a temporary staff surgeon. He will treat illness and injury but not on the forward lines."

"Ah." Mr Stead's pale grey eyes were impassive. Mary couldn't help thinking he was looking through, rather than at, her. "But *if* your husband were to join a battalion," he said, "he would be well protected."

If: was there something in his emphasis?

"Our troops fight in a square, with the medical corps at its centre. No enemy on earth, especially one as primitive as the Dervish, could break a British square."

Mary gave the bell another impatient shake and, in the narrowing of Mrs Ferguson's beady eyes, read disapproval of her disorganized household.

"And what of your husband's practice in Wimpole Street?"

"A colleague of John's, awaiting a board appointment to the Middlesex Hospital, has kindly agreed to act as caretaker."

"That must lessen Dr Clarke's burden."

Had John been burdened? It hadn't seemed so to her. But, then, perhaps he had tried to spare her. Turning away from her visitors' inquisitive eyes, she looked out of the window. How pale the winter light was, not like where John must be. She saw how the colour had leached from the sky. It would soon be dark. And still they'd had no tea.

"In the manner of the Atrocitarians . . ." she heard.

A skip in the conversation. A dislocation in time. The kind that increasingly overcame her. She must go to Betty. She made as if to rise.

"Stay with us, Mrs Clarke," Mrs Ferguson's high-pitched tones rooted Mary to her seat, "so that we might share with you the reason for our visit."

"The reason?"

"We are exposed, Mrs Clarke." This from William Stead. "Although our support is heartfelt, we are here on a different mission."

"A mission?" She sounded like a parrot.

"We came to ask for your help in our campaign to save General Gordon."

"Of course." She spoke clearly enough even as she registered the welling of the inner disturbance that often overcame her these days and not at moments of her choosing.

She wanted more than anything to leave the room and . . . no — she could feel Mrs Ferguson's beady gaze on her . . . she must not think of that. "I don't see what I can do." Would they notice the tremor in her voice?

William Stead, at least, seemed to register nothing out of kilter. "We are planning a movement, Mrs Clarke. A campaign modelled on Mr Gladstone's successful agitation against the Bulgarian atrocities. I was one of the prime minister's supporters during his Midlothian campaign when he enlisted the public's outrage to right a terrible injustice."

"What a fine role you played there, Mr Stead," Mrs Ferguson trilled.

"You are too kind, Mrs Ferguson, and we must give credit where credit is due. Mr Gladstone led that charge. Which makes his foot-dragging on the matter of General Gordon all the more incomprehensible."

"Indeed it does!"

How Mary disliked the sanctimonious Mrs Ferguson with her gushing interruptions.

"Our intention is to recruit the public's indignation — as the prime minister once recruited it — against the abandonment of General Gordon. We will strengthen the hand of our allies in the Cabinet so that they might do everything in their power to ward off the general's capture or, even more unthinkable, his death. It is in the service of this noble campaign that we have come to recruit you. We need you, Mrs Clarke."

What she needed was a moment to calm herself. "Of course." She got up. "I'd be happy to subscribe. If you'll excuse me, I'll fetch my purse."

She took a step in the direction of the door.

Mr Stead was also on his feet and, although his expression was bland, he had positioned himself in such a way that, should she carry on, she would walk into him. "No, Mrs Clarke, it is not a subscription we seek." The sinews on his stout neck bulged, suggesting that should she try to bypass him he would likewise match this move.

"Although we would not refuse one." This, accompanied by Mrs Ferguson's tinkling laugh, Mr Stead ignored.

Mary was trapped.

"I am preparing a pamphlet on Gordon's plight," he was saying, "in the manner of the Bulgarian pamphlet. It would be greatly enhanced by the inclusion of short extracts from your husband's letters."

Ah. Mary exhaled. Since John's letters had been disappointingly impersonal, she could see no objection to her visitor publishing them.

"That, at least," Mr Stead continued, "was my original idea. Since then, however, I have had a better one. We must hear from you."

"From me?" Her alarm was evident to them all. "What could I say?"

"Everything, Mrs Clarke. Or, at least, everything important."

"But I am not important."

"On the contrary. The view of a loyal wife, such as yourself, on the high motives that led Dr Clarke to take part in this mission of mercy would stir the public imagination."

"But, Mr Stead —"

When he held up a hand, she couldn't help registering how creased and mottled its flesh was, and she couldn't help feeling that, in his undiminished enthusiasm, something about him made her recoil.

"I understand your reticence, Mrs Clarke. You are un-accustomed to the limelight. But think of your husband and how he must be counting on your support."

"Indeed — but what can I do?"

"A great deal, Mrs Clarke. A great deal. My lengthy — and I hope you won't think it immodest if I add successful — apprenticeship as a newspaperman has taught me the power of ordinary stories to stir the imagination. Your thoughts, your words and your sweet support would speak directly to the people on whose support your husband, and men like him, depend. All you would need do is answer a few questions. My pen would accomplish the rest."

She tried again: "I don't think —"

"Forgive me for interrupting, Mrs Clarke, but if I may continue? We will also be organizing a series of public meetings to counter the impression that certain members of the Anti-Slavery Society have misguidedly formed of the general. It would add immeasurably to our platform if you would consent to lend us your presence."

"In public?" Mary's heart skittered.

"Yes, indeed, Mrs Clarke. In public and on a platform. At my right hand."

Such a strange request. She could not take it seriously.

The fire, she saw, was burning low. Betty must bring more coal.

"You must excuse me." The strength of her anxiety gave her the courage to brush past him. "I will go and fetch the tea."

As she opened the door for her maid, and followed her into the room, Mary took pleasure in the tray Betty had prepared.

With its white fringed shawl, the silverware polished to an unblemished shine, the bone-china teacups, the tea cosy, the sugar tongs, the milk in a small jug, it was lovely. As for the cake stand, it bore more sandwiches and slices of cake than any three people, even if they were starving, could possibly have eaten, and there was also a chafing dish, with hot buttered crumpets. True, Betty did have an awkward way of going about things, and she placed the tray down rather clumsily, but the sound of cups rattling did not seem to disturb her visitors.

Mr Stead had his back to them. His pent-up energy must have launched him across the room, dodging the large centre table and the silk-covered chairs, to the window where he was now standing by the birdcage. "It was Evelyn Baring's opinion that the Sudan needed to be evacuated," he was swinging his arms as he spoke, "and since Baring is Her Majesty's representative in Egypt, and Gordon her loyal subject, Gordon did his utmost to fall in with this plan. But there are good intentions, and there are events as they unfold."

"How lovely this looks," Mrs Ferguson chirped.

"We had to relieve Kandahar before we evacuated Afghanistan. We may now have to relieve Khartoum before we evacuate the Sudan."

His arms were so frenetic that Mary thought he would knock the birdcage off its hook. And, yes, one hand did catch the edge and set it swinging. She started forward but there was no need; he braked the motion of the cage. "If we relieve Khartoum, our forces could drive the Mahdi back to his base in Kordofan."

Although she still had no idea whether or not what he was saying was true, she no longer cared. She would give them tea, she thought, then find a way to get rid of them.

"This bird, Mrs Clarke," Mr Stead was looking at the canary, "has it been long in your possession?"

"A few months. It was a present from John."

"Pleasant company for you, I am sure."

"He doesn't sing."

"You feed him with your own hand, and when you do, you comfort him, stroke his soft breast, do you not?

She nodded.

"But if you were to unlatch this gilded door and carry the cage to an open window, the bird, no matter how much he has valued your womanly soothing, would fly away. That is in his nature." He pushed a stout finger through the bars of the cage.

Mary felt an echo of her earlier reaction to his fleshy hands. She shivered.

Withdrawing the finger, he said, "General Gordon is also caged, in Khartoum, and without a loving woman to tend him. But what sets the general apart from this canary, as well as from any other bird or beast, is that were you to open the door to his cage, he would not fly away. The general is pure nobility, not only of breeding but, more importantly, of purpose. In telegrams and messages smuggled out of his imprisoned city, he has made it clear that he will not leave until every man, no matter how humble his station, who has expressed a desire to be free of the Sudan, may also leave."

Gordon again, Mary thought angrily. Would he not stop? She felt rising inside her the annihilation of what she was, and what she said, and feeling this she heard herself say loudly: "My bird never sings."

He frowned. Mrs Ferguson stirred uneasily in her chair.

John's right, she thought. There is something wrong with me. And now her visitors knew it. She felt embarrassment rouging her cheeks. She looked down.

"Perhaps the bird doesn't wish to sing." Mr Stead sounded sanguine.

"Why would he not?"

"He will. Give him time and he will." He smiled sweetly, making Mary realize he was an essentially kind man. Her overwrought imagination had led her to misjudge him.

"But, you, Mrs Clarke," he said, "you do not have the same luxury of choice. You are not a canary. You are a woman whose husband is risking all for his country. Please, Mrs Clarke, consider my request."

He was gazing at her so intently that he made her feel quite small. Is this, she thought, how his hero General Gordon — whose bright blue eyes were legendary — looked at those he commanded?

"Your presence would add greatly to the strength of our platform."

The fire was low, Mary thought: she should have asked Betty to put on more coal.

"Gordon cannot be described by any formula," Stead was saying. "He must be classed by himself as one whose life is dominated by the principles of Thomas à Kempis. He was due to give me his copy of *The Imitation of Christ*, you know. I would have numbered it among my most valuable possessions."

"Milk?" she asked.

When he nodded, a gesture that the watchful Mrs Ferguson aped, Mary carefully poured milk into the cups, then tea. The laudanum she had taken had begun to work its magic. She'd been right to leave the room when she did. Now that she was back, and the drug was settling in her, she felt as if she had come home.

"As leaders of the world," she heard, "we British have had to assume responsibility for Egypt's commitments in the Sudan."

"Sugar?" she asked.

Mrs Ferguson declined, while Mr Stead confessed to a sweet tooth and a liking for three lumps, which Mary supplied. She could feel the hard cold grip of the tongs in her fingers. She watched her hand transferring the sugar to his cup. Everything careful if a little slow.

When Mr Stead came to take it from her, she walked past him, and took his place at the window.

"For the sake of British honour," his voice was distant now, "Gordon agreed to rescue the Egyptian garrisons from almost certain death."

Her beautiful canary — how kind John had been to give it to her. She put a finger through the bars of the cage. The bird had, at last, grown used to her. It did not shy away. When she began to stroke its soft yellow neck, it leaned into her touch. She could feel the pulse of its tiny heart.

"For the good of the Empire," she heard, "and to preserve our reputation for honour, which is, justly, second to none, we had no choice but to intervene."

She thought, Yes, for the sake of British honour, and for his own, John had had to follow.

It was not as late as she had previously assumed. The sun was only now going down.

How fresh and sparkling everything looked. The bare branches of the beech were filigreed with ice that shone through the tawny moss grey of branch and trunk. She saw how the falling rays of the sun had pinked the last of the snow, as if the tree was sealing itself until spring revived it.

And then, below the outstretched branches, something peculiar. A vision that she knew could not exist and that, somehow, she had created in her mind. A boat. Almost a rowing boat, but larger than any she had seen and hooded as no rowing boat ever was. In her garden. Impossible. And there was something else. Some strange animal on the boat? If she concentrated hard

74

enough she might be able to identify it. If she stood long enough it would shape itself to her vision, would answer the question it posed without her having to try too hard. Except . . . She didn't have to work everything out. She could merely let things be. She breathed in and then out, in a long satisfied sigh. Her limbs were heavy but not unpleasantly so. She felt herself . . . She felt herself so right, so cocooned in the company of her visitors.

"We have imposed on you, Mrs Clarke, for too long," she heard Mr Stead say. "This being, in my view, the most important issue of our time, I may have pressed too hard. I understand, of course, your refusal and I —"

She turned. "On the contrary, Mr Stead, I have no intention of refusing your request." She had not meant to say this, but it felt completely natural, particularly when she added, "I will do as you ask. I will attend your meeting. I will sit on the platform beside you and, in that way, I will lend my support to my brave John."

TO THE EDITOR OF THE TIMES

Sir, — Your readers will have been amused by Mr Bartholomew's outlandish rendering of recent history. In particular, they will have been entertained by Mr Bartholomew's description of the Mahdi as Chosen.

The false prophet, Muhammad Ahmed, declared himself the Mahdi, and presumed ruler of the Soudan, without election. He is backed by his right-hand man, the brutal Abdullahi, who supports the so-called Mahdi so as to smooth his own path to power.

General Gordon has treated the Mahdi to every courtesy. Once in Khartoum, he sent greetings along with the gift of a ceremonial tarboosh and an offer to appoint Muhammad Ahmed Governor of Kordofan. The so-called Mahdi replied by dispatch of a filthy Dervish coat which, had the general accepted it, would have made Gordon his subject.

From the outset, General Gordon made it clear that he did not want charge of the Soudan. Having found that there could be no reasoning with the Mahdi, he requested the installation of a Soudanese official in his place. This was refused.

What choice was left to an honourable man other than to share the fate of the men whom he had gone to rescue? It is for this reason that honour demands that General Gordon be rescued, no matter the cost.

I and others will not rest until this has happened. I am therefore pleased to announce that we will be holding a series of country-wide Public meetings. We are honoured to be joined on our platform by the wives of some of our brave men presently risking their lives for the sake of England's honour.

I am, yours faithfully,

18 Dec. W. T. STEAD

CHAPTER
SIX

Dear John . . .

The gas chandelier lit the ceiling more effectively than it did the desk. As Mary's hand moved across the paper it created dark shadows. She pulled the oil lamp closer and read what she had written.

Dear John . . . No, that would not do. She took up a fresh piece of paper and dipped her pen into the ink.

My dearest John . . .

Her dearest John. She put down her pen.

The library, with its red walls, its flickering fire, its tables piled with books, its leather-bound collection on the shelves, and its polished desk on which she kept her ledgers, had once been her favourite room. She had liked to sit there in the early evening doing the household accounts, one ear open for her husband who, on his return, would always come to join her. And after supper, especially on cold nights, they would wander back to the library and settle themselves on the embroidered chairs at either side of the fire, sometimes to talk, sometimes to read or, in her case, to sew, and sometimes just to enjoy each other's silent companionship.

That had once been their routine. But after John had opened his Wimpole Street consulting rooms and run them alongside home visits and attendance at the poorhouse, he had come home so exhausted that he had sunk into a chair in the drawing room where he would stay until supper time. If, after eating, they had retired to the library, he had made straight for the desk. He was an ambitious man, determined to keep up with all the latest developments. He would read scientific papers and write notes with such concentration that it was as if he had forgotten her existence until such time, that is, that he had raised his head to tell her he must go to bed.

Was this, she thought, why the library no longer afforded her much pleasure? Because it stood as a symbol for her growing comprehension that in John's life there were things more important than her? Or was it just that her tastes had changed?

When they were first married, she had taken such satisfaction from the framed pictures of her favourite flowers, the stuffed birds under their glass domes, the bust of Admiral Lord Nelson, the collection of different paperweights that stood beside it, the roses made of shells, and the ornamental glass. She'd spent hours placing and re-placing them until each was in the perfect position. Now the sheer weight of these things seemed overwrought — they even crowded out the thoughts she had planned to write to John.

Their possessions closed in on her, worsening her claustrophobia. And Betty had banked the fire too high. The room was far too hot. She was suffocating.

She could not bear it. Not for a moment longer.

* ★ ★

It was terribly cold in the dispensary. She pulled down the sleeves of her blouse and ruffled the line of her high collar. At least she was calmer, more capable of thought.

She would go back to the library and complete her letter. She knew now what she would write: she would tell John about William Stead's interview with her (it had gone, so Mr Stead had told her, awfully well) and then she would share with him her apprehension at having to appear on a public platform. That was what she had originally planned to write, but somehow she had mislaid the intention. How fortunate that she had left the library. She could go back now and write her letter.

She took a step deeper into the dispensary.

No. This was not what she meant to do. Not every night. Or, at least, not tonight. She was sleepy. She would write her letter, then slip easily into bed. No need.

The voice that said, "No need," was wrong. She could feel the need building. And she would address it.

What harm? she thought. What harm?

She was in her skin and, at the same time, out of her body. Seeing herself from on high, so neatly dressed, a strand of brown hair free of its ribbon and softening her forehead. She could hear her own quickened breaths and the rustle of her skirt as she went to the imposing mahogany cabinet that stood against one wall.

Her mind was made up. Had been long before she could acknowledge it. She would take a draught of laudanum, just a small one. It would help her write and it would help her sleep. Tomorrow she would forgo the pleasure if only to prove that she could.

She withdrew the small key from her skirt pocket, slipped it into the lock and unlatched the top doors, which also freed the wide set of drawers below them.

She pulled open the second drawer and took out the small box. Another key — she had that as well — opened the box and there it was, resting snugly in its carved slot, the bottle containing the tincture of opium.

It wasn't long since laudanum had been commonly prescribed against cholera and dysentery, for earache, stomach cramp and flatulence, as well as being included in many patent medicines. John had given it to her when she was agitated, and had even left her some. He was a doctor. He knew what he was doing. He had just not realized that he would be gone for so long or he would have left her more. How could there be any harm in helping herself?

It being rather late in the evening, she would take only a small amount. Enough to help her sleep. And write. She tilted the bottle this way and that.

To her annoyance, the tilting produced only the faintest ripple. So faint she might have imagined it. She uncorked the stopper. A drop but not enough.

Something fluttered inside her — the familiar bodily rebellion of which, once she let it out, she might easily lose control. There was an experiment John had shown her: the kicking of a frog as a result of what he had called electrical animation. Except, in this case, she had become the frog with her animation the beginning of despair. She couldn't manage without the security of knowing there was enough laudanum, should it be required.

She didn't need it all the time. But . . .

If she hadn't had so much trouble composing a simple letter.

If she hadn't thought to leave the library.

If she wasn't so alone.

If John hadn't gone.

Now all of this had happened. There was no going back.

She would not be defeated. If the tincture was finished she would have to make her own. She had watched him do it often enough. She knew how.

From the cupboard she drew out a bottle. She took a vial — John was so neat, everything in its rightful place — and poured a little brandy into it. Not too much, for she remembered John telling her that excess alcohol caused excess stimulation, which wouldn't do: she wanted to sleep. Carefully, she weighed out a few grains of powdered opium, then added them to the brandy.

Last step: agitate. That was what John did. So that was what Mary did. She agitated so that she might stop her agitation.

She could not stay in bed a moment longer. She lit a candle and got up, put on her dressing gown and left the bedroom.

A floorboard creaked. She stopped. The house was so quiet it seemed to be holding its breath.

The thought that a house might breathe made her laugh, and the sound of her laughter made her laugh the more. Too loud. She stopped herself laughing, saying, "Sssh." She laid a finger over her lips as if someone was there for her to quieten. "Which there is," she said. "There's me." Then, realizing she had spoken aloud, she wagged the same finger in reproof.

She was in such a happy mood. She wished there was someone with whom she could share it. Betty was there, of course, tucked up in bed, but Betty would not do, not even for the entertainment to be gleaned from her startled face "That would be cruel," Mary said, hearing herself saying it.

It was probably better not to stand on the stairs talking to herself. She would go downstairs and choose a room, any room, go in and close the door. Then, if she was driven into translating further thought into speech, she was less likely to disturb Betty.

Down she went, tripping lightly to the drawing room.

The fire had burned itself out and the room was very cold. She considered clearing the grate, laying the fire and lighting it — Betty would be surprised to find it blazing in the morning — but the thought wandered away and by the time it came back to claim her, she was no longer so cold.

For a while all she did was roam the room picking up objects, examining them, then putting them down. It was an interesting enough activity as long as she was engaged in it, but it palled. What next?

She wished there was someone with whom she could hold a conversation.

She wondered whether the canary was ever lonely. Of course. She could talk to it.

Picking up a lit candle, she made her way to the cage. She took away the material with which, nightly, Betty covered it. Even in the dim candlelight she could see the bird perched on one leg, curled up, with its head tucked in. Such a delightful sight. So sweet a ball of fluff. How kind of John to present her with it. She poked a finger through the bars. The canary gave a little shake, then folded itself into an even tighter ball. "Wake up," she said.

The bird did not move.

"Wake up," she said again, louder. She poked the canary hard enough to knock it off its perch. It righted itself, shook its feathers and blinked furiously. The sight amused her — or she thought it had. She gave a laugh, but it sounded more like a sob.

She remembered then what William Stead had said about the canary. About its flying away when General Gordon would not. She checked and, yes, the door to the room was closed, the curtains drawn. She opened the cage. "Come." Her voice was gentle. "Come out and explore." The bird backed away. When she put in a finger to coax it, it backed away even further. It was, she saw, still half asleep. She remembered how, instructing her on its care, John had told her that canaries liked their sleep and needed it: it was cruel to disrupt it. "I'm sorry." She closed the door and re-covered the cage.

The room seemed hot, crowded and uncomfortable. She was the one who was truly caged. By the house. By its emptiness, and John's absence. By the barrenness of her life. She was seized by the urge to escape its confinement. She needed to get out.

She stood at the open front door. The night was still, the moon high and round. It cast an eerie white light over the garden and the street. The air was cold and sharp — her breath would be coming out as steam. How clean it felt. How clear. She ached to step outside. To go over the mat and down the path, through the gate and — even in her dressing gown — on. She yearned to walk where her fancy took her and for as long as she wanted. To stop only when she was inclined to do so, without regard to what anybody might think. She imagined herself doing it — yes, there she went: she could see herself going down the path and into the street, rounding the corner, and then she was gone, perhaps, and this she thought with elation, never to return. She was going to do it. She was.

In that moment of her certainty a great chattering seemed to rise. Voices that filled her head. John's, Betty's, her parents', the neighbours' and, above them, William Stead's forbidding her to step out. She heard them ringing: a united chorus of condemnation that seemed real.

Once, as a girl in the country, she would have stepped out. Now the prospect scared her.

She went inside. She closed the door. She was defeated. Like the canary, she would not leave her cage. And, like the canary, what she needed, more than anything, was sleep.

More laudanum. And then . . . to bed.

★ ★ ★

My dear Mary . . .

The flickering lantern on John's table made it hard for him to see his paper.

It was cold outside his tent. He pulled his borrowed great-coat tighter.

My dear Mary, he wrote, the repetition of the greeting pleasing him enough to continue: *It is certainly strange to be so far away from home*. And not easy, although he didn't write this. He didn't want to worry her. She'd not wanted him to leave — he'd known that even though she'd not said as much — but he had felt compelled to follow his desire. He shouldn't further burden her by telling her his troubles. And, besides, he would soon acclimatize.

Everything is so very different here, he wrote, *and that includes the practice of my profession* . . .

Too serious. He'd begin again. He'd write not about his difficulties but about the countryside. Mary, being country-bred and not widely travelled, would be interested in that.

He looked out at the encampment. The glittering of distant fires and lanterns made it seem festive, which was fitting, so close to Christmas.

That gave him an idea. He'd write about the view, about the magical elements in such a vast gathering of men. And he'd write about what he could hear — the murmuring of the men, the creaking of the camels' harness, and the reassuring tread of sentries on the perimeter sands. He could even write about the Egyptian contingent — that would surely amuse her: they spent the whole night calling to each other.

"Number one, all's well," they'd call, and the next, "Number two, all's well," and on until they reached the last (number thirty-six) when they'd start the sequence again, this comforting litany sending John to sleep and buoying his dreams.

My dear, dear Mary, he wrote. *This is a harsh land, but at night it is truly beautiful.* Next sentence. He would describe the sense of space he felt, and the huge immensity of the heavens. He would say —

A footfall. Slightly ashamed of his relief, he looked up.

How quickly and how quietly that stolid figure, silhouetted against the lamp, had arrived. "Tom?"

"The colonel's still at supper. Can you come?"

"Of course. Let me fetch my bag."

The patient had one leg tied up in a lint roller.

"A camel kick did for him," Tom said, "but there's something else not right."

Even by the dim light of flickering kerosene John could see the man's skin was pasty and slick with sweat. Gently he lifted the blanket off the affected limb — not gently enough to stop the man shouting out.

"I'm sorry, old man, I'll try to be more careful," he said, and then to Tom: "How long has he been like this?

"He came on bad a few hours after the colonel set the fracture."

"Was carbolic used to clean the wound?"

"That it was. The colonel fair ladled it on."

Which, judging by the white deadness of a vast patch of skin, was true.

"We could none of us catch our breath."

"Pass me my bag." The area around the roller was inflamed and hot to the touch. John took his stethoscope from its leather case, and laid the bell gently below the point of the roller.

As he had thought. "The roller is too tight. There is no pulse below the wound." On top of that, John thought, but did not say, the colonel (the bloody carelessness of the man) had applied poultices to the open wound in such a way as to stop it draining.

"Will you recommend loosening the roller?"

"Yes. And we'll get rid of these poultices too. They've done their job." John glanced up at Tom. "May I leave it to you?"

When Tom's expression didn't change, that sense of being awkwardly out of step assailed John. He should have remembered that an officer did not ask an army man to do something, he told him to do it. And he did not tell a junior to do something that would annoy the man in charge. "On second thoughts," he said. "I'll see to it." He set to, loosening the roller and retying it about the leg. When he took away the poultices the foetor was so unpleasant that it was an effort not to gag. He couldn't help glancing up at Tom, who was unmoved. Of course: a bit of purulence would never trouble an old soldier who had witnessed so much death. John patted the patient's arm. "Fetch me if he sinks any lower."

"I'll call the colonel."

Right again. This man was the colonel's patient.

"It were a complicated fracture," Tom said.

He sounded almost apologetic — and well he might, even though what had happened was not his fault. The injury that had resulted from the tremendous kick would indeed have been difficult to treat. The fracture was comminuted, the bone having broken into several pieces with one fragment penetrating the skin. But the poor patient had had the added misfortune to be treated by a doctor whose main qualities, as far as John could tell, were a combination of instinct, bravado and unarguable self-belief. The colonel was not just old school: his lack of skill in the administration of modern antisepsis technique and anaesthetics meant that if he were now to amputate he would have to excise the whole joint.

"If it deteriorates further, as I believe is more than likely, the colonel," he could not keep the anger from his voice, "will need to perform a secondary amputation. He should do this only after the suppurative stage is established and when the violence of the inflammatory symptoms and sympathetic fever has abated."

"I'll tell him so, shall I?"

Was Tom being sarcastic? John sighed. He knew better than to ask. "How's the enteric doctor?"

"Dying."

"I'll look in on him."

He sat in the dark with a candle to watch the juddering rise of the patient's hollow chest. The man's spirit was fighting a battle it could not win.

"I'm sorry," John said, not for the first time, to the unconscious man. He shifted on the little camp stool.

His words were unnecessary. The colonel had been right — there had been no other option. John had done what he had had to. If in the process he had caused a dying man some pain, well, that was in the nature of the job. He laid his hand on the man's wasted arm.

The patient was burning up. His time was almost upon him.

On countless other occasions John had sat with the dying. It was a matter of pride that he maintained the necessary distance to do this without losing sensitivity. Why then did this death feel different? Was it because the patient was a doctor? Because he was young, like John, with a wife back home? Because he was dying in a foreign country? Because John had wronged him?

"I'm sorry." The words issued involuntarily, but they were true. He *was* sorry. Not necessarily for what he'd done but because this brave young man — the men of his regiment had attested to his courage — was dying before the campaign had even half begun.

Two seconds: the man breathed in. Four: he let out his breath. Soon the pace of his breathing would accelerate. Then there would be a lengthening pause between breath and exhalation until at last what had been a man was gone.

TO THE EDITOR OF THE TIMES

Sir, — It appears from his last letter that the swelling of Mr. Stead's head may have cut off the oxygen to his brain. He seems to have forgotten that even before General Gordon reached Khartoum, the Mahdi's forces had control of Kordofan. How then could that province have been in General Gordon's gift? As to the tarboosh hat: how could this symbol of Egyptian oppression be taken as anything other than an insult?

It is a mark of the forbearance of the Mahdi, as well as testimony to the existence of a sense of humour, that he returned the compliment with a simple patchwork coat similar to that worn by himself and by his followers.

Mr Stead complains that General Gordon's suggestion as to his replacement as Governor General was refused by Her Majesty's Government. Your readers should know that the man proposed by General Gordon was none other than the notorious slave trader Zebehr Rahma Mansoor.

What an extraordinary suggestion! It was General Gordon who, during his first sojourn in the Soudan, sent Zebehr into exile in Cairo. It was General Gordon's former deputy, the Italian Romolo Gessi, who, with Gordon's full approval, killed Zebehr's son. On hearing the news of this son's demise, Gordon is even reported to have said: "Thus does God make gaps in the ranks of His enemies."

Leaving aside the question of the sanity of a man who would choose as an ally the father of a son he has had killed — and in a country where vengeance against killers of one's own clan is not merely expected but obligatory — how can an anti-slaver, as General Gordon professes to be, give charge of that unhappy country to one whose immense wealth is derived from the sale for profit of his fellow human beings? Mr Gladstone was right to veto this prospect.

Sir, yours obediently,

A. BARTHOLOMEW
Chairman, Huddersfield
Anti-Slavery Society

19 Dec.

CHAPTER
SEVEN

In the brightness of the day, the general glared at his boy. "You will not bring him."

"Yes, General, I shall."

The general continued to glare at the boy, who was no longer behaving like his boy. Will stood, nonchalant, as if he didn't care, although if the general had looked closely he would have seen how the leash was trembling in the boy's hand. The dog felt it, and looked up anxiously at his master.

"If Frankie isn't allowed, then I won't come."

"Suit yourself." The general marched off in a south-easterly direction along the bank of the Blue Nile. The boy followed with his dog.

Another peaceful day, clear and blue. Frankie pulled at the leash, straining to get to the river, after a water rodent or even, brave and foolish as he was, a crocodile. When Will restrained him, Frankie raised his head and yipped, not in anger or aggression but for the sheer joy of being outside, his mouth open in a semblance of a grin and his wiry legs jiggling up and down.

"Quiet that animal before the Dervish do." There was such a murderous expression on the general's face that Will reined Frankie in.

"That's better." The general smiled. "I trust you brought a pencil." He led the way into the arsenal.

In the darkness of the cavernous building Will wrote numbers as the general called them out: *1,042,000 rounds Remington ammunition, 364 rounds Krupp, 3,423 rounds mountain gun ammunition.* Alongside these, he noted the general's estimate of the remaining food: *402 ardebs wheat, 60,428 okes biscuit.*

Plenty of ammunition but little food. That spelt their doom. All a wily enemy — and the Mahdi was showing every sign of being that — need do was keep out of range of the general's guns and Khartoum would starve. Will looked at the general, who merely said, "To Burri."

It had been hot in the warehouse but it was even hotter out. The sand burned through the holes in Will's shoes. Dragging his feet, he followed the general along the banks of the broad Nile and to Burri Fort on the south-eastern edge of the city.

The fort was manned by a contingent of Egyptian troops. They had been sent to Sudan on punishment duty for rebellion or similar crimes and after a year of being besieged in a city they hated, and whose inhabitants hated them, the only thing keeping them at their posts was their terror at the fate that might befall them should they leave the general's protection.

They were not, however, frightened enough to keep order. There should have been a sentry on guard outside the fort. No such sentry was apparent. Even after the general called, "Rounds," no sentry appeared to demand the password, and give the reply. When he raised his voice and bellowed the word, an Egyptian officer appeared. His uniform was crumpled, as if he'd been sleeping in it, his shirt unbuttoned, his *tarboosh* askew. He executed a crooked half-salute, then turned to grin at his men, all equally dishevelled, who had come tumbling out behind him.

"These people are enough to break one's heart," the general muttered and then, to the men: "Wipe those vacuous expressions off your pug faces."

Most of them understood a little English. They scowled and muttered darkly among themselves. Will pulled Frankie closer.

A fizzing sound: an enemy shell whistled through the air. Grabbing Frankie, Will threw himself to the ground. He heard the scuffle of men scattering, then a bang as the shell exploded. No cry — no one hit — only silence, which Will withstood, holding his breath against the next incomer. Sure enough, there it was, this one so close it created its own Dervish sandstorm, sending up fragments of sharp stone to embed themselves in his leg.

"Am I to fire back?" This from the officer in charge.

Will peered up and across the distance that separated him from the general, who was still on his feet. Dust, thrown up by the impact of the shell, had settled on his polished boots. "If you dare ask again for permission to fire," the general was saying, "you're really going to catch it." There was no mistaking the menace in his voice. "Play them with the *mitrailleuse*."

His order was soon executed. Now Will could hear the fast drilling of the machine gun and the soft popping-out of spent cartridges.

The sun was at its height. Its heat cut deep into Will's bones. The hand he had run over Frankie's back and under his belly had come up dry. His dog was unhurt. "Sssh, boy." Will tried to calm him. "Sssh." He could feel the ground burning through a tear in his trousers that left his knee exposed. The dust smelt a little sour but mostly of the dryness that befits a soil in which nothing ever blooms. He could feel sand in his eyes and mouth. He bit his lip.

Rat-a-tat. The machine gun spewed out bullets, then paused as if to pay tribute to another thudding shell. Will braced himself. Everything so very bright. A drop of blood that his teeth had worked free from a blister on his shredded lips fell darkly onto the sand. The brown and yellow of his dog, now quiet beside him. The impassivity of the general's boots. A man who had no fear of death. Not like Will. He felt the fear deep inside him. Come on, he told Death. If it's going to happen, come on.

"*Allahu Akbar.*"

The chant was followed by the general's "That's enough. They're moving away their gun."

It was their time for prayer. Will heard it five times a day, and still he could not block it out: *Allahu Akbar* sung out four times, and then the change, *Ashadu an la illaha, Ashadu an Muhammad rasul Allah*, and against this the cheering of the general's troops, as if they'd won a victory.

From across the river, the rising of another call: *La ilaha illa-llah*. There is no God but Allah. *La ilaha illa-llah*. It swelled up into the bland blue sky.

The hot ground was a comfort to which Will cleaved. He wanted, more than anything, to keep lying there, his dog safe beside him, never to have to get up.

"Here."

The general's face loomed. In his hand, Will blinked, something white. A handkerchief. "Up you get."

There was no refusing the general — not for the first time Will registered how strong he was — and in an instant Will was on his feet. A tug, and the general had hold of Frankie's leash.

The general had been right: Will should not have brought his dog. He had endangered Frankie. He could feel the blood on his lips and the wet heat of his face. He used the general's handkerchief to wipe away the moisture.

"In the Crimea," the general had bent down to pat Frankie, "to duck in the face of fire was considered mean. In a position of command, one learned to avoid it. But there is no fault in it. On two occasions, when shells came close, I bobbed or I would have lost my head."

The consolation forced out Will's sob. He swallowed. "I was getting out of the way of our sights, General," he said. "Like you taught me to."

"If I had died in the Crimea," the general's voice was dreamy, "the Foreign Office's only comment would have been 'and good riddance'."

Will had done with the general's handkerchief. He made to hand it back.

"You can keep it."

"*La ilaha illa-llah*," Will heard. "*There is no God but Allah. There is no God but Allah . . .*" A sound that could have eaten his insides out.

"Listen to them." The general was looking at the enemy encampment. "They are not afraid to meet their Maker." His expression was full of yearning as if he ached to cross the river and join with the enemy, not only in their chanting but also in their wishes.

"Time to go." Will pitched his voice hard.

The general shook himself out of his reverie and began to walk, heading south-west, to continue to trace the perimeter line.

There is no God but Allah.

All Will could think was that he did not want to meet his Maker. He did not want to die.

From Burri Fort by the Blue Nile, they walked to the other side and the White Nile. Now they were opposite the hill where the second Dervish encampment was sited. It also being at prayers, the general was free to inspect the parapet and ditch that were Khartoum's first line of defence. The bottom of the ditch was paved, its sides a forest of spear heads, and there were crow's feet every hundred yards to stop the Dervish breaking in.

Will raised his eyes to the hill where the hostile multitude was camped.

"If they were foolish enough make a dash from there," the general said, "we would cut them down. But the Mahdi is a sophisticated strategist." He was talking as if Will was a fellow general. Will knew that he was really talking to himself. "The Mahdi will have worked out," he continued, "that we are at our most vulnerable on the flood plain." He stretched out a hand. "There, at the end of the parapet." He was pointing across the Nile at the third encampment.

"They'll press through when the river's at its lowest." The general's blue eyes seemed to mist, but what he said was, as ever, practical: "We have to keep it mined and guarded. If the wire entanglements are twenty yards in depth mixed with earth mines, only a continuous bombardment of days will destroy them."

Kneeling, Will let the dog nuzzle his face.

"Get up," the general said, "before that animal gives you a disease. We'll go to see if we can rustle up an extra portion of wheat for the Christmas meal."

TO THE EDITOR OF THE TIMES

Sir, — It is my concern for General Gordon that persuades me to answer an unreasonable correspondent who prioritizes radicalism over decency, and doctrine over reality. Even this, however, cannot persuade me indefinitely to continue. May I therefore make it clear that, no matter the provocation, this will be my last word on this matter in these pages.

Mr Bartholomew trumpets his no doubt hard-earned anti-slavery credentials as proof of his righteousness. He states, correctly, that Zebehr was once a slave trader and therefore an enemy of General Gordon who, along with Sir Samuel Baker, did more than any other man to put an end to that iniquitous trade in the Soudan. What Mr Bartholomew does not say is that, during his prolonged stay in Cairo, no further stain has attached itself to Zebehr.

General Gordon is a God-fearing man who lives by the teachings of our Lord, Jesus Christ, the first of which is forgiveness. It is General Gordon's saintliness and not a lack of sanity that led to his offering Zebehr the chance to redeem his sins by steering the Soudan to peace.

In conclusion, and this will be my last word, your readers should know that the Mahdi keeps slaves. He has gone on record saying that his religion permits this. Yours in finality,

20 Dec.   W. T. STEAD

TO THE EDITOR OF THE TIMES

Sir, — I tremble for our security now that Mr Stead has taken a vow of silence.

Who else is so supremely confident in his own judgement, he thinks he has the right to tell us not only how we should behave, but also what we should think: and this includes the choice of a hated slave trader over a popular leader to rule the unfortunate Soudan?

I remain, sir, your most bewildered, obedient servant,

A. BARTHOLOMEW
Chairman, Huddersfield
Anti-Slavery Society

22 Dec.

PART TWO

Following the mass meetings in Hyde Park and Manchester and the subsequent pouring in of subscriptions, notice is hereby given of a meeting to be held in London on Christmas Eve in aid of General Gordon. The editor of the *Pall Mall Gazette* Mr W. T. Stead will speak on the necessity of increasing funding to the mission to rescue General Gordon. Also present will be wives and representatives of General Wolseley's Gordon Rescue Expedition including Mrs John Clarke whose recent words in support of her brave husband have stirred much admiration.

Pall Mall Gazette

CHAPTER
EIGHT

The singing pulled Mary from her reverie.

While shepherds watched their flocks by night
All seated on the ground . . .

She looked out of the window of her hansom cab
and saw a group of lone women, capped or bonneted
and holding lighted candles. Above their heads, brightly
coloured halos flared out into the darkness.

The Angel of the Lord came down,
And glory shone around.

Was she imagining them?

She swallowed and her throat convulsed. Her right
hand was trembling, which seemed peculiar since the
left was perfectly still. She laid the left on top of
the right and closed her eyes. She would count to ten
and then she would open her eyes and look out. If the
women were still there, she would know that she had
not conjured them.

She counted to ten and opened her eyes. The women
were still there and so were their halos, not

supernatural but caused by fog floating through the spreading rays of gaslight. And the women were not alone. People surged past them, up a flight of broad steps and into the imposing . . .

Where was she? She'd neither followed her route, nor could remember where she was meant to be.

Blood seemed to knock against the walls of her veins, surging so fiercely she could almost feel it, dark and viscous, bulging at the fragile pulp of her pounding heart. What if it broke through?

She pulled her gloves tighter. The silk cut into the creases between her fingers.

"Mrs Clarke?" William Stead, who had appeared from nowhere, was stretching out a helping hand.

She let out her breath. "How kind of you to meet me."

"You are our most important guest." He helped her out of the cab and guided her past the singing choir towards the entrance. "There are many here anxious to make your acquaintance."

They climbed the stone steps, merging with the crowd, the draught of which seemed to pull her to and fro. Soft silks, satins, velvets and harsh calicos blurred her vision as her ears rang with hearty greetings that she couldn't quite take in.

She felt herself adrift, her most dominant thought that she did not belong here, among these people. She was seized by an urge to flee their cloying geniality, and the stench of their perfumes, which seemed to burn her nostrils, or if not to flee then to push through rudely until she had left them far behind. But Mr Stead was continually held back, not so that people might be introduced to her but so that they could win acknowledgement, and a few kind words, from him.

"What a wonderful gathering." His fleshy lips were close to her ear. "That is thanks in large measure to your contribution to our pamphlet. You have inspired them."

She nodded and kept to herself the thought that any inspiration his readers might have garnered from the interview had less to do with what she had told Stead than with the way he had embellished it. He had given resonance and solemnity to sentiments she couldn't remember expressing.

Despite Mrs Clarke's modest and womanly insistence that she could not speak for a husband who is so far away from home, it was with the greatest sympathetic animation that she described Dr Clarke's courageous decision to risk his life to defend British honour and for the good of the Soudanese people.

The article had continued, as if in her voice, to describe John's admiration for General Gordon (had John ever spoken to her of the general?), and her confidence in John's courage under fire. And this even though she had told Stead, on more than one occasion, that John had promised he would not be going into battle.

There was a bottleneck at the door. Each inadvertent push against her seemed to press the air from her. She was a hollowed thing, about to crumple in on itself.

108

"We will soon be inside." She felt the slight touch of his hand against her waist as he guided her through the doorway.

Straight into the mêlée they pressed. Such a squash. A sour heat rising. All those women, beautifully dressed in tight-fitting cuirass bodices with pleated and flounced skirts, wafted in on the arms of smart men, while others, less formally attired in loose, flowing robes, spoke loudly, all ignoring the roughly dressed working men also coming into the hall. In their midst, Mary was ill at ease in the outfit she had chosen, which she now judged to be rather too provincial and much too formal.

To think that she was going to be on the platform where they would all be staring at her! She felt the oppression of them, their voices far too loud. Sound blatted through her, a great wave of it, threatening to overwhelm her. She was aflame, her body, especially her fingertips, tingling.

"We have set aside a room where you can partake of some refreshment."

That was precisely what she needed: a moment to collect herself.

"Ah, there you are, Mrs Clarke." The officious Mrs Ferguson opened the door to Mary to reveal a room full of quietly chatting women. Not for them the fashions of the audience outside: their high-necked, neatly constrained, muted costumes proclaimed their quiet respectability and yet, as she looked at them, they seemed to bare their teeth, a snarling group of women, led by Mrs Ferguson, preparing to rip her to shreds. The sight provoked in Mary such a visceral urge to flee that she might have done so, had not Mr Stead's voice — "Ladies, may I introduce you to the courageous Mrs Clarke" — rooted her to the spot.

She closed her eyes and wished herself away. This is just a dream, she thought. Not one of the luscious waking dreams that the laudanum usually fostered, but still a dream. She breathed in, feeling her chest expand. She breathed out, letting go of her agitation. When I open my eyes, she promised herself, they will all be gone.

A soft pattering, slapping sound washed over her. It took her a moment to identify it. They were clapping.

She opened her eyes.

As Mr Stead excused himself, she looked around the room. She felt herself relax. Now she could see the women for who they were: a group of respectable matrons, sensibly dressed, who spoke in quiet tones and wanted only to make her acquaintance. The first to approach, and the others deferred to her, had soft, downy skin, big bright eyes and brown hair framing a wistful face.

"It is my privilege to introduce Mrs Josephine Butler." Mrs Ferguson was fairly bustling with pride. "You will have heard something of Mrs Butler's tremendous contribution to the plight of fallen women," reminding Mary of the admiration with which John had spoken of the brave woman who had led the successful campaign against the Contagious Diseases Act.

Such a pity he wasn't there. He would have taken such pleasure from hearing Mrs Butler complimenting him (*your valiant husband*) and also pride at her praise for the manner in which Mary had sacrificed her privacy to secure General Gordon's rescue (*not an easy step for any wife*). And this, Mary decided, was correct. Mr Stead might have elaborated on, and expanded, her answers, but an inner core of truth ran through what he had written of which she should not feel ashamed.

"How clever of Mr Stead to arrange this meeting on the night before the birth of our dear Lord," Mrs Butler was saying.

Of course. It was Christmas Eve. That was why they had been singing carols.

How could Mary have forgotten? The blood pounded in her ears, a rising inner sea.

Mrs Butler linked an arm in one of hers. "Allow me to present you to our other friends."

The waves retreated, leaving Mary beached in calm. She was a little embarrassed to have forgotten it was Christmas Eve but, she told herself, that was unimportant. She felt warm, accepted, as Mrs Butler led her round the room, effecting introductions. There was the queer, crumpled kindness of Mrs Booth who, with her husband, had founded the Salvation Army, and the portly Mrs Warrington, who gave service as a rent collector at Katherine Buildings, and her companion, the reedy Mrs James, who had opened her house to fallen women (*Mrs Clarke really must come and visit*) and more, all of them grand philanthropists. Mary had never dreamed they would trouble to listen to her, and all were so complimentary about John's dedication that she almost wished she had not extracted from him the promise not to go into battle. How they fluttered around her, these ladies, like soothing moths. She felt herself cosseted in their winged approval and by their gentle strokes.

"And here," Mrs Butler's voice cut through her languor, "is our latest recruit, Rebecca Jarrett."

The silken fabric of the security in which Mary had been enfolded was rent.

"Rebecca, this is Mrs Clarke."

It wasn't only the use of the Christian name. Rebecca Jarrett's dress, plain to the point of dowdiness, could not hide the heavy fall of her blonde hair and the confident swing of her hips, despite, or perhaps because of, her pronounced limp. Her manner, too, was different: not for her the murmured pleasantries of the other women. She didn't speak. She offered her hand, as the others had, but her grip was harder, her skin, unprotected by gloves, much rougher than theirs, and though the look she shot Mary might not have been entirely unfriendly it was searching. There was insolence in her eyes, Mary thought, and in the upturned tweak of almost indecently full red lips.

"Rebecca has recently been rescued by the Salvationists," Mrs Butler said, "and has taken temperance to her heart. We have great hope that she will be instrumental in saving other suffering Magdalens from the inequity of alcohol and the harsh life of the streets."

So that was who Rebecca was — or once had been. And yet, how strange: instead of disapproval, Mary found herself thinking of the other with a kind of fellow feeling. It was almost as if, having been introduced to Rebecca, she already knew her and liked her very much.

What would John, who had always been careful to protect her from his rougher patients, think of Mary's empathy for a fallen woman, even if the admirable Mrs Butler had made the introduction?

There was no time to pursue this line of thought. Mr Stead was back and murmuring in her ear. "Our meeting is about to begin. Let me escort you to the hall."

Ushered on to the high wide stage and seated at Mr Stead's right hand, Mary gazed down at a sea of people, several hundred of them, who, as she and the other dignitaries filed on, had fallen into respectful silence. She was discomfited by the artificial quiet and by finding herself the focus of their attention. But once Mr Stead had placed himself in the centre of the stage, and once he had silenced the pattering applause with a graceful dip of his head, her anxiety diminished.

She sat with a straight back, a smile to mirror those of her fellows, and wondered what kind of person came out on Christmas Eve to a meeting. They must, she thought, be very virtuous. And yet they looked — at least in the front ranks of corseted, bustled dresses and feathered bonnets — not so much virtuous as smug.

"While others might have despaired," Mr Stead was saying, "General Gordon, trusting to God, has not."

As the front row nodded its agreement, Mary noted several of the women she had just met. They were not smug. She berated herself. They were merely driven, as John was, by a desire to do good. Pulling back her wandering thoughts, she looked at Mr Stead, who was saying: "There is a man, known to us all, in whom hope shone as a pillar of fire after it had gone out in other men."

Cromwell, she thought, this confirmed by an echoing shout. "Cromwell."

"Cromwell indeed." Mr Stead turned over a page of his speech.

"Are you comparing Gordon to Cromwell?" This, too, issued from the back of the hall.

Mr Stead peered over the heads of the dignitaries, and Mary with him, into the hall's shadowed depths where the working men were seated.

"I am," he said, "for just as Cromwell shaped the future of our country, so Gordon guards our honour. Our connection to Suez has made the Egyptian troops in Sudan our responsibility. By saving them, Gordon rebuts the charge that England forsakes its dependants. In fact," he glanced down, as if to check that his feet were sufficiently well planted on the wooden stage, "it is as if King Arthur has come back to life, nerved with the faith of Cromwell, to serve England in the Sudan." Despite his evident determination to stand by this grandiosity, it provoked from the back a burst of laughter that wasn't entirely friendly.

Mary shifted in her seat, her restlessness mirrored in other members of the audience.

"Gordon's contribution to peace in China is well known." Although Mr Stead had raised his voice, he still sounded calm. "While superintending the fortifications of the Thames he did God's work on behalf of the guttersnipes and street Arabs of Gravesend. He will not be forgotten by those poor unfortunates who reaped the benefit of his ragged school, many of whom became sufficiently qualified for admission to the Merchant Navy."

Rising discontent was now evident in the bobbing of heads and the lifting of hands, both of which Mr Stead seemed determined to ignore. Even the people in the forward seats, who had been motionless until now, were turning to look back. "As in Gravesend," Mr Stead's raised voice summoned them, "so in Khartoum."

"Not so." A man had jumped up and was illuminated by a gas lamp. Mary could see that, contrary to her expectation, he was respectably dressed, his fawn waistcoat tightly buttoned, matched to his trousers and his jacket, while his accent suggested education. Even so, he sounded very angry. "In Gravesend," he called, "Gordon said nothing of his support for slavery. But in Khartoum his very first act was to post an order — a *firman* — permitting those who so desired to keep slaves."

Mr Stead peered across the rows. "Mr Bartholomew?"

"Why do you ask that?" Even from so far away Mary could see that the man was grimacing. "My name is not Bartholomew."

"Could be Christopher Columbus for all we care," someone shouted. "Answer the charge. Why should our troops risk their lives for a slaver?"

"Gordon is no slaver." That Mr Stead's calm had deserted him was made clear by the flush rising above his collar and up his neck.

Mary's interest quickened.

"In his first sojourn in the Sudan," his face had reddened almost to puce, "he did more than any other man to put a stop to that iniquitous trade."

"Yes, and on his second sojourn," Mr Stead's opponent was being egged on by people around him, all nodding, some offering vocal support, "he tried to install a notorious slave trader, Zebehr, as ruler of the Sudan."

Mr Stead's hands were crumpling the pages of his speech. "Having a Sudanese in charge," his voice had lost its calm, "was necessary. Zebehr was the only credible candidate."

"Shame."

"And let us not forget," Mr Stead raised his voice another notch, "the Mahdi himself uses biblical texts to justify slavery."

"Then why not name the Mahdi a Cromwell too?" This, from the back of the hall, was met by loud guffaws.

"Gentlemen." Throwing his speech down, Mr Stead held out his arms as if to embrace the audience. "Can we not debate this in a civilized manner?"

"Slavery is not civilized."

"We live in the real world, and Gordon is a realist. No matter who wins in the Sudan, the slave trade will continue."

"Shame," the cry echoed. "Shame." What had once seemed a gathering united by common purpose fractured into its disparate components: disapproval was tutted in the front ranks in tune with the censorious shaking of heads, while deeper in the hall those around their spokesman were urging him on, some with hearty claps on his back, adding to the jagged disagreement and disruption that Mary absorbed into herself. She could feel again her heart against her chest, like the fluttering of a bird, trying to get out.

"If the Mahdi wins," Mr Stead was shouting, "the Sudan will be lost to barbarism. Worse, opposition forces in Arabia and Syria will be galvanized."

"Not our business."

"If the Turks then step in, as I can assure you they will, it will become our business."

Mr Stead's thunderous statement animated his supporters, whose cries of "Hear, hear" clashed with a repeated chorus of "Not our business."

Above it Stead was shouting, "If Russia responds to Turkish intervention, there may be another war. The Empire of our beloved queen would be threatened. India — yes — if the rebellion spreads, I warn you, even India might fall."

The audience had all taken sides. From the front ranks came a rousing "Hear, hear," accompanied by demands for those at the back to hold their tongues, while from the back physical posturing seemed to threaten violence.

And there on the stage sat Mary.

Her gaze was drawn to a single woman in the middle of the front row. Unlike those around her, she was looking neither to left nor right nor the back. She was looking forwards, but not at Mr Stead now shouting, "The Mahdi is a false prophet. A fraud . . ."

Rebecca Jarrett was looking straight at Mary.

". . . who hides his evil intent behind the banner of his religion."

Meeting the other's eyes, Mary again experienced a strange sense of familiarity. It was as if she could see through Rebecca to who she really was.

Rebecca, she thought, is not who the Salvationists think she is.

"And if he is a fraud? At least he belongs to the country."

Another thought, equally clear: She knows. She knows what I am.

"Not like that madman Gordon."

She knows what I have taken.

Could Rebecca help her to buy more opium?

CHAPTER
NINE

The officers' Christmas meal had included platters piled high with eggs, chickens and orange pumpkins mashed with lashings of butter, and afterwards, double helpings of plum pudding, slightly glutinous for lack of suet, and sweet melons washed down with champagne, of which there seemed to be no end. From outside came the sound of men singing. Inside the officers' mess the conversation was raucous.

"You're almost empty, Doc." A freshly open bottle hovered into view.

"No, thank you." John laid his hand over his glass. "No more for me."

"Good man. Someone needs to keep their wits about them," John's neighbour sloshed champagne into his own glass before passing on the bottle, "to carry us to our beds." With the orderlies removing the debris of their meal, the officers settled down to some serious drinking.

Glancing along the rows of trestle tables, John thought that the men squeezed together on makeshift wooden benches were a good lot. Cheerful, accustomed to each other's company, tolerant of each other's foibles and raring to go, even as they remained patient in the face of fearsome logistical problems.

"A toast." A portly, curly-haired officer tottered to his feet. "To more camels."

The others raised high their glasses and "More camels" reverberated gustily, a lack of camels to transport food and water being the major obstacle to their venturing further into the Sudan.

"I'll drink to that. Although the day I see the back of those beasts won't be a day too soon." This sentiment was seconded by the thumping of cutlery against the wooden tabletop. A pause while more champagne did the rounds, men pushing back their chairs to give themselves more room. An officer started softly to sing a carol but, thinking better of it, let it die. Too late: it had already changed the mood.

"There'll be carols at home," someone mused, and from another: "My children will have dressed the tree."

Conversation faded as longing blunted the hard edge of drunkenness, thoughts turning to families left behind. John's as well. He wondered how Mary had spent her Christmas evening. He hoped she had been able to mute her loneliness.

The thought shifted so uneasily in him that he was relieved to see one of their number clamber to his feet. "Why so grim, chaps?"

"Hear, hear!"

"And who's holding on to the champagne?"

"More."

"More."

"To we who are going into battle."

John joined the refrain, "To us," sipping what was left in his glass as he saw his superior, Colonel Watson, rise.

"Let us not forget those who are to stay behind."

The colonel was not talking about his family. His gaze was on John, and although he was smiling there was something cold in his expression.

"Men such as our fresh-faced surgeon here," he said, "who has turned our hospital into such a beacon of modernity. When we are marching into battle, we'll be buoyed by the thought of the calm, quiet, *safe* order he has here overseen."

It dawned on John that he was being damned with faint praise. The awkward hush that resulted suggested others might be thinking something similar, but when one joined the colonel on his feet to say, "To all who remain behind the lines," the toast was so genially drunk that, if not for the colonel's sudden frown, John would have assumed he had imagined the slight.

As he made his way to his tent, John chanced upon a group of men who, lit by candle and gas, were sitting on the ground. He paused when, from their midst, a lone voice rang out: "While shepherds watched their flocks by night . . ." Except it wasn't that. The tune was the same, but the words were different.

When ten years ago I 'listed, lads,
To serve our gracious Queen,
The sergeant made me understand,
I was a Royal Marine . . .

A group of Blue Jackets was gathered around a fire that had almost burned down, their faces orange in the glowing embers as they watched the man whose angelic voice belied his comic text.

I've rode in a ship, I've rode in a boat
I've rode in a railway train
I've rode in a coach,
and I've rode a moke . . .

A pause, drawn out for dramatic effect, until the line, *And hope to ride one again* was met with wolf whistles and cheers. The man bowed low, then straightened up for his finale:

But I'm riding now an animal,
A Marine never rode before
Rigged up in spurs and pantaloons
As one of the Camel Corps.

There was an eruption of hurrahs, bottles clinked and insults from army units. John laughed with the rest until a man, spotting him, called out, "Evening, sir," provoking a silence from the group into which another's "And a very merry Christmas to you" sounded half-hearted.

As an officer, John didn't belong in their company. "Merry Christmas," he said, and moved on. As he made his way to higher ground, he could hear sergeants calling time and warning of dark punishments that would result from the failure of any man to spring up at the first note of reveille. Him as well. He should also go to bed.

With the fires mostly out, and the men in their cots, John might have imagined himself alone. But the air was so clear and dry that even the slightest sound, a man coughing, another turning restlessly, a third muttering in his sleep, as well as the endless calls of the Egyptian contingent, seemed to take place right beside him. He sealed the letter he had finally written to Mary. He looked up to the vast, hammocked web of glittering stars, so bright they seemed to bulge within touching distance. How Mary would have loved this sky, he thought.

In that moment he seemed to see her, not as she had been and probably still was, waiting in the library for his return, but that other woman. The one he knew of in another place, and — yes, he would allow the thought — the one he knew of in bed, her raven hair disordered, her eyes glinting in the darkness, her cheeks flushed with the heat of his desire and hers. He shivered. Since leaving England he had thought of her only as she had been on his departure, fighting to contain her nerves. He was now remembering the flamboyant Mary who flourished in the dark, not just in the privacy of their bedroom. She had loved to walk out at night, something they had often done in the first flush of their marriage, another activity that had ceased because he had been so drained by his work.

He missed her. Or that was what he told himself because that was what was expected. But another part of him knew he had needed to get away from her.

She had started to want too much. Not only those after-supper strolls, for which he had been far too fatigued, but also his attention. Although he had never told her so (why hurt her feelings?), the disparity between her need for conversation and his for rest had grown so great that he had had only to step over the threshold to be overwhelmed by the weight of her expectations. Even if she wasn't there to greet him, he seemed to feel her demands pulsing through the library walls. Like a spider she was waiting every evening in the same chair, if not to entrap him then to make him talk. She didn't seem to notice that he was too tired to tell her he was too tired to talk. And so he had begun to steer clear of the library, or to hold his tongue when he was with her, his exhaustion made worse by her innocent, if unspoken, accusations and the corresponding waning of his desire.

He laid the letter to one side and looked up. He saw a shadow separate itself from the darkness.

"Major Clarke?" He recognized the man as a member of General's Wolseley's staff. "The general sends his compliments and asks if you'd be kind enough to pay him a call."

Sounded like a medical matter. "Are you sure he wouldn't rather consult Colonel Watson?"

"The colonel is temporarily indisposed."

So it *was* a medical matter. And the colonel was drunk. "I'll come straight away."

"The general's private quarters." John's escort swung his lamp in the direction of the largest in a group of fenced-in tents from which floated the sound of whistling.

"He sounds cheery enough."

"Does he?" The officer pulled aside the tent's flap. "Go in, sir."

There was only one man in the spacious tent and it was Wolseley. He had his back to John but hearing his aide's "Major Clarke, sir," he turned. He was still whistling, or his lips were pursed as if poised to carry on with his merry little tune, but he looked far from cheerful.

The commanding presence of Garnet Joseph, Viscount Wolseley, who would stride out to urge on his men, or dash into the desert on a magnificent white camel, or inspect lines of troops he'd had pulled from bed for an emergency drill, was absent. In that man's place stood someone more ordinary, prematurely aged, his face almost grey in the gaslight, his shoulders stooped. Only his mind seemed sharp. Reading John's reaction, he said, "I always whistle when I am most dismayed. To hoodwink the men. Not that I think it does." He sighed and composed his face, the powerful commander taking up residence once more in his features. "I'm sorry to have called you out so late on Christmas Eve but I have little time to spare during the day. And the men must never think that there is anything wrong with their general. Not that there is much wrong. Like most military men, I'm blessed with a strong constitution. But I thank you for responding to my call. I trust you dined well?"

"Very well, sir."

"Our staff certainly did us proud. Served two fat wild geese they'd bagged during one of their forays. The meat was dark and strong. Extremely tasty." Wolseley started whistling again but then, looking guiltily at John, he stopped.

"How can I help you, General?"

"Spot of bother with my eyes."

"Are they sore?"

"They ache a bit, and they itch like the devil."

"May I examine you?" John turned the general's head towards the light before gently rolling back each eyelid in turn. "It's conjunctivitis. We've seen quite a bit of it recently. Nothing to concern us."

"Is it akin to ophthalmia?"

Some patients liked to be in the know and Wolseley had that look about him. "Ophthalmia is a disease attributable to insects and dirt," John said, "which is most often preceded by the presence of raised vesicles, called sago-grain granules, on the inside of the eyelids. None of these being present in your case, I deduce that yours is a mild irritation — conjunctivitis — caused by the ingress of sand. Bathing in cold tea will bring relief. But you should take care not to aggravate the condition. Always wear goggles outside."

"Impossible. The men must see their general's eyes."

"Then wear them when you're riding. It will set a good example to the men, who should be wearing theirs."

126

"Thank you. That is most helpful."

The words sounded like dismissal, but there was something so uncharacteristically tentative in the way they were pronounced that John did not pick up his bag. His suspicion was confirmed when Wolseley, whose self-assurance and certitude were legend, started to wander aimlessly about his tent, eventually pausing by his bedside table from which he picked up a book. As John stood waiting, Wolseley opened it. He lifted it to the lamp and read a line or two, before looking at John. "Byron," he said. "I take comfort in his work. He was eccentric but I admire his vigour. He speaks of a courage that is peculiar to man and, specifically, to the men I command. Do you read him?"

John nodded to hide his surprise and pleasure that Wolseley valued his opinion. "I find myself more drawn to Browning."

"Really? Can't stand the man. Sickly meanderings of a schoolgirl. Feminine without fibre or soul. Better one hour of Byron or Tennyson, in my opinion, even though it be criminal, than a cycle of Browning's bread-and-butter missishness." The general drew himself up as if to say he was a man accustomed to being obeyed in all things, even in his taste in poetry, which John took in his stride. The powerful were sometimes compelled to assert themselves in front of their doctors, especially if that doctor was inferior to them in station. And this man was truly powerful. With his hand-picked ring of allies, he had a reputation as such a stickler that the phrase "all Sir Garnet" had already inserted itself into the English language.

"Can I be of further assistance, General?"

"Oh, don't be such a stuffed shirt. Sit." Wolseley shoved a chair at John, nodding impatiently at him. "That's better." Wolseley also sat down, stretching out his legs. John's instinct had been right. The general wanted to talk.

"I've not had time to get to know you," Wolseley said. "I regret this, particularly since Colonel Watson speaks so highly of your work."

"I'm glad of that," John said, although he in fact was surprised.

"Not easy to be away at Christmas," Wolseley said. "You have everything you require?"

"More or less, given how far we are from civilization."

"Good, good." Wolseley drummed his fingers absently on the table. "You will let us know if there's anything more we can do to assist your work?"

"I will, thank you."

"No need to thank me." Tap, tap. "My job is to ensure that the men are well cared for." Tap, tap. Tap, tap. As if, John thought, he were tapping out a message. At the same time the uneasiness that had been evident in Wolseley's expression when John had first stepped into his tent had seeped back.

"Is something else ailing you, General?"

"Ailing me? Nothing." Wolseley's bark of laughter was so devoid of amusement that he seemed to catch his own false note. His expression softened. "Well, nothing bodily. It's the waiting. Can't abide it. Never have been able to. It's the way with us military men. Come upon us on the battlefield, bullets flying, swords

128

flashing, men dying, and you'll find us not the least perturbed. But in the anticipation of a battle . . . well, that's different. Gordon's the same. No sooner did we persuade him that he should go to Khartoum than he had to leave that very night. Went straight from Whitehall to Charing Cross. I had the privilege to carry his belongings, such as they were. If his nephew hadn't dashed up at the last minute with his uniform case, he would have gone without it. As it was, he had no money. I emptied my pockets, gave him my spare cash, my watch and chain, while Glenville did a quick whipround at the clubs." Wolseley smiled at the memory. "He raised about three hundred guineas. Came back just in time to find the Duke of Cambridge holding open the carriage door for Gordon and Stewart — poor devil, what a dreadful death his was, deceived into stopping on his way to get help and cut down by cowards — and we wished them God speed."

Wolseley's fingers were now drumming such a storm that John felt he had to say something to break the tension. "I'm sure, General . . ."

Wolseley's fingers stopped mid-tap. "Hush."

Then John heard what the general had already registered — the heavy huff of a hard-breathing camel.

"I wonder," Wolseley said, and John seemed to see hope in his expression, battling with the fear of bad news.

They could hear the creak of a saddle and the phlegmy, grunted instruction that Arab drivers used to their animals, someone pulling the camel to its knees so

129

its rider could dismount. Next came the sound of feet padding across sand.

"Come." Wolseley was on his feet before his tent flap had shivered.

A gaunt officer, dust-covered from head to toe, entered, saluted and held out a tiny piece of paper. "From General Gordon, sir."

"At last." Wolseley strode over to take it. "At last." In a flash, he had it open. He read what was written there and then said, "Everything all right." His apprehension seemed visibly to melt away. "This is good news." He looked up, smiling, at John. "It means we still have time on our side."

Out of the corner of his eye, John saw that the officer was shifting uneasily.

Wolseley did not appear to notice. "Champagne, I think. Call my orderly, will you?" John nodded and began to get up but Wolseley snapped, "Not you. The major here." He whirled round to face the man. "Either that, or tell me what's on your mind. Be quick about it."

The officer took a deep breath. "It's the messenger, sir."

"What about him?"

"It's odd, sir, what he told us."

"Do you doubt the provenance of his message?"

"Not that, sir. We are satisfied it was given him by General Gordon. The seal confirms it."

"But?" Wolseley stamped his boot down so hard that the whole tent shook.

"It's the story he had to tell us, sir. He speaks no English, nor has he had much education, so it took some time to extract a clear account from him. But the essence of what he has to say is that there is no food in Khartoum."

"That's no surprise."

"No, sir. We already suspected it. But, according to the messenger, and he was very insistent on this, the situation is worse than we have so far assumed. He says the city is in imminent danger of falling. He was fairly specific. I'd go so far as to say that he insisted on it."

"But this says: 'Everything all right.' " Wolseley waved the paper in his officer's face. "As clear as day. And written in Gordon's hand."

"I know, sir."

"Do you think the messenger is lying?"

"That was our initial conclusion, sir, but when we questioned him further he was equipped with facts and figures. Told us, down to a fraction of an *ardeb*, how much food remains, as well as the numbers of enemy massing at the gates."

A fleeting uncertainty passed across Wolseley's face and when he said, "It would be just like Gordon to have thoroughly briefed his messenger," it was almost as if he were trying to convince himself.

"Indeed it would, sir. But the rum thing is that the man insists the figures were supplied to him not by General Gordon but by the general's batman."

"What batman?"

"Precisely, sir. None that we know of. But the messenger, no matter how we cross-questioned him, stuck to his story. He said General Gordon was watching from a short distance away while his batman supplied the figures."

"What do I care," Wolseley barked, "whether Gordon supplied the details personally, or permitted someone else — who has awarded himself batman status — to do so? What I want to know is this: in your opinion, and don't beat about the bush, is this messenger telling the truth?"

"Yes, sir. Our interpreter agrees. He knows the man. Says he doesn't have the wit to invent such a complicated story. He added that General Gordon does a regular inventory of stores and ammunition."

"As Gordon would." Wolseley glared down at the piece of paper. "But why would he write that everything was all right?" There was a long pause. "Could the messenger have been intercepted by the Mahdi and fed this contradictory nonsense?"

"It is possible, sir, but given that the figures tally closely with what we know about Khartoum's stores and her supply chain, we think not."

A long, quiet beat. John held his breath, as did the other officer, while their coiled spring of a general silently sifted the conundrum posed by these conflicting messages. To him, and him alone, fell the task of making a decision in the knowledge that, depending on what he decreed, some men would live and others would certainly die.

He pursed his lips and began to whistle, the tune coming to John along with the words: *While shepherds watched their flocks . . .*

132

The whistling cut off abruptly. "You are certain this is Gordon's seal?"

"Yes, sir. We are."

"Hmm." Wolseley crossed the tent and turned. He crossed it again, and once more. Suddenly he stopped. "Ah, now I understand." His voice was resonant with certainty. "Gordon thinks of everything. Having sent his cipher books with poor Stewart, he could not write to us in confidence. He must have written down this bland message here," he waved the paper in the air, "so that, in the event of the enemy capturing his messenger, they would be deceived." He laid the piece of paper on the desk, smoothing it almost absently. He was no longer thinking about what was written there. He was considering what he would do about it. "We must assume that the messenger is right and that Gordon is almost out of time. We will have to redouble our efforts. Have the 19th Hussars left to join Brackenbury at Merow?"

"They go at first light tomorrow."

"No longer. Send someone to rouse Buller and tell him there has been a change of plan." Wolseley began again to pace. "I was counting on having more time but, transport camels or no transport camels, we must send an early contingent across a hundred and seventy miles of desert to Metemma, where Gordon's steamers are waiting. My compliments to the chief of the Hussars and ask him kindly to attend. There must be no delay in testing the camels for battle readiness." His pacing having placed him adjacent to John, Wolseley stopped. He frowned as if he couldn't remember who

John was or why he was there. "Thank you, Major." He nodded curtly. "You may go."

On his way out John crossed paths with members of Wolseley's staff who, in various states of undress, rushed in. They stepped aside to let him pass, several acknowledging him with a nod, but their intent was such that he knew they would soon forget he had ever been there. Caught up in the uneasy conviction that he was leaving behind real men to do a real job, he slowed his pace.

"If the worst comes to the worst," he heard Wolseley saying, "I hope Gordon dies in battle. Far better than the ignominy of being taken. I know Gordon. He would not want to live in captivity."

CHAPTER
TEN

The Governor General of the Soudan, Gordon Pasha, has received confirmation that General Wolseley's Expedition has left Korti and will soon be within sight of Khartoum.

Gordon Pasha has commandeered four houses near the Palace for the English officers. Compensation will be paid in notes signed by Gordon Pasha, and redeemable in Cairo.

Similar compensation will be offered in exchange for the compulsory purchase of furnishings necessary to bring these houses up to the standard befitting an English officer.

Khartoum wall newspaper, 2 Jan. 1885

The men were so weakened by lack of food that they had barely managed to carry in the divan. No sooner had they put it down, though, than the general demanded it be moved. "They're *English*," he barked, "*officers* with delicate skins. Put it," he raised his whip hand, "over there, out of the sun."

The men might not have been able to understand what he was saying, but they had learned how to follow the direction of a *kourbash*. They half carried, half dragged the divan to its appointed place.

"That's better. You may go."

This the men clearly understood. They left as fast as their weary legs could take them.

The general surveyed the room. Dressed in his white ceremonials, feet apart, one hand wielding the whip that he had previously banned from use, he had the appearance of a powerful commander inspecting his troops rather than a general without an army, surveying the room of a house that, with four others, he'd had furnished in preparation for the arrival of a rescue expedition in which he did not appear to believe.

"What do you think, Will?"

"Very good, General."

"It will have to do." The general marched up to the divan and, with one booted foot, pushed it straight. He held up his left hand and stuck up a thumb. "Napkins," he wiggled it, "and napkin rings. Silver." This was marked by an index finger that joined the upraised thumb. "Dinner service." Another finger went up, and the fourth was poised as he frowned. "Glasses?" He dropped his hand. "Everything they might want." A pause. "All I ask is that they don't invite me to dine with them."

With his tongue, Will probed the deepening sore that, having worked its way into a crack, had begun to spread along his lower lip.

"I'd sooner live like a Dervish," the general was saying, "than have to endure the pomp of an English dinner."

136

Will looked down at Frankie.

"We'll move out of the palace as soon as they get here."

"Where will we go?"

"Once they claim for themselves the victory whose foundations I have laid, we can steam home."

Home. A word Will no longer permitted himself. Now he bent to whisper in Frankie's ear, "Hear that, Frankie? Home. We're going to England." The dog, whose coat grew thinner and more ragged with the passing of each day, obligingly wagged his tail.

"You won't be able to take that animal." The general was moving towards the door.

Frankie wagged his tail again and then, at a tug of his rope, trotted after Will.

Outside, the enemy drums were thudding as they had been incessantly for days.

"If only they'd stop." Will's voice shook.

The general took no notice. His attention was focused on two Egyptian soldiers, who had accompanied them to the house and whom he had ordered to wait outside. Now they were sprawled in the shade of a palm, their mouths slack and wide to reveal blackened stumps of teeth and reddened gums, with one snoring loudly in syncopation with the drums.

The general went to stand directly over the men. When neither moved, he raised his whip.

The land that lined the river, at least on their side, was no longer the focus of activity as it might once have been. Hunger and hopelessness had sunk into the city's pores and everyday activities had largely been suspended. If anybody had asked Will, he would have said that, on emerging from the house, no one, apart from the sleeping soldiers, was about. And yet, as the general raised his whip, he knew, without doubt, that they were being watched. From dips below the bank, perhaps, or from other houses, or by men camouflaged with dust where they lay in a stupor, from which Gordon's upraised arm now roused them. Eyes burned fiercely into Will's back, anger spiking through his spine.

In that moment Will knew that if he were to turn round he would see no one. He knew — just as once he had been told he had imagined the sightings of his dead father — that the general would say his watchers were imaginary. But, also, unless he stopped the general whipping the soldiers, one of the watchers would stir the last of his energy and attack the general. This Will might be disinclined to prevent, except that if the general was killed he would be too.

To save himself, he must save the general. Will grabbed the whip arm.

"How dare you?" The general's eyes blazed with a fury that would once have withered Will. "They're my soldiers. They need to keep discipline."

It was almost over. They were almost dead. What was the point of Will holding his tongue? "They're not your soldiers and they never have been. They were just posted here to die. They're tired and hungry and they won't stop sleeping no matter how much you beat them." But they will come and slit your throat one night, Will thought, and mine as well. He tried to swallow the thought down a gullet so desiccated by heat that he almost vomited.

The general narrowed his eyes, whose whites, in the flare of the yellow sun, were stained by a spreading redness. He stepped away from the two soldiers and, without taking his eyes off him, from Will.

The air so thin. And dry. And clear.

Will looked at the general. He saw, as if for the first time, the low droop of Gordon's brown moustache, emphasizing the downturn of his lips; the sideburns streaked with grey; the head erect on the short bull neck. Finally he saw that the general's hair, too, was turning grey.

"Mutiny, is it?" The general drew out his revolver.

Will stood. And looked. Perhaps for the last time.

"No longer scared?" The general cocked his gun.

Still Will stood, and still he looked. Somewhere at the periphery of his vision, something seemed to move. Father's come to save me, he thought, the absurdity of the idea making him sad.

"On second thoughts." The general lowered the gun and aimed it at Frankie.

Will pulled his dog behind him. Frankie yelped.

"Out of my way."

The general's voice was whiplash hard and in contrast Will's reply, "No, General, I won't," sounded oddly gentle.

"I'm going to shoot him."

Will did not blink. His brown eyes were as mild as ever, his mouse-brown hair sticking wet to a head on which small scabs had congealed. "Go on, then." His jutted chin did not waver.

Silence and the drum. The drum from the enemy camp.

The general's outstretched hand trembled as the air seemed to snap and curl. His index finger twitched, and the twitching spread upwards and intensified, making his whole arm shake. He let it drop, and also his head. He put the gun back into its holster. The drumming ceased.

Will let out his breath. He had known the general wouldn't shoot. Hadn't he?

The general was looking at the boy. Kindly. Something in his expression reminded Will of that night in Gravesend, when the general had stopped his carriage to ask the despairing boy if he was in need of a meal and a place to lay his head, both of which could be provided, as long as Will was willing to hear God's words and to learn to read them for himself.

The general turned his gaze on the sleeping soldiers. "In exchange for only a tenth of their produce, the Mahdi has said he will rid his people of these dogs." He smiled. Calmly. Almost serenely. "A most captivating programme. No wonder they are flocking to his side." He turned on his heel and strode off along the bank of the Nile.

CHAPTER
ELEVEN

The sense that they were in the middle of nowhere, waiting for something that was never going to happen, had gone. Lethargic routine had turned into purposeful intent as new men poured into the camp at Korti to gather in groups, their belongings laid in front of them.

"They're riders from different regiments, picked to join the Camel Corps," Tom told John, as they passed one such group. "They're being camel-trained before they set off."

John stopped.

"In front of you," their burly sergeant was saying, "you will find your rifle, your sword, your bayonet, your bandolier, your belt, your pouch, your frog and sling and your haversack." He walked along the line, picking up one or other of these items, turning the swords so they flashed in the sun. "You will be issued with fifty cartridges, which you will keep in your bandolier over your left shoulder."

"Shall we go on?" This from Tom who, in response to John's "I should like to watch", stayed where he was.

"You will place in your haversack your goggles, your veil, your drawers, your cholera belt, your prayer book,

141

your housewife spurs, a spare pair of boots, shirt, and socks. Come — what are you waiting for?"

As the men scrambled to shove their possessions into their haversacks, the sergeant walked up and down with barely concealed impatience. When, having finished packing, the last of the men snapped to, he picked up one of the stiff leather skins that remained. "This," he held it up, "is your most important piece of kit. It's a native waterskin — they call it a *mussak*. It will keep your water cool. Immediately we fall out, you are to fill your *mussak* with water. Watch it carefully. Any leaks you are to sew up. You will then grease the hide. Take care. Without water in the desert, you will die."

Many of the men were frowning at the strange object, none, however, displaying any perturbation at the mention of death.

The sergeant gestured to an Arab who, in wide white pantaloons, a white shirt and an elaborate white turban, was holding a camel. "Now for your animal. They're bad-tempered brutes but, like your waterskin, they are your lifeline."

The animal, its surprisingly dainty head encased in a black leather headstall, was led up to the sergeant. Its rubbery lips were bared to reveal sharp teeth, to whose power many of John's recent patients could attest. It had large eyes with thick lashes, a welcome barrier against sand, and bushy eyebrows, which helped to keep its eyes clear of the diseases that had plagued the men. An odd animal, deserving, at least in appearance, of the suspicion with which the men were regarding it.

"The first thing to note about your camel is that he is no horse. Once he's on his feet, there is no way to mount him. You have to bring him down." The sergeant seized hold of the long rope whose other end was attached by a chain to the animal's lower lip and hauled on it. He was not a small man, but although he pulled, and pulled again, the animal neither budged nor gave any sign that it was ever going to. The men appeared to be looking straight ahead, but several didn't trouble to hide their smiles.

The sergeant looked to his helper, who loudly cleared his throat while tugging sharply at the rope. In response, the animal folded itself down to its knees. Laughter broke out.

"Wait till you try," the sergeant said. "Settle down. You've had your fun. If you don't watch, you won't learn. You don't learn, you die." He turned to the camel. "Once your animal is down, you will hobble it." At a nod from the sergeant his helper deftly tied a rope around one of the camel's forelegs. "Looks easy, but takes practice. You'll be getting plenty of that. Now you load it. In the fore pommel here," the sergeant hit the camel's front flank, "you are to keep your camel's rations. Like this." His helper hefted a huge sack into place. "Twenty pounds of corn." The sergeant turned to glare at his men. "Make sure you have every bit of it. If the camel doesn't eat, it will die. If it dies, you die."

Another slap, this one on the rump. "The aft pommel is where your waterskin goes. It must be well secured. There will be no sharing and no spares. Lose your *mussak* and you die. No matter how tired you are, you are to keep it greased. If it leaks, you die. Got that? Not suffer. Die." The sergeant nodded as if this prospect gave him satisfaction.

"Next, you place this blanket," he hefted one, "over the saddlebag. On top of this, you put your saddle." He threw up the red leather saddle. "It's padded. With the distances we're to cross, you will be grateful for this small mercy. Now here is the point of all this: mounting your animal."

The sergeant reached over and pointed to a bucket attached to a saddle. "Your Namaqua rifle is stored here." He shoved one in. "Like this. Butt foremost. You must have it in your possession before you mount because, once up, there will be no bending down for it. But if you were to attempt to mount with the rifle in its bucket . . ." The sergeant nodded at his helper, who put one foot on the stirrup, then made as if to swing the other leg over, stopping just before it hit the rifle. ". . . that will happen. Do it in a hurry and you will break your leg. Or if your camel takes it into its head to rise suddenly — and what these animals don't suddenly get into their heads to do is not worth thinking about — you will fall off and break your neck, so remove the rifle from its bucket and sling it over your left wrist, like this, where it will remain until you are properly seated. Only when you are safely in your saddle will you put your rifle in its bucket. Got that?" A murmur of assent along the line of men. "Right. Let's get to the point of this demonstration. Mounting the bleeding thing. You untether your animal." His helper freed the camel's foreleg. "Then you take hold of your rein like so —"

144

"Aren't you going to show us, Sergeant?"

"Yes, come on, Sergeant, show us how it's done."

The sergeant glared at his men until they fell silent. He turned to the camel. He looked for a moment as if he was about to carry on, but something in the ranks behind him indicated that the shouts might not have been entirely friendly. He took the rope from his aide.

The men stood watching as the sergeant pulled on the rope to shorten it. That done, he stepped away at an angle to the beast. "The camel's a bloody contortionist," he said. "It's capable of lifting its back leg and kicking you in the arse while you're astride it. But it has its limitations." He hauled again on the rope, pulling the head of the now protesting camel back and jamming it against its own rump. "And the one that will be most useful to you is that, with its head back like this, it can't get up." He gave another tug. "Make sure you have tight hold of the rope. Once you have the head secured, you will sling the rifle over your left wrist, put one foot in the stirrup, and throw the other over. Now you can slot the rifle, butt up, in the bucket." The rifle went down. "Be careful. If by some ill chance you have let slip the camel's head and it starts to rise, as it will, then grip on tight until it's up. Only then swing the other leg over. If you have managed, by some stroke of ill-deserved luck, to keep control of its head, now's the time to release your hold." As soon as the sergeant loosened the rope, the camel, which had been bellowing, snapped its head forward. "Lean back," the sergeant barked, "and hold on for dear life." The animal was already levering itself up, its human cargo immediately diminished as it roared and swayed until, at last, it was on its feet and the sergeant mounted. His achievement was greeted with loud applause and whistles. "Funny. Very funny." The sergeant was shouting so loudly he even out-bellowed his animal. "Not so funny when you try it. And try it you will. Over and over again. In battle if you can't do it right, and fast, you know what will happen. You will . . ." The sergeant waited for his men to complete his sentence.

They did so loudly and in unison: "Die."

CHAPTER
TWELVE

Will's legs were jelly and he was breathing quickly, in and out, in and out, as he registered the beating of the drum. It would never stop. Not until it had pounded them all to death. He pulled Frankie up. The dog's head was scabbed and he could see sores through the thinning tufts of hair on his back.

"You'll be all right." At the sound of Will's voice, Frankie looked up, not trustingly, Will thought, but rather as if he understood what Will had said and did not believe him. "Come on."

Even though it was the hottest part of the day, the system of message conveyance, whose workings Will had never been able to fathom, had been activated. With the general on his way, the space that had previously been devoid of activity was filled with people doing what the general had ordered them to do, although at half the requisite pace. Everything and everybody, save the general, had slowed to the heavy beat of the sun. In a line, soldiers passed wires from hand to hand; an ox, its ribs poking out, the sagging skin of its empty belly hanging down, dragged a water wheel in a dismal circle. The warm water slopped thickly into a channel to be scooped out by a slave, who staggered off with a clay pot on his head. Even the white sails of the small sloops crossing from Tuti island seemed heavy, their keels sinking into the grey water, although their hulls were almost empty of grain. And still the drums kept on.

"What are they up to?" The general had stopped so suddenly that Will almost ran into him. He was pointing with his whip at a line of soldiers who were moving lethargically through the heat between the armoury and the palace.

"They're laying lines," Will said.

"On whose orders?"

"Yours, General."

"I never issued such orders."

A small but audible voice inside Will told him to leave this conversation, but somehow he could not. "You did." He heard his voice ring out. "You said they must lay lines so that when . . . *if* the enemy broke through, you could blow up the palace."

"Blow up the palace?" The general snorted, as if in amusement. "Why, for goodness' sake?"

"To stop us being taken prisoner."

"To do what?" The general looked at Will. "Are you mad? I would never have ordered such an action. It has the taint of suicide."

Will blinked.

"It is not for us to say when and how we die. That is in God's hands. With His help I will continue to do His work and, if need be, suffer and die for my beliefs."

And blinked again . . .

"Like Christ before me, I will refuse a numbing potion. Our Lord would not abate, by mortal means, the slightest pang of His passion: Matthew twenty-seven, verse thirty-four."

. . . to stop the tears that had sprung to his eyes leaking out.

The general took off, shouting, "Shoo. Get away from there." His frame was stick thin and black against the brightness of the sun as he ran full tilt at the soldiers, who scattered in alarm at the sight of their commander charging them, arms wide. "Run. I tell you, run!"

The general's voice had dropped, but he continued running to the place the soldiers had recently occupied. He was going in circles wrenching up lines from the empty dryness. Eventually he stopped, bending almost double, wheezing with the effort of his run.

His suit was stained with perspiration and dust. His face was so pale it seemed almost featureless. His moustache hung limp and wet while on his cheek there were two dark red spots. As the soldiers stopped running and turned to face him, he teetered forward.

Will ran to him. "Come." He took hold of the general. "Lean on me."

CHAPTER
THIRTEEN

They had walked only a mile from the camp, and already John was desperately thirsty. He wondered how much water the *mussak* held, and then where more water would be found. Ahead he could see the solid back of Tom Jennings, who walked steadily on, the dark, damp patch that had spread across the back of his shirt the only sign that he was also feeling the heat.

They hadn't gone far before the strip of green that ran along the edge of the Nile faded from sight. Now it seemed hardly possible that there could have been anything fresh or green so close to this ugly stretch of beige sand whose only distinguishing marks were outcrops of sharp black rocks. What scrub there was was spindly, grey-green and so wind-beaten it was hard to understand how it was still rooted.

They were walking uphill, a dreadful effort in the heat. Already the sand was infiltrating John's throat and, despite the goggles, his eyes. And this, he knew, was only the start. If he were to go with the soldiers — and it was still only *if* — how would he manage?

Tom waited for him to come abreast. "Not much further. Just over the crest here."

Such a small climb, yet the effort caused sweat to pour down John's face. No wonder he was thirsty.

"Careful." They were making their way across a particularly concentrated patch of stones. John watched his every step, which was why he didn't realize they had reached their destination until it was upon him. Even then, he knew it only by the sound.

His hearing, which had been filled previously by his own hard-won breaths, was invaded by the yells of many men.

Tom was standing a little ahead. "What a fucking sight."

And so it was. Stretched out before them was the desert's vast monotony of greys and browns, of sand drifts broken by mounds of rocks that, in the far distance, grew into dull grey hillocks. Such an immense landscape, it seemed to shrink the group of mounted, helmeted, yelling soldiers. "Hussars," Tom said as, sabres drawn and pointed forwards, the men dug their spurs into their horses and rode in formation across the sand, shouting hurrahs, dust whirling as they closed on a group of seated camels at which their sabre points were aimed. They rode straight at them, only at the last moment to swerve away.

"Would you credit it?" The dust began to settle, as the jubilant Hussars galloped into the distance, creating fresh dust storms. "They didn't so much as blink."

"The Hussars?"

"The camels. The Hussars were testing them to see how they'll function in the heat of battle. From what we've just witnessed, once they're down they won't budge, no matter what you throw at them. That's just as well, because you see there?" Tom pointed across the sand to where, in the distance, they could see orderly lines of soldiers. They were so far away they looked like toys, many of them holding on to camel halters. "That lot there is drilling for an attack." A miniature officer raised his sabre. "That's the order to close over." The men began to move.

To John, it was like watching a boyhood fantasy: a British square assembled with tiny toy soldiers. None of the exuberance the galloping Hussars had displayed, but the same ruthless efficiency was everywhere in evidence as camels were pulled down and hobbled, then the men moved away to slot themselves into the four sides of the square, four perfectly straight lines that soon sealed in the sitting animals, the front row diving down until they were prone while, behind them, two further rows of men formed up, the first kneeling, the second standing, all with guns outstretched and ready to fire.

"One minute twenty seconds," Tom said. "Not bad. And over there — you see where the camels are in the centre of the square?"

John nodded.

"That's where we'll be. The Bearers Company will bring the injured to us. We'll patch them up as best we can and load them on to cacolets — two for each camel — to keep them safe until the enemy has been driven off. By we, I mean . . ." Tom looked at John ". . . if you decide to come with us."

"I've decided," John said, and he had.

It was time. Mary must write to John. Now. Before she changed her mind.

My dearest John, she wrote.

She hesitated. Laid down her pen. She was writing to tell him of her unassuageable need for laudanum. She had decided she must. Yet only now, after weeks of indecision, did it occur to her to wonder how he might react. She had no idea. He was her husband, yet she didn't know him.

The wonderful icy numbness of the dispensary was calling to her. Go on, a voice inside her urged. Go on. Solve today's problem. Tomorrow's can take care of itself.

She shook her head violently. That voice was not her friend. It was her enemy. It was trying to lead her astray. It belonged to a different woman. A woman John had not met, and who, if she wrote to him, he might never meet.

She picked up her pen and dipped it into the inkwell.

There is something, my dearest John, she wrote, *that I must tell you.*

Such a contrast at the river's edge. Such a different landscape from the desert, which, once breached, might turn out to be the last landscape John would ever see. He pushed away the thought. He was a surgeon, not a

153

soldier. As Tom had shown him, he would be protected. Yet he was frightened — and excited.

He took in the sight of the grey-blue water, the still silhouette of spiked palms that, in the distance, seemed to merge into blue. He looked up into a sky that had been tinted red-gold by the waning sun. Everything, the banks, the men, the air, was so very quiet and still.

He worked his fingers absently at the crumbling grey-brown riverside rock, his hands covered with dust. Another presage, if one were required, of what lay beyond these banks.

A fluttering of wings, and there, almost within touching distance, was a bird, as big as a thrush. It had alighted on the shore and stood, its emerald feathers quivering slightly in a soft breeze that, in the desert, would become the harsh whip of a wind.

He glanced down at the paper in his lap.

How to explain to Mary that he had volunteered to go with the Camel Corps? How to make her understand that he hadn't meant to break his word? How to tell her he had to go? Not because they needed surgeons, although it was true that they did. Not — although this was also true — because he was unable to let brave men like Tom Jenkins ride into battle without the medical service they deserved. And not because it was his duty or because pressure had been applied. There was another reason, which hovered so vaguely at the edge of consciousness that he could barely put it into words. It was half a thought: he had to go for himself.

154

He looked across the river where green tree tops were flushed by rays from the setting sun at the same time as the pink of the sky deepened to crimson. It would soon be dark. He had to write to her. And he had to write to her now.

My dearest Mary, he wrote. *There is something that I must tell you.*

PART THREE

EGYPT AND THE SOUDAN
(BY EASTERN COMPANY CABLES)

KORTI 1 Jan
A messenger who arrived here from Khartoum last night brought a small piece of paper, bearing only the words. "Khartoum all right. December 14 — C. G. Gordon." The messenger says that General Gordon told him to say that Khartoum could not be taken by the enemy. On the occasion of the last attack the garrison had disabled one of the Mahdi's guns.

LATER
There is no doubt of the authenticity of the above message, which is both sealed and signed. The messenger adds that General Gordon has occupied two palaces, placing a gun on the roof of each. He goes up to the top of one every morning, and looks round the country with a telescope, and he spends the day in one or the other. At night he goes round the works. He still has cigarettes, for he offered the messenger one on his coming away.
The Times, 2 Jan., 1885

CHAPTER
FOURTEEN

The general was running through mist so thick that, should he have looked down, all he would have been able to see were the nubs of his toecaps appearing and disappearing. He could hear the long bridge creaking. He was engineer enough to know it was on the brink of collapse. His fault. By demolishing an arch to let his steamer through, he had set off a chain reaction that would do what centuries of wear had not achieved.

He was running — but from what? From death? What point? his dreaming self kept asking. What point?

Boulders that the ages had held together fractured, pieces breaking off and tumbling down, stone supports sliding into the river while the wafting silhouettes of darkened willow branches bore silent witness to its destruction. And now he was running on water, his face ablaze. The summer palace was burning — roomfuls of coloured silks, screens and ebony-lined walls had liquefied, later to congeal into an unsalvageable mass. A punishment for betrayal. A punishment too far.

"No," he shouted, as he ran. "No. Stop. No!"

"No," the general kept shouting. "Stop it. No."

"You must, General." Will tried to spoon Warburg's tincture into the general's mouth. "You told me you had to."

The general closed tight his wrinkled lips. He turned his head away. He was delirious, insensible but not insensate.

Each time Will inadvertently touched his fever-heated skin he flinched. "No." There was such pain in his voice that he no longer sounded like himself. "Stop it. No."

"You have to, General, or you will die. And if you die . . ."

The general flung out an arm so suddenly and forcefully that the back of his calloused hand sent Will flying. He landed on the hard stone floor, head smacking against the wall, and there he lay, a rag doll of a boy.

"No," the general said, softly now. "No." He lapsed into quiet.

Will opened his eyes to find Frankie licking his cheek. He elbowed the dog away. Felt the back of his own head, sticky with blood.

When Frankie came back into focus, Will batted him off. The dog yelped.

"There's a time, Frankie," Will said.

He realized he was lying in a corner of the general's suite, his head against a skirting board. The general was also in the room, unmoving on his bed. Groaning, Will pushed himself up. "General."

No answer.

"General?"

The general's doing. He had shoved Will away, just as Will had shoved his dog.

"Frankie." When he tried to click his fingers they squashed, like jellied eels, against each other. Still, Frankie came up, slowly and tentatively, to lick his master's hand. "Good boy." His dog's tongue cleaned the blood from his hand. "Good boy." No longer dog and owner, they were brothers now.

Something hard against his lips, and Will's "Drink this, General." He opened his eyes. "I was dreaming."

"Drink some water."

"About China." It was dark outside. The last thing he remembered, before the annihilation of his fever, had been a light too brilliant to face.

He manoeuvred himself upright and saw his white suit, freshly cleaned and pressed, hanging on the back of the chair. Had he imagined wearing it before? Had he imagined running at the soldiers? Yes. That was it. Like the demolition of the bridge, it had been a dream. "How long have I been out of commission?"

"A few days." Will had barred the door to the general's room and spread the word that he was planning the fight back against the Mahdi and should, on no account, be distracted. "It's almost New Year."

"I was dreaming." The general leaned back against the pillows, which Will had plumped for him. "About the bridge at Patachow. Something that happened when I was there."

"Take a sip."

"I demolished an arch so the *Hyson* could pass through and the bridge collapsed."

"General, you must drink."

"She was a thing of beauty." The general's hand trembled as he took the glass. "Or she was beautiful before I came along. Scores of arches and they all fell, one after another. Like a tempest ripping through a concertina. There was nothing we could do to hold them back." The general's hand shook so violently that the glass slipped from it and shattered, fragments skittering across the stone floor. "My God . . ."

"It's easily cleared."

"Why have you forsaken me?" The cry stolen from another man's lips. He slipped down in the bed and let darkness overcome him.

The light from the oil lamp played against the stone and was reflected back by the shards of glass. Sweeping it away, Will heard the general clamber awkwardly out of bed and pull out his pot. He heard him fumble with his buttons and then, after a pause, straining.

The general groaned.

Will imagined himself out of the room, out of the city and — why not? — out of the country. He placed himself in a public house. He put Frankie at his feet. He conjured a foaming tankard of beer as accompaniment to his succulent hot fish — he tossed a piece to the ecstatic Frankie. After that, he thought, they might share a nice bit of mutton and some lobster claws, or a bloater, or a herring with a twist of — Hold on: he'd never been able to stand the smell of herring.

He propped the rush broom against the wall and made his way to the general's bed.

Gordon had clambered back in. Will bent down to get the pot from beneath the bed where the general had kicked it.

"Leave it."

"But the smell . . ."

"Leave it, I say." The general patted a space on the bed beside him. "Sit. I want to talk to you."

"In a moment, General." Will picked up the pot and carried it out. Then he made his way back. He did not sit on the bed. He drew up a chair.

"Is the glass swept away?"

"It soon will be." He made as if to rise.

"Don't do it now." The fever had drained the blood from the general's face. "You need to rest."

Will frowned.

"Before my first tour of duty in the Sudan," the general said, "Ayub Pasha's sister was so incensed when she heard I was to take her brother's place as governor general that she broke almost every pane of glass in the palace and ripped up all the cushions. They had a devil of a job setting the place to rights before my arrival." He sighed. "She'll have her revenge now, won't she? If she's still alive."

Will shifted in his seat.

The general's voice was almost dreamy. "I've broken a fair number of windows in my time. The men at the royal arsenal would fashion crossbows for us boys. We used heavy screws for ammunition."

Will smiled. It was strange to think of the forbidding, praying, commanding, ranting general as a boy. Then his smile faded as it dawned on him that his chance of living to be a man and remembering himself a boy was getting smaller by the minute.

"I'm thirsty," the general said.

Will got up, lifted the cloth from the jug and poured water into a fresh glass. He took it to the general, making sure to place it carefully in his hand.

"The rescue expedition is on its way." The general closed his other hand over Will's.

"Yes, General." Will extracted his hand.

"Here." The general held up the glass.

When Will bent to receive it, the general laid a hand on his head. "What happened?"

"I slipped." Will ducked out of the way.

"In this climate, you must prevent wounds festering. Go and clean it."

"Yes, General."

Will turned away but the general's "I'm sorry, Will," halted him in his tracks.

"You didn't mean to," he said.

"Not for that. I'm sorry for bringing you here. It was selfish."

How many times had Will lain outside the general's door, and thought about bursting in to demand an apology for the cruelty with which the general had played him? He must have known, when he had first offered Will the treat of a trip to London, that they would send him to Khartoum, but he hadn't said a word. And when he did deign to tell Will what he was planning to do, he had presented the trip as an adventure no red-blooded boy would refuse. Not once had he made reference to any danger. And although poor Stewart had tried to warn Will, poor Stewart had been no match for the general.

"I wanted your company," the general said.

Will felt the surge of a ferocious rage. Was he some plaything to be brought here to die just because the general had a fancy for his company? It was nonsense, anyway. All the general wanted was someone to empty his pot and wash his suit, to nod and smile when he complained about others.

What had given him the right? That thought swept through Will, too, not in fury now, he was too weak to sustain it, but in grief: he felt it welling, gripping his throat. He bunched his fists. He wouldn't cry. He wouldn't.

"I promise you one thing," he heard the general say. "At the end I'll look after you. You won't feel any pain."

CHAPTER
FIFTEEN

The rasp of the saddle against his skin made John grit his teeth. His camel walked on doggedly, as the moon cast its white glow over the long caravan and the stony wilderness that surrounded it. Nothing much to look at. John looked ahead.

He was soon mesmerized by the sight of the long, ridged U of a neck that lay beneath the baggy, tawny skin. He watched the neck shifting that implausibly narrow head with its unearthly knobbles from side to side as the camel trod in the footsteps of the animal ahead, on and on, as far as John could tell, into eternity. The bump and sway of the relentless forward motion lulled him. He couldn't stop his eyes closing. Without knowing it, he slumped in his saddle and —

"Watch where you're going."

He jolted upright.

He had no idea how long he'd been asleep, or if it had been his camel that had strayed into another's path. But no, when he looked across, he saw that one of the pack camels, tied head-to-tail in strings of three and led by a single man, had collided with the column.

"Keep your animals under control." A private struggled to disentangle his camel from the interlopers.

167

He pulled desperately against the prospect of being left behind — which was already happening because other riders were circumventing the tangled beasts and moving on.

John drew abreast. "Can I help?"

"No, you can't." As if from nowhere Tom had appeared. "Or you'll be left behind."

"But someone must."

"They'll bugle for him later." When Tom gave a brisk tug on John's camel's mouthpiece, it slotted itself back into the moving column and plodded on.

Tom was right. Every now and then there would come the faint sound of bugling from the rear. It was the signal for the column to halt and wait for stragglers to catch up, thus also allowing a merciful fifteen-minute break, which many of the men used to slip off their camels and sleep until, always torturously too soon, the order came to move on.

They were all so thirsty, the wells they had passed having been nothing more than funnel-shaped holes with a meagre supply of dirty, brown water that they'd quickly exhausted. They must reach Jakdul urgently: there, they would be able to refill their waterskins and let their livestock drink.

As the march stretched on past a hundred miles, their water diminished and still they did not reach Jakdul. John could not have been the only man whose thoughts strayed to tales he had been told of Hicks's doomed expedition, and of Hicks's army zigzagging the desert, crazed by thirst, so that when finally they were attacked, most of the men did not even bother fighting back.

He must not think of it. The two situations were nowhere analogous. While Hicks had made simple mistakes, Wolseley was a master tactician who had had time to prepare — and who had infinitely more resources. And while Wolseley's troops had been hand-picked, all Hicks had had at his command was a bunch of disaffected Egyptians. Besides, the Mahdi was at the gates of Khartoum: he would not have been forewarned of this expedition and therefore would not have blocked the wells as he had done to Hicks.

Even so, they had to keep on moving and John with them.

"Thank you," he turned to say to Tom. But Tom had already gone.

It had taken so much courage for Mary to write to John that she had assumed somehow that she would be instantly rewarded, so that at least a week had passed before it dawned on her that, even if he had received her letter, he would not be able to come and rescue her. In the meantime, her need had increased.

She had long used the store he had left her — why had he been so mean? — and had had to plunder his dispensary stocks. Each time she did so, she had told herself the lie that it was the last time, and since it was, she should indulge herself.

Now the full extent of her folly was laid bare.

She had known the stock was running low. She had known it for a while. Yet every time she had made the trip to the dispensary she had failed to register how few grains of opium remained. Only now, as she stirred the last specks into some brandy, did she face the fact that they were indeed the last. And, as well, while her stock had diminished her desire had increased. She no longer felt safe in the old stand-by with which she had reassured herself: that she could stop at any time. Without laudanum in her system, she was permanently unwell, her head pounding, her body aching, and this even though she spent most of her time on the sofa turning the pages of a book she could not read.

That day had been the most punishing so far. Beads of perspiration had kept breaking through her skin, although she had felt so cold that even a double layer of blankets, and the fire banked as high as Betty could make it, could not stop her shivering.

Betty had wanted to fetch a doctor. Mary had forbidden it. John's colleagues were jealous of his success: he had often told her so. She must not expose him. And, besides, she couldn't bear to reveal to a stranger how low she had sunk, and to see in the eyes their judgement that John had been right to leave her.

Still, she needed opium and soon.

She stood in the dispensary overwhelmed by an unbearable physical impatience. Some dark thing seemed to beat inside her, trying to batter its way out. She stamped her foot. "Think." She said the word out loud. "Think."

Her thoughts were as clotted as syrup pudding but she did have one: there had to be more. The longer she cleaved to this notion, the more convinced of it did she become. He must have another store. Of course he must. He was a careful man, mindful of the urgency of his patients' needs and reluctant to share his business with the nearest apothecary.

An image came to her of John packing to go.

She had stood in the dispensary and watched him gathering up the medicines that he had thought he might need and the army not supply. If she stood still now, she could expand the memory and force it into an appearance of reality, like one of her waking laudanum dreams. She made herself stand still.

His hazy outline seemed to solidify in the frigid air, his familiar taut physique moving from drawer to drawer as he spoke the names of the medicines he was seeking, not for her benefit but for his. And, yes, her memory was not at fault. She could see how, finding insufficient quantities in the lower drawers, he had started to explore the less conveniently accessible upper shelves.

There had to be more laudanum. Of course there did. All she had to do was find it. And find it she would.

She breathed out, letting go the tension. She fetched the high ladder from the storeroom and, having lodged it against the wall, hoisted her skirt and began to climb.

She was falling.

She was at a great height and falling so slowly that John had time to calculate the angle of her descent, to place himself at the right spot, open his arms and break her fall.

He would save her. That was what he wanted to shout out to her.

She was hurtling down. He braced himself for impact, his legs steeled so fiercely that they hurt.

She was coming too fast. The prospect of her smashing into him filled him with such terror that, even as he told himself to stand his ground, he stepped aside.

He cried out: "Mary!"

The soft brush of air as she slipped past.

"Mary!"

Her frown of disappointment as, raven hair flying, she continued to fall down into a deep well. Soon he could no longer see her, even in outline, could only hear the splash of her body plunging into the oily water. Gone. The rim of blackened liquid would have parted to receive her and she, who had never learned to swim, would have been sucked down, deeper and deeper, until the dark, moist, sludgy silt at the bottom sealed her in.

"Major," he heard. "Major Clarke, wake up."

He opened his eyes to find a bearded, filthy Tom shaking his shoulder. The dream dissolved. He was on the ground where he had dropped as soon as the order to halt had been given. He was just as filthy as Tom and, despite the blanket Tom must have thrown over him, his teeth were chattering with cold.

"We'll be off soon," Tom said.

All around, shadows of men were yawning, stretching and getting up.

"You'd better warm yourself."

Still trying to shake off the dream, he shifted closer to the fire of dry grass and mimosa that Tom had built. He pulled the blanket tight around himself.

"Here." A steaming cup of cocoa was pressed into his hands. He took a sip, luxuriating in its sweet warmth.

"Better?"

"Yes. Thank you." A falsehood. The awful image of Mary falling was still embedded in his mind. "I was dreaming."

"So I heard. About Mary. You were shouting her name." With his back to John, Tom was getting something from his pack. "She your wife?"

"Yes." He thought of her alone in London. "I dreamed she was falling."

"You wouldn't be the first to have a dream like that."

"I couldn't catch her."

"It's only natural, us being so far away and all." Tom busied himself, not looking John in the eye.

Was Tom right? Was it just the distance between them that had triggered his fears? He wanted to believe it, yet was unconvinced. The longer he had been away from Mary, the more powerfully had the conviction grown in him that something was wrong. Something, and this thought, too, kept recurring, from which he had run.

Struggling to collect himself, he croaked, "What about you, Tom? What do you dream about?"

"About my damn camel, that's what."

"You don't have people back home?"

A frown on Tom's pockmarked face. "I did once," he said. "A wife and son. Long ago. They're gone." He thrust something at John. "Eat this."

"This" was a half a tin of cold bully beef that, when heated by the sun, turned into a soupy red mass of stringy worms. At night it solidified back into a respectable-looking chunk. John dug in his spoon. "Mmm." He was surprised. "It's even beginning to taste good."

"Everything tastes good when you're hungry." Tom laughed. "Me, I liked it better when they issued us with salt pork and salt beef. More flavour. And, strangely enough, no matter the quantity of salt in them, we didn't used to get so thirsty."

The older man was sitting close, his short, stout back as straight as ever. He had such stamina. While John's energy was almost entirely used up in not falling off his camel, Tom kept an eye on the medical supplies, made sure the newly trained bearer companies stuck to their section of the column, and was always available when John needed him. All of this on much less sleep than John had.

"Why don't you get some rest?" John said.

"No point."

"I'll watch out for you."

"We'll be leaving soon."

The moon was bright enough to light the vast sprawl of their temporary camp. Everywhere men were being shaken awake, while others were packing away utensils and putting out fires.

"Best to stretch your legs."

With a great effort, John clambered to his feet. As he did, the pain that sheared down his leg was so sharp, he gasped.

174

"Here." Tom handed him a small, dented tin from the medical supplies. "It'll help if you rub it in."

John felt beneath his trousers and drawers to where the saddle had rubbed his inside leg. The skin was wet and oozing. As gently as he could, he massaged in some of the glycerine.

"I laid some on your camel as well. He's got galls where your saddle's digging into him." Tom threw sand on their fire. "Your average native doesn't use a saddle and now we know why." He stamped on the embers. "They're also inclined to bury their waterskins in the sand. Maybe that's what we've been doing wrong."

He was referring to the disaster of the *mussaks*, whose leather skins, even though they were greased, were liable to turn damp and flabby with leaking water until eventually they shrivelled up. Only the Blue Jackets with their supply of india-rubber bags, and the Medical Corps, with its extra rations for its patients, had a half decent supply of water, and even they, having ridden through the heat, were beginning to feel the torture of a thirst that could not be slaked.

A rustling among the ranks. In the day, orders were conveyed by flag or heliograph, but at night they were passed verbally from one section of the corps to the next. Now the wave of sound that fluttered through the ranks told them to "saddle up". Men began to separate from the earth amid the yowling of camels being mounted. Soon the column had reformed and moved off.

Mary had started her search carefully enough but as time went on she grew increasingly slapdash. The crash of a bottle brushed aside in an attempt to see what might be hidden behind it sounded loudly in the silence of the night. She knew she should stop and sweep up the glass, then give up the search and go to bed.

She could not, would not, stop. Not until she had found what she was looking for. But the longer she looked and the less she found, the more furious she became. Much of her anger was directed at her husband. Why had he left her? He must have known she hadn't wanted him to go.

She thought of all the excuses he had made, the most frequent of which was that, as a patriot, he had had no choice. What arrant nonsense. There were countless doctors in London, including the colleague who was looking after John's practice — and he was unmarried — who could have gone in his stead. But, in the name of virtue, John had insisted on being the one to go.

He wasn't virtuous. He was vain. And selfish.

She swept her arm across a shelf, deliberately disrupting his meticulously ordered array. Such satisfaction as the bottles fell. Such splendid mayhem. She swung her arm again, glorying in the smashing vials of powders and potions, pills and liquids of every colour and viscosity. What intense satisfaction. For the first time in days she was actively enjoying herself.

"Ma'am!"

With a flickering candle in her hand, clad in a long flannel nightdress and dressing gown, her hair plaited down her back, Betty was standing in the doorway, staring in open-mouthed amazement at the havoc Mary had created. In that moment, Mary saw herself through

Betty's eyes and she also saw the dispensary. No wonder Betty was shocked: even Mary could not believe that she had orchestrated such chaos. And although the voice that told Betty, "Don't move, you may cut yourself," sounded like hers, when she had descended, she caught sight of her reflection in the mirror, and did not recognize herself: her dark hair was disordered, her brown eyes had pooled to black, her cheeks were blanched white and her lips stained an unnatural red. "I was looking for something," that wild woman told her maid.

"You should have asked."

"I told you to go to bed."

"I was waiting for the bells."

As if on cue, they began to toll, softly at first, St Andrew's traditionally ahead of the others, but by the time the count had risen to ten, and the last two notes were struck, the sound had gathered momentum and the sonorous pealing filled the room as the minute hand on the wall clock that Mary could see in the mirror joined the twelve. Midnight. In that moment, she had a flash of inspiration. Of course. She knew now how she would get what she needed.

"A new year," Betty said.

Why hadn't she thought of it before. A solution? Not possible now. But tomorrow. A new year — and she would be a new woman.

The sight of Betty's lower lip trembling brought home to Mary how young her maid was and how shy. "Go to bed now, Betty," she said gently, shaking her head when Betty looked set to protest. "You can sweep this up tomorrow." Then as an afterthought: "Happy new year."

When Betty turned obediently Mary saw her thin back quivering. "Don't worry," she said. "I am perfectly well." She knew, with a calm certainty that had eluded her for days, that even if this wasn't quite true, it soon would be.

Through the darkness, a soft rolling in of sound.

Should auld acquaintance be forgot,
and never brought to mind?

Men singing, each part of the column picking up the refrain from the one in front and relaying it back.

Should auld acquaintance be forgot,
and auld lang syne?

And John joining in the chorus, his voice one with those of the other men:

For auld lang syne, my dear,
for auld lang syne,
we'll take a cup o' kindness yet,
for auld lang syne.

The tension of his dream drained away. Now he thought fondly and without fear of his beloved Mary, tucked up safe and well in their Barnsbury home.

THE ADVANCE ON KHARTOUM

With the movements begun last week the Khartoum Expedition entered upon a new phase, and one which will be followed with intense interest by the country. The probability of the desert route to Metamneh being adopted by a portion of the expedition was always recognized, but ignorance as to the number of available camels precluded certain forecast. The advantages of the short cut are obvious. Even if the most favourable estimate of time for the flotilla to round the vast bend of the Nile is accepted, the gain by the desert route will be very marked. In distance from Korti the difference is about 200 miles, but the boats cannot nearly maintain the camel's average, and the saving in time will be in a much greater proportion. But, besides this, the moral effect of the desert march and the sudden descent on the river between Berber and Khartoum will unquestionably be considerable. Under the circumstances, therefore, the element of time being so important, no commander of Lord Wolseley's genius would hesitate for a moment to accept a certain measure of risk. And that there is some risk to be faced in the next move cannot be denied.

The Times, 8 Jan., 1885

CHAPTER
SIXTEEN

In Khartoum, the first hopeful sign for days: the general was out of bed, dressed and at his desk. At the same time a not-so-hopeful sign: he had spent almost the whole day at his desk and there was no evidence that he'd been doing anything. He had nothing but the Bible to read but he hadn't been reading it. He had no paper, so he couldn't have been writing. He had no interest in what the men were up to. Every time Will entered his suite, and he'd found several reasons to do so, the general had been in the same position, staring out — not as he might once have done, in search of the rescue expedition, but dully, as if he knew it wouldn't come. He was caught up in what he called his "doles", his worse-than-Colorado-beetle disease that had held him so firmly in its grip that he'd not even objected when Will had brought Frankie to keep him company.

Frankie's bushy tail wagged madly at the sight of Will. He whined and strained at the rope by which Will had tethered him. Although he was less active than he used to be, he hated being tied up, a precaution that Will, who didn't trust the general's mood, had thought worth taking. Will bent down and opened his hand — "Here, boy" — to reveal a minuscule piece of bread, which Frankie almost inhaled, before sniffing him wildly in search of more. His liquid black eyes, Will saw, were larger than ever, something Will had noted in himself.

"If you keep giving that dog your food, you'll starve," the general said, "and then someone will catch and eat him."

"They've laid on an extra ration to celebrate the new year," Will said.

"Which new year?"

"Ours, General — 1885. I told you so not an hour ago." An hour before that as well.

The general shrugged. "Well, it isn't theirs." He inclined his head in the direction of the window as if Will wouldn't otherwise have guessed he was talking about the enemy. "Their new year falls on the twenty-first of October. Our 1885, their 1302. Two years after 1300 — the coming of their Mahdi." His voice was low and without inflection.

A leaden depression weighed down Will's limbs. "I saw you on the roof," he said.

"Went up for some air. Forgot where I was. No air to be had. But there were white kites with ragged wings and hawk heads, just by the confluence, crying plaintively. And a man visible in the Mahdi's camp throwing dust into the air. He looked like Shimei calling up David — thou bloody man. Probably one of mine gone over to the other side." He sighed, then seemed suddenly to brighten. "Well, he won't have long to wait. David will come out soon enough." A transitory cheer that was driven away by the morose, "It is our lot to be like Him, who, from His birth to His death, was miserable."

"But we've had a messenger, General. The relief is on its way. It will soon be at Jakdul."

"Jakdul?" A flicker of what might have been amusement twitched at the general's downturned lips. "If Wolseley hadn't spent so long luxuriating in Shephard's Hotel in Cairo, he would already have been here. But no. He leaves too late, attempts the river route, which any fool could have told him was the wrong choice, before gallivanting his troops around the desert setting up supply chains. It's one thing to dispatch a regiment of the best across the desert to surprise the Mahdi, quite another to traipse your camels this way and that. I dare say that somebody must have forgotten to point out to him that this is the Mahdi's country."

"You must go and tell your troops they're on their way. They need to hear it from you."

"Why should I bother?"

"They keep asking where you've got to."

"I cannot face them."

"They need you, General."

"I have taken such a dislike to those blacks — I cannot bear the sight of them."

That's mutual, Will might have said, but instead he took what he'd been hiding out of his back pocket. "Look." He thrust it at the general.

Gordon's surprise when he said, "Is that paper?" was unmistakable.

"I found it in the armoury."

The general's expression darkened. "Why would I want paper?"

"You could write your journal."

"There'll be nobody to read it."

"Then you could write one of your messages to the city. You know those always cheer them up."

CHAPTER
SEVENTEEN

Mary sat at her dressing table, looking into the mirror, and waited for time to pass.

Her eyes, she saw, were their usual placid brown and some extensive pinching of her cheeks had given them colour; the iciness of the air — it had snowed overnight — had helped too. And while her bodily jumpiness still plagued her, her thoughts were calm. She had made a plan and was determined to see it through. Her resolve supplied her with a great surge of energy that almost lifted her out of her seat. It being too early, she resisted. For her plan to work she must stay calm.

She sat for what felt like a lifetime until, at last, she heard Betty getting up. Still she sat, listening to Betty sweeping the dispensary, and laying fires. A soft trundling outside, then, "Milk-ho," heralded the arrival of the milkman's cart. The eager pattering of footsteps — could Betty be keen on the milkman's boy? — then the maid's high voice, his bass reply, the slosh of milk passing from pail to jug, the clink of a coin, and another, softer, exchange before the door was shut. More footsteps: Betty putting the milk in the larder, and finally Betty making her way upstairs to tap on Mary's door.

184

"Come."

"Your water, ma'am." Betty, who was holding a steaming jug, had, as usual, addressed herself to the bed. Finding it empty, she wheeled round so abruptly that water slopped on to the carpet. "Are you still unwell, ma'am?"

"Thank you, Betty. I am much improved."

"I could've helped you dress."

"I was up early so I did it myself. Have I done wrong?"

"No. You look lovely, ma'am."

Which was as planned.

"I'll lay your breakfast in the dining room," Betty said. "Then you'll be wanting to run through the menus."

"Not this morning," came Mary's even reply. "They will have to wait. I shall visit Dr Clarke's consulting rooms." She had decided to tell the simple truth and leave it at that, but Betty's obvious bemusement wrung from her "My husband asked me to do so." The lie tripped off her tongue. "I shall go after breakfast."

"Yes, ma'am." Betty gave an awkward bob. "Will I call a hansom?"

"I shall catch the omnibus. There is one that goes from Islington to Regent Circus, is there not?"

"Yes, ma'am, but —"

"I shall take it."

She pushed aside her yearning: it would soon be sated. With that in mind, she negotiated the omnibus competently enough. But the pavements, once she had left the omnibus, seemed impossibly crowded. She was buffeted from every side. Young men — clerks, she guessed — with flowers in their buttonholes and polished sticks swinging, strode past in the confidence of their belonging, undaunted by the chill, the dirty slush through which they stepped, and the lines of carriages and hansom cabs that swished past. All of this was so unfamiliar. She was completely out of place. Doubt flooded in. It did not matter that she had put on her finest day dress, with its soft blue folds, high bustle and train: she was a stranger here and vulnerable.

She felt someone take her elbow. She whirled round.

A man jumped away. "Forgive me, Mrs Clarke. I didn't mean to startle you. I called you but you seemed not to hear me."

"Mr Stead." She felt the heat rising to her face.

"Are you here on business?"

She nodded.

He looked at her, and she could see that he was waiting for an explanation. "I am on my way to my husband's consulting rooms."

"Let me, please, accompany you."

"I shall be quite all right. I haven't far to go."

"But I insist. Come." He hooked his arm, offering a nook for her hand, which she knew she must take.

In her imaginings she had made this journey alone. Now, with an acquaintance by her side, her determination wavered. It was as if she were a small child aching to cry out. No, that was too strong. The child was too small even for that. It wanted to bleat, and in that way to summon back her husband.

She swallowed the sound. John was gone. She was convinced of it, despite his promises. He would not come back. She blinked away tears and took the proffered arm.

"Your destination?"

"Wimpole Street. Over there."

"As you said, not far." He led her across the road, telling her that he had just come from observing the debate at the House. "Questions were asked." His fervour was, if anything, fiercer than she remembered it. "The country is united in our support of General Gordon. His example has galvanized us. By his determination he has given us direction in a time of uncertainty. Even Mr Gladstone is now praying for the general's safe return. I am confident that he will be saved. Our forces will soon be in Khartoum. Those nay sayers who have been so critical of the route chosen by General Wolseley will have to eat their words."

So caught up was he in his own narrative it didn't matter that she was barely listening. She was grateful for his prattle. It stopped her thinking about John's desertion and her own desperation. One foot in front of the other, she thought, and that way reached John's consulting room. She thanked her companion and turned away from him, went through the door and up the stairs. She pushed him, and everything other than her mission, from her mind. She wasn't going to think again until she had what she had come for.

The moment she stepped into John's consulting rooms, she was a woman transformed. Smiling and engaged, she gave her name before going to sit and thumb graciously through a periodical.

When the doctor appeared she did not look up. He called her name. She smiled but did not move. He came to her side. Younger than John, he cultivated the look of a much older man, his dark suit, sober waistcoat and the gold watch on its fob chain over a substantial stomach adding to this impression. "I apologize for having kept you waiting, Mrs Clarke." He took one of her hands and clasped it in both of his. "Do come in." He escorted her to his — John's — surgery.

If she had been an ordinary patient she would have seated herself in the chair that stood before the desk. As it was, she merely stood and looked at him, smiling. She was John's wife, sure of herself, and of the righteousness of her purpose while this doctor was so poor and unconnected his only hope was to be awarded a position in a hospital. If she played him correctly, he would do her bidding.

He drew an armchair closer to the fire and, having made sure she was comfortably ensconced, fetched his chair from behind the desk and seated himself to face her. "I trust you are well?"

"Very well." She invested her lips with the suggestion of a tremor. "Although I do miss my dear husband."

"I can only imagine how much," he said. "And now that the Camel Corps has set off across the desert, you must be concerned for his safety."

She nodded and, without comment, looked down.

She seemed to see herself through his eyes, the very image of a perfect wife. Not even John could have

188

guessed that this was a copy rather than the genuine article.

"I can show you the books now," she heard the doctor say. "You will find everything in order."

Oh! He thought she was John's spy — she almost laughed — come to check he was not pilfering from the business. The lie she had told Betty had become the truth.

"I will put aside a desk where you may examine them at your leisure."

"That will not be necessary," she began, before it crossed her mind that she, who always did the household accounts, might enjoy looking over the business ones. But not now: now was reserved for something much more important.

Unless . . . Why not, she thought, have both?

"Perhaps you will send the books to Barnsbury," she even half believed that this was indeed the reason for her visit, "where I can look at them."

"Of course. I will see it done."

"Thank you." She was surprised by how much she was enjoying herself.

"Your husband is a fortunate man," the doctor was saying, "to have not only a beautiful wife but one who takes such an interest in his profession."

The perfect line. She seized it. "You are too kind." She managed a blush. "Naturally, I would want to help him in any way I can."

"Of course, Mrs Clarke."

"I am even occasionally called upon to issue medicines from the dispensary, at John's instruction."

She gave a deprecatory laugh. "You don't find that too presumptuous, I hope?"

"On the contrary." He was her grinning fool. "If I were fortunate enough to have a wife as intelligent as yourself I trust she would do the same for me."

He was gazing at her with such admiration that she was reminded of how John had once looked at her. At least marriage had not completely dulled her. The confident, carefree girl she had been, the one with the power to turn men's heads, still existed.

Time for that girl to take command. Now. Before her courage deserted her. "Which brings me to the further reason for my visit," she said, "if I may?"

"Of course, Mrs Clarke."

"My husband has a particular patient, rather well connected — I hope you will understand if I do not name him — who prefers to be treated away from the public eye."

"Yes, indeed. We all have such patients."

She knew that he did not. Her courage rising, she said, "My husband left a series of packages for this patient. I have been issuing them at intervals, according to his instructions. But, John having been away rather longer than anticipated, they have now run out, which has put this patient in particular difficulty."

"You could send him to me."

Too fast. Too eager. She had him. "I would certainly have done that, but he is particularly chary of meeting anybody new. I had hoped you might help him through me. I would naturally inform him of your co-operation, which might persuade him eventually to consult you directly."

"If I am able to assist, then I am at your service."

"How very kind."

"What is the nature of his requirement?"

"John gives him laudanum."

"I see. Laudanum."

Was that scepticism she could see in his grey regard? She drew herself up to meet his gaze. She must not show any nervousness, and neither would she break the silence. She was, anyway, indifferent to him. What he might be thinking might have worried Mrs Clarke but she was no longer just Mrs Clarke. She was the girl Mary she had once been.

"Until the Pharmacy Act of 1868," the doctor held her gaze, "laudanum was freely available. It was much misused by the lower classes — hence the Act. Although the illegal trade has not entirely been stamped out, only pharmacists and doctors are permitted to issue it. Modern practitioners favour newer mixtures — laudanum's paregoric, for example, the camphorated tincture of opium or morphine. I am a little surprised your husband has not considered changing the treatment."

"I wouldn't know about that." A perfect answer because why would she?

"Some patients are most averse to change." He sounded as if he might be trying to convince himself.

Her smile concealed the clamping of her teeth on her tongue. A fine balance. She must not say anything to disturb it.

"Well, Mrs Clarke." He leaned forward and returned her smile. "This is what I propose."

Such a contrast between the woman who had stepped into the surgery and the one who stepped out. She was no longer the Mary who had almost cried for John on her way in.

As soon as she was safely out of sight, she had sipped some of the laudanum he had given her. Already it was beginning to relax her, slowing the pounding of her leaden heart, the laudanum vibrations stroking her from within. Even her breathing was orchestrated by a new luxurious softness.

She was able to take in sights she had previously ignored. The gloriously blue sky, bright and hard. The white magnificence of the buildings. What before had seemed jagged was now smooth. She slotted into the moving crowd and flowed with it. True, there was something to be concerned about in the future — he had not given her nearly enough — but why worry when her easy steps matched the blissful languor that had assailed her limbs? She smiled. Her cheeks lifted and her jaw softened. She felt . . . wonderful. She had done something without John. His going away had been good for her.

CHAPTER
EIGHTEEN

Jakdul: as the word passed down the column the mood was transformed. Jakdul in sight. John bent to repeat it — "Jakdul" — to the patient strapped into a cacolet.

The man's bearded face cracked open. His swollen lips parted to emit a feeble cheer. He was very sick, his skin so badly burned that parts had peeled off to reveal a raw, red underbelly. He was also extremely brave. Each bump of the camel against the increasingly stony ground must have been agony, but he had not once complained or even groaned.

John dropped water into his open mouth.

As the man tried to swallow, those close enough to see some precious drops regurgitated involuntarily flicked out their tongues to moisten lips smoked by the sun into hard, dry strings. A desperate longing seemed to consume them. Not, John knew, because they begrudged water to a dying man. It was just that water had become their sole obsession.

"We'll soon be there," he told his patient.

The man nodded, and stretched his gaunt face into another imitation of a smile, neither he nor John saying what both must have been thinking: that Jakdul had, in all likelihood, come too late to save this man.

No time to worry about that. Jakdul was nigh. Each step took them a little closer. Hope flared in breasts even as men told themselves not to hope too much. Rumour had it that Kitchener had scouted the place and found water there, but that was only rumour and could not be relied on. Not dependable, either, were the Arab guides who had boasted of the bounteous wells: how could one trust the word of a man who had been press-ganged into coming on this march?

As they jolted closer to Jakdul the path began to change. Soon they were moving down a wide, dried-up channel that must once have been a river. To both sides, spindly mimosa and blue-green grass gripped thinning sand. The bulbous outcrops of anthracite that had been scattered through most of their journey had increased in number and size, and joined up to form two natural walls that grew higher and higher as well as closer together, forcing them into single file.

The merciless sun burned down, its light turning the walls an ominous shining jet black. The path began further to narrow. The column was now hedged in on both sides by walls that appeared, in the near distance, to merge.

"Good place for an ambush," said a man in front of John.

He was cut off by a curt communal "Hush."

They were too thirsty to talk. Too thirsty to fight. Too thirsty, almost, to ride on towards Jakdul. Besides, the Hussars had gone ahead to reconnoitre. The buglers had sounded the all clear. There would be, could be, no ambush.

194

But what if there was no water in Jakdul?

Don't think of that either. Keep going. If not Jakdul, then Metemma after it.

On they went, in single file, a handler leading the patient's camel, while another walked by his side to stop him banging into the rock. The walls of stone were now so high they cast shadows over the moving march. On and on. Would Jakdul turn out to be a mirage? Not a mirage but a phantasm created by their officers to keep them going.

Then, at long last, a chain of ricocheting voices turned desire into reality. Each man transmitted the message to the man behind him: at the point where the two walls of rock seemed to meet there was a cleft, so well concealed that it must be true; the magician Kitchener, in his flowing Arab robes, must have been the one to find it. And through this cleft there lay Jakdul. A dead-end waste of sand and pools — this news passed along as well — most of which were dry. But not all. There were three cisterns, worn into different levels of the rock. Three natural wells. And each contained water.

Water and it was near. It was all they could think of. How agonizing to think of it and not to see it. To know it was there and be unable to drink. On top of this one voice rose into the thin, hot air, like a nightmare: "Do not drink," telling them what they could not contemplate: "Listen. Do not drink."

Forward the column went, camel after camel passing through the narrow gap. Into a kind of hell.

High, dark walls of stone formed the perimeter of a huge dry bowl, trapping a cacophony of sound. Camels bellowing, Arab voices urging them on, British sergeants sweating and swearing, and that same unrelenting cry: "Listen, men." Real and not imagined: "Do not drink."

"Unload your camels over there," a sergeant roared, while to his counterpart on the other side of the opening fell those impossible words: "Do not drink." But now that they had come closer, they could also hear a merciful qualifying, "Do not drink from the lower pool. The water's tainted. Use the tanks."

The restraint that had stopped the men torturing their plodding camels snapped. Knowing how close their animals were to collapse they nevertheless dug the sharp ends of their boots into the sagging sides. "Forwards!" they shouted, only to find that, sure-footed as they were on sand, the camels were slithering on the stone. And still, "Forwards!" the men yelled, as their camels groaned, rumbled and reared their heads. They, too, were maddened by thirst. They bared their teeth as they slid towards the dismounting station. It was so slippery there that, no matter how hard their riders pulled on their halters, the camels, whose hoofs could not grip, would not be coaxed down. Eventually the riders had to slide off their animals, their curses mixing with the camels' mad bellowing. And all the while pumps worked noisily to push water from the upper pools down the hundreds of feet of pipe the engineers had laid into large tin boxes, which had once contained biscuit but now were nowhere near big enough: these reservoirs were continually being emptied by the press of thirsty men, and there were always more who needed water. Flaking lips were licked in the agony of being so close and yet so far away, tongues swelling in anticipation, as riderless camels made for the lower pool, "Animals only." The same terrible refrain. "Do not drink from the lower pool." Into the lower pool the camels waded, there to stand and suck, their humps, limp and flabby, gradually gaining definition as their riders, receptacles in hand, waited their turn, John among them.

"Here." Another of Tom Jenkins' miraculous appearances, this time with a waterskin.

Without a word, John tipped it to his lips.

The water that streamed into his mouth was cool and utterly delicious, flowing through him like a blessing. Tears — moisture that he had assumed had been baked from his body days ago — sprang to his eyes.

"I'll make sure the patient's unloaded," Tom said.

John was still drinking.

"We've set up base over there, under that mimosa. Near the guards' mess."

John did not spare the place a glance.

"Drink, then go and see. It's a wonder."

When John had started to drink, his tongue, thickened, fibrous and seeming to fill his mouth, was an obstacle to swallowing. Soon, however, both it and the roof of his mouth — how could it have grown so hard without his noticing? — softened and the water flowed through. He drank himself into a drunkenness more intense than any he had ever previously experienced.

He was not alone in this. All around him men laughed uproariously and shouted sentences that made no sense but expressed the joy that could be got from drinking water while others, grim-faced, stood and watched and waited their turn.

At last John had drunk the last drop. His stomach was rock hard. After days of deprivation he had most likely drunk too much, but should Tom have arrived with a second waterskin, he would have drunk that as well. The water surged inside him.

How privileged he was. How lucky to have Tom. A long line of men, silent and intent, eyes focused on the tanks, queued to get their share. Others, disobeying orders, were scrambling up the sheer rock face to reach water for themselves.

"Go and see", Tom had said, and John, feeling invulnerable now, thought, Why not? No matter that he had once been uneasy with heights. The privation of the march had done its job. It had made him stronger. Tougher. Less afraid. He joined the row of men climbing up the steep escarpment.

When her driver leaned across to open her door Mary, feigning a confidence she did not feel, stepped out smartly. "Thank you. Wait here for me."

She crossed the cobbled road on to a pavement so filthy she had to hold up her skirt. There was a knot of people ahead, and their eyes were on her. She took a deep breath and walked towards them. They quietened at her approach and moved out of her way, but she could still feel their stares as she made her way to one of a long row of high, narrow houses.

Since her visit to Wimpole Street she had been so full of energy that the thought of being cooped up at home until John's return made her want to scream. She had to find something to occupy her time. She went up a short flight of steps and pulled the bell.

The exterior of the house was neat, and inside its damask curtains gleamed. It was smarter than its neighbours, but even they were respectable enough, nothing like the dark slums of her imagination. No matter that her mother would never have dreamed of venturing into Spitalfields, especially unchaperoned. Times had changed, and Mary with them. She felt herself relax. She had done the right thing. There was no reason for anxiety. This thought was confirmed when a young girl opened the door and, seeing Mary, curtsied.

"I'm Mrs Clarke. I sent a note."

"Oh, yes, ma'am. They're expecting you." The maid stepped back to reveal a clean, if somewhat bare, interior.

Ahead was a steep staircase, and to one side, a parlour, into which the maid gestured. As Mary was about to go in, the sound of hurried footsteps on the landing made her look up. She saw a woman who, carefully holding a basin, moved hastily, but also very quietly, across the landing. There was something familiar to Mary in her purposeful walk and dignified gravity.

"If you'd wait in here, ma'am."

Alone in the clean, plain room Mary sat on the edge of a chair and gazed around. The room was respectable if also rather bare, with no pictures on the wall, and no ornaments on the side tables. It was, she thought, a room of duty rather than of the heart, with no sense of home. And, despite the quiet, agitation seemed to flutter in the air, fed by pattering footsteps, low voices and, she imagined, shaking heads.

"Mrs Clarke."

It was Mrs Ferguson. Mary's heart dropped.

"We are delighted to have you with us."

The sight of this overbearing woman with whom she always felt wrong-footed, combined with the portentously grim edge of Mrs Ferguson's smile, told Mary what a bad idea this had been. Never mind. "I'm afraid I've come at a difficult time," she said. "Is someone ill upstairs?"

"Yes." The smile stretched and simultaneously chilled. "One of our girls. She was never very strong and then she caught a chill. The inflammation has settled on her lungs. She is breathing with great difficulty. We fear her time is near."

"It would be better, then, if I came back on another day." She would leave and never return.

She had reckoned, however, without Mrs Ferguson's determination. "I will not hear of it, Mrs Clarke. We shall be sorry to lose Lizzie but we take comfort in returning one of our own to God, and in welcoming you to our refuge. Please come upstairs and make Lizzie's acquaintance. She will like that."

They went into a horrible plain room, the only furniture a narrow iron bed and, above it, a large wooden cross. A figure lay on the bed and a woman knelt by it, her head bowed in prayer.

Mary was accustomed to sickbeds — her husband was, after all, a doctor — but something about this scene provoked in her a ferocity of feeling that was not so much fear as rebellion. I have to leave, she thought, and would have done — but she could feel Mrs Ferguson's breath on her neck. If she were to try to escape, this portly meddler would be there to block her.

"Here is Mrs Clarke," Mrs Ferguson said loudly, and with great satisfaction.

The kneeling woman, whose stern black dress seemed a reproach to her kind face, got up. She stepped aside to reveal on the bed a white wraith whose emaciated arms lay, unmoving, on the coverlet, while her straggly hair flowed out beyond the pillow. The sight pulled from Mary an involuntary "But she's so young."

"As far as we have been able to reckon it, Lizzie has only just turned twelve."

"How dreadful."

"Dreadful indeed." This from Mrs Ferguson. "She was thrown out into the streets by her despoiler. Without protection, she was bought and sold like a slave until at last, God be praised, she found her way to us. Stories such as hers are commonplace. That is why Mrs Booth founded this refuge." Mrs Ferguson went over to the bed to lay a proprietary hand on the girl's arm. "How are you, Lizzie?"

The child, whose breathing was laboured, did not respond. Undaunted, Mrs Ferguson continued: "This is Mrs Clarke, Lizzie, come to give you comfort," and to Mary: "Draw nearer so she may greet you."

An image reared in Mary's mind. Not this young girl but another of the same age. Her sister. It was a memory she avoided revisiting. It filled her with horror.

"Come, Mrs Clarke."

"It would be an intrusion. She does not know I'm here."

"Only God can know what she knows." This from the woman who had been praying and now approached Mary. She took her hand. "Come. Greet her. It will comfort her to know that you are here to join our growing band."

The top pool to which John had climbed was large and very beautiful. Its green waters — oddly cold — touched lightly against rocks covered with glutinous dark weeds. The air was cool and dry, and dragonflies, their wings glinting scarlet in the waning sun, skittered over the surface of the still water where it deepened and darkened almost to black. It was also very quiet. The tanks being full, even the pumps had stopped so John could hear the men far below who, having pitched camp, were frolicking in the lower pool, washing away the sweat and grime of their journey. Others stood by the water's edge, shaving.

How wonderful to be in their company. To be alive and so full of life.

202

He thought of Mary, of the vivacity and vigour of her welcome when she had met him on his return from work. Now, looking back, he saw how aloof he must have seemed to her. He would make it different in the future, he thought. He would enfold her in his arms and listen to her. When he got home. He would talk to her about the things he had learned.

He was so tired. He stretched out across the surface of stone that, with dusk only just falling, was still warm. How wonderful to rest. He put his arms behind him, making a pillow for his head, and closed his eyes against the scarlet sun.

Mary kept her eyes closed as she knelt beside the other women, all three praying for the dying Lizzie. She had begun in great discomfort but, as time passed, she relaxed. There was something reassuring about the company and their prayers.

"Fear thou not," Mrs Ferguson intoned, "for I am with thee. Be not dismayed, for I am thy God."

Mrs Ferguson wasn't a malicious woman, Mary thought. She had done Mary a favour by insisting she stay.

Something shifted on the bed. Could it be? She opened her eyes. And, yes — her heart soared. She had not imagined the movement.

She had been right not to give in to panic and run away. She would remain in this company.

Mrs Ferguson's rising "I will strengthen thee" seemed to resonate inside her. "Yea, I will help thee."

The girl lifted an arm.

"Yea, I will uphold thee with the right hand of My righteousness."

The girl's eyes opened — they were green and startled — then her clear child's voice rang out, "Hallelujah!" Her hand slapped down on to the sheet. One last, long sigh. Such finality. She was done and death slackened her mouth, while what little colour she'd had was already waxen with life-lessness.

"She's gone."

Mrs Ferguson's thick hands closed the girl's eyes. "She is with God now. Let us pray. 'Our Father, which art in heaven . . .'"

Mary had no voice to lift in prayer. She was capable only of registering the tears coursing down her cheeks. She was weeping without meaning to, and for a child she had not known.

She was feeling . . . No words came to her when she tried to name it. She could only acknowledge it as a feeling.

The sunstroke patient died as he had borne his illness: without fuss. John leaned over to close his eyes. "We should have called the chaplain."

"He didn't ask for one." Tom laid a thin shroud over the corpse. "If it's special pleading God's after, there'll be plenty of that at daybreak when they bury the poor devil. They'll pray up a storm then, although, him being a private, they won't mark his grave." There was an uncharacteristic hint of bitterness in Tom's tone but, meeting John's enquiring glance, all he said was, "We should take something to warm ourselves." He went to

204

the pile of medical supplies, took a half-empty bottle of brandy from the stores and said, "Come."

John followed him, both men picking their way gingerly past knots of sleeping men, most of them huddled in blankets, others squeezed against their animals in an attempt to ward off the icy wind that, sweeping down the high-stacked stone surroundings, had caused the temperature to plummet.

"Let's get clear away." Tom led John to the water's edge, his keen eyes helping him to pick out some smooth rocks on to which they both settled. He used his teeth to open the bottle and spat the cork into the water. He took a long draught. "That's better." He wiped the neck of the bottle and handed it to John. "Here."

The hit of brandy against the back of John's throat felt so good that he took another, longer, swig. Good. He passed back the bottle. For a while it moved between them as the deep snores of animals and men rose up into the night with, as counterpoint, the soft tread of sentries on their circled watch. Every now and then a muffled curse rang out as, without lights, they skinned their shins on the edges of the rock.

"I don't know why they're not allowed to sleep," John said. "There can't be anybody out there."

"It looks empty enough, I grant you, but to them that understands this country, there'll be nooks and crannies to hide in."

"You think the enemy knows we're here?" John shivered.

"They'd have to be deaf and blind not to, thanks to Wolseley's brilliant plan. First he sends us up the Nile and through all those cataracts, and all because he once won a war by sending troops upriver. When he finally grasps that this river is different from his last one, he changes his mind, opts for the desert route, marches a whole contingent to Jakdul to check for water and then, like the grand old duke of York, back to Korti to fetch us. We might as well have telegraphed our whereabouts to the Mahdi and saved him the trouble of sending scouts." Tom took another gulp. "Bleeding officers. You should hear them boasting, when they're in their cups, about what a glory it is to die in battle. They don't think of us, though, do they, who are meant to die with them?"

Looking out at the dark water, a mirror to the blackness of the night, John wondered what had made the habitually taciturn Tom so suddenly garrulous.

"And you know the reason for all this toing and froing? It's because we're short of pack camels. And why are we short of camels? Because gentlemen officers, like Sir Redvers blooming Buller, in charge of buying camels, is using forty-six of them to carry his champagne. Veuve Clicquot," the name so bitterly pronounced it sounded as profane as any swear word, "is the one to which he is particularly partial." Tom spat on the ground.

John was thrilled by the man's confiding in him but, as an officer, he felt beholden to put the other side. "You don't like the army," he said.

"I like it well enough." Tom gazed out moodily across the water. It was still and dark. John thought again of the upper pool in daylight. So different from the deep, dark, undrinkable undertow through which Tom was swimming.

"It's the officers I can't abide," Tom said. "Bunch of crooks. Not all of them. They say Gordon knows how to fight. Stewart too. You'd be okay with *them* if it came to a scrap. But as for the rest." He spat again and took a long swallow of brandy. Then, with exaggerated care — He must be as drunk as I am, John thought — he set down the bottle. "If we'd had more water, that man would have lived."

"Perhaps."

"No perhaps about it. Some ninny with friends in high places issued us with waterskins that don't hold water. Have you ever heard anything so stupid? They think so little of us that they risk our lives for nothing."

"The kit could have been better." John shrugged. "But men do die."

"You think I could have been so long in the army without knowing that? We're soldiers. Dying is what we do. What I can't abide is losing one for no good reason."

"It could have happened at home."

"A man die of sunstroke? Not likely." Tom picked up the bottle. "I hate to witness an unnecessary death. Somebody's son has gone and for no reason." He was speaking so softly John had to lean in to hear him. "It fills me with regret for my wasted life." He drank deeply, finishing what remained, then inverted the bottle. No drop fell out. He was a dark shadow in the night, gazing at the empty bottle.

"I had a son once," Tom said. "I couldn't abide his mother. I left them both when I signed up." He threw the bottle into the water.

PART FOUR

THE ADVANCE ON KHARTOUM

The force which left Korti on Thursday, the 8th, reached Gakdul on the 12th, and after a rest of two days started on Wednesday last for Metammeh. Thus, the second journey from Korti to Gakdul occupied considerably more time than the first, while both men and animals appear to have suffered from want of water. The proper allowance for a desert march in the cool season is a gallon a day for each man, and it is clear that either the wish to carry as many stores as possible led to the provision of too small a reserve of water, or a greater rate of advance was calculated upon and the capacity of the Howeiyat wells was overestimated. The hardship was no doubt partly caused by the fact that the men have not yet all learnt the hard self-discipline involved in sparing the water as much as possible; but it is specially stated that the waterskins "proved utterly deceptive through leakage", and the column suffered, therefore, from that want of a proper desert equipment which was foreseen and foretold. The force which left Gakdul at 2p.m. on Wednesday consists, according to the telegrams of Saturday, of the Guards-Marines Camel Corps (380), the heavy Camel Corps (350), the Mounted Infantry (400), a squadron of 19th Hussars (90), a half-battalion Sussex Regiment (say 175), Royal Artillery camel battery (three guns), Royal Engineers (30), Naval Brigade (50, with one Gardner machine gun), making a total fighting force of 1,475 men with three guns. If the light Camel Corps is present, the total strength would be 1,825.

News from Gakdul requires nearly three days to reach London ... Even with the special arrangements which have doubtless been made, it seems doubtful whether the information so anxiously awaited could reach London before tomorrow.

The Times, 19 Jan., 1885

CHAPTER
NINETEEN

By the narrow passageway through which they must all pass, half a dozen Sudanese guides were guarded by a contingent of 19th Hussars with instructions to shoot them, should they show signs of bolting. Behind them was arrayed the rest of the Camel Corps. They were about to leave Jakdul.

How smart they looked. More than fifteen hundred men, and their officers, freshly shaved, spick and span in their yellow ochre cord breeches and dark blue puttees (or, in the case of the officers, long field boots), their grey serge tunics toning them to the desert, while their white pith helmets glinted in the sun. Their brown bandoliers were hugged tight to their chests, puffed with bullets.

When the order came to mount, the men expertly unhobbled their camels, wrenched back their heads and then, in silence and synchronicity, leaned back in their saddles and jerked on reins causing their camels to dip and sway as they lumbered to their feet without protest and in record time. Soon the whole company was lined up to go. Such a different atmosphere from their first setting off. Then their easy camaraderie had lit the atmosphere. Now something darker and much more determined took over. There was the same eagerness, but it was shot through with deadly intent. They were heading into what, in all likelihood, would be a battle whose terrain and terms they could not dictate. A reason for anxiety, yes, but they were the cream of the British Army. With the disasters of the Crimea behind them they were still the best. The undefeated. They had no doubt that victory would be theirs.

A bugle call. The first of the camels began to plod out of the safety of Jakdul.

They were starting late, their departure having been delayed by the necessity of ensuring that each man and each beast was sufficiently hydrated. The next watering hole was deeper in the desert at Abu Klea, the only possible stopping point before they reached the Nile at Metemma where Gordon's steamers would be waiting to take them on the last stretch of the journey to Khartoum. As the column moved off, a fresh order was passed along: the men must drink only when so commanded.

Such a picture of manly resolve, and John in its midst. Confident on his camel, and surrounded by the members of the bearer companies with their supplies, their cacolets and litters, he flushed with pride. His uneasy night of awakening to find himself shivering, not from cold or fear for himself but from the fear that he might let the men down, had left him. At this moment of their setting off, in the baking heat of mid-afternoon, he felt at one with the other men. He glanced down at hands so weathered by the sun they no longer looked like his. He saw them shaking, again not from fear — it wasn't that, he told himself — but from exhilaration.

"You've nothing to worry about, laddie." It was the harsh voice of Colonel Watson, who had steered his camel deliberately close. A white Arabian breed, it was taller than John's, which allowed the colonel to look down on him. His gaze alighted on John's hands. "At the first hint of trouble, get well inside the square." There was insolence in his tone, heightened by his next remark: "The men will have better things to do than look after you." He steered his camel away.

How dare the man?

"Take no notice." Tom had witnessed the episode, as he seemed to witness everything. "As brusque as he is, I'd as soon have him guarding my back as any other soldier." He gave a tug on John's camel's headstall, which set the beast plodding in the hoofprints of the string of camels that stretched out far into the distance. "Stay close." He narrowed his eyes against the bright sunlight as he steered his animal in front of John's.

When Betty came into the sitting room to say, "There's two," Mary didn't, at first, understand but when Betty added, "He says it's three and fourpence," she realized that the maid meant there were two letters from John. Her arm was heavy as she counted out the coins.

Slow footsteps, Betty's tread to the door and then slowly coming back, by which time, Mary could no longer contain herself. She snatched the envelopes. "Thank you, Betty. That will be all."

Mary sat down, dropped the letters into the folds of her dark blue skirt and looked at them. She was frightened by the thought of what they might contain.

She tried to work out when she had written to John. If she could do that, she would be able to guess whether there had been enough time for him to have received her confession and sent back his reply. She counted backwards and forwards. There couldn't have been enough time.

Why, then, had he written two?

Unable to sit still, she made her way to the library where, it being early, the fire had not been lit. She sat at the desk, telling Betty who had followed, "Leave me. And please close the door behind you."

Alone at last, she wasted a little time in moving aside the surgery accounts, the desultory inspection of which had become her nightly activity. In their place she laid the envelopes. She smoothed them, first one and then the other. Then she slit them both open.

She had meant only to glance at the dates on each so she could be sure to read them in sequence. But the first she looked at, which turned out to be the second he'd written, was shorter than its fellow and she couldn't stop her gaze skimming to the end. Relief — he had not had her letter — knocked against a darker emotion. It tugged at her, making her want to read the letter again, more slowly. But no. She turned the paper over, seeing its other side blank, then applied herself to the first.

It was written to the same formula as his previous letters. To begin: admiring praise for the men with

216

whom he had found himself; next, descriptions of sights seen, and sounds heard, so many of them that his high looped handwriting was packed tight across the lines, through the margins and up the side of the page, where he had signed off in abrupt shorthand almost at the point where he had begun, his hurry necessitated, he wrote, by the need to catch the mailboat before it steamed away. After which, and almost as an afterthought, he had hastily scratched what might have been protestations of love but his words were now so tightly crammed she couldn't be sure.

It was, in short, an ordinary letter, the kind Mr Stead would cheerfully have reproduced in his *Pall Mall Gazette*. It told her nothing of the man she knew. Or, at least, of the man she had once believed she knew.

She laid it to one side. Delaying the moment when she would reread the second letter, she looked around the library.

It had changed. She had rearranged the furniture to create more space, removing ornaments once painstakingly amassed, throwing away fringed lace mats, and ordering Betty to polish the wooden surfaces until they gleamed. The room was now much brighter and lighter. So much more up to date. It delighted her.

There was still above the desk that daguerreotype of John. She looked up at it. Back he gazed, and sternly. He was, she thought, practically glowering. Perhaps she would have the portrait moved.

She picked up his second letter.

Korti, Soudan, January 1885.
My dearest Mary,
　　There is something that I must tell you.

How odd that they had had started their confessions in almost identical fashion. She read on:

News having reached Korti of General Gordon's deteriorating circumstances, General Wolseley has ordered the Camel Corps across the desert.

　　The Expedition has insufficient surgeons. There being no time in which to await more, I cannot, in all conscience, refuse to volunteer my services. I have therefore resolved to travel with the corps.

　　The officers are confident that the resistance of the Mahdi, whose forces are concentrated around Khartoum, will melt away in the face of our advance. I have even overheard several of these brave men regretting that they might succeed in their mission without ever having the opportunity to engage the enemy. You may therefore rest assured that I will not be in any danger.

　　We are imminently to depart. I must dispatch this letter forthwith. Once our march begins, there will be few opportunities for mail collection. Do not therefore be alarmed if it is some time before you receive further news of me.

　　In haste. Your loving husband,
　　John

★ ★ ★

And that — she turned the letter over to take in the blank page — was all her loving husband had to say to her.

She laid down the letter and stepped away from the desk. She noted absently that she was shivering. The room was very cold.

She looked up at the picture of her husband. The forbidding doctor gazed back. Not a hint of a smile in his expression or any of the gentleness she had once associated with him.

If he does not return, she thought, this will be my remaining image of him.

She caught the thought and held it to herself.

It was what she had feared from the first when he had told her he was thinking of joining the expedition. "I have not yet made up my mind," he had said, but she had read in his expression the lie that lay beneath his words. He *had* made up his mind. He had been asking, without having to say the words, for her permission, and she, who had never been able to refuse him anything, had given it. With one proviso, that he would not go into battle — which he had willingly conceded.

And here he was, writing as if her fears, and his assurances, were trivialities to be ignored.

There is something that I must tell you.

As she thought back to her confession, the shame that had been building in the weeks since she had dispatched it washed over her. It was one thing, if he had been here, to talk to him, but to have written so baldly of her weakness . . .

If only she had not sent him her letter. If only . . . if only something would prevent it getting through. He had gone into battle: he might die.

If he did, would they read her letter? "No," she said. "Of course they won't." They would send it back with the rest of his effects. If he were to die, she would be spared his disgust and then, before she could bite it back, there came another thought: Maybe it would be a good thing if he did die.

She was revolted by herself. She stumbled forward, crumpled into a chair and dropped her head into her hands. She closed her eyes, wanting simultaneously to blot out her thoughts.

She found herself embracing a vision that would not leave her. That frail figure on the bed. Not the stranger, Lizzie, but her sister.

The angry flush that had stained her sister's face was fading to white. Her father stood at the threshold, as if something was stopping him coming in. Mary knelt beside her mother at her sister's bedside, and prayed — this was how it was and would always remain — prayed shamefully not that her sister would live but that she, Mary, would not die. Please, God. Please, God, don't let it happen to me.

And now she might lose John too.

She seemed to see him then. Could she not control her wayward thoughts? His hand, stroking her face, belied the puzzlement in his expression at the intensity of her desire. She had frightened him, she knew she had, even though he denied it.

220

She sat in the dark, abandoned place where he had left her. She continued to sit as the sun slipped into the horizon, and the grey light that had filled the room darkened. Unthinkingly she sat, unaware of the chill creeping into her bones. And then, after a while, thoughts began to glimmer. Slowly they came, thoughts she had not had before and which, at first, so muddied her mind that she blocked them. Still they nudged her, growing stronger with the dark, until there could be no denying them.

It was not her fault, she thought, that Elizabeth had died. Her prayers had not killed her sister. Such an evident truth, yet this was the first time she had grasped it. As she did so, the icy cold of her grief began to lift, giving way to a rebelliousness that rode in on another thought. If John isn't here, I must make my own decisions.

CHAPTER
TWENTY

"Come on, Frankie." Will tugged at his dog's leash. "Up you get, boy."

Painfully thin as he was, Frankie was still capable of resistance. He dug his thick yellow claws into the stone floor. Will could easily have dragged him up — one yank would have lifted him high into the air — and Frankie knew it. He gave a soft whine, more cat than dog, looked up at his master and seemed to shake his head.

The sight almost made Will cry.

What Will wanted more than anything was for Frankie to behave as he used to. To beg to be let out of the room as once he would have done. But Frankie no longer had sufficient energy to be that dog, and Will lacked the heart to force him to it. He let go of the leash.

Frankie's bony frame sank to the ground.

"Come on, boy."

Frankie slapped down his tail.

"Come on." Tears springing to Will's eyes. "You can't give up."

Although Frankie's eyes were moist to match Will's, and his tail was still wagging, he stuck to the floor. It would be cruel to force him up.

Will patted his dog's head. "I know. You want to, but you can't."

When Frankie licked his hand, Will felt how dry his tongue was. He went to the door and poured water from a jug into a bowl. In one last effort to persuade the dog to his feet, he nudged the bowl forward. "Here, boy." Frankie didn't move. Sighing, Will took it to him, putting it down close to his head. Still Frankie did not move. "Come on, boy. You'll feel better if you have a drink." Frankie's head drooped.

Will scooped water into his curved palm and held it up to the dog's mouth. Frankie's tongue darted out to lick it.

"Good boy." Will gave him another palmful of water, then lifted the bowl and held it up to him.

When Frankie raised his head high enough to lap, Will's spirits soared. There was hope. There had to be. "That's right." With one hand steadying the bowl, he used the other to stroke the dog's head.

Frankie's wiry hair had thinned. It was as soft and smooth as wet silk. But if Will had applied any more pressure he would have felt bone.

Frankie stopped drinking but at least he'd had a bit. And he did look brighter for it. "I have to go and find the general," Will told him, "before he comes to find us."

Frankie's tail thumped but he dropped his head on to his paws and closed his eyes. He wasn't going anywhere: he did not have the strength.

"You sleep." One last stroke of Frankie's skeletal back. "Keep your strength up." Then Will whispered, "I'll find you some food, I promise."

Down the corridor Will went, past all those shut and deadened doors. He would have passed Stewart's room as well, but the man's ghost seemed to tug at him. He opened the door.

"Hello," he called, as he always did. As always, there was no answer. He stepped inside.

The first thing he noticed was the layer of dust that had settled over everything in the room. The second was the feeling that he was not alone. He told himself that hunger was making him imagine things, yet now he seemed to see, by the desk and framed against the light, a shadowy figure. His heart thudded and his teeth clenched. Nobody ever came into this room.

Could the enemy have broken in?

But no. The wavy outline of a man was not behaving as an enemy would. It merely occupied the space, unreal, and yet it seemed real to Will. "Who are you?"

The figure of a man turned and its featureless face seemed to break out in a smile.

Despite the long years of their separation, that pockmarked face was unmistakable. Will started running to the father who he knew could not be there. And who was not. He found himself utterly alone by the desk.

His run had cost him dear. He doubled over, struggling to catch his breath. His head spun and his chest hurt. Stupid, he thought. So stupid. Like the general's, his sanity must have been eaten away by lack of food. Some trick of the light, and some trick of starvation, had embedded his father in his mind.

"Stupid," he said. His mother had been right: in dying, his father had left him unprotected. She had been right about Will too: he was a wastrel, who couldn't even concentrate on doing the one thing he had to do, which was to save his dog.

CHAPTER
TWENTY-ONE

Having tied the triangular bandage tightly round the soldier's bloody, blistered foot, John dismissed him with a nod. He had been treating men in the night air — mostly saddle sores and foot problems — for hours, and all of this after a punishing march. He was very tired. He corked carbolic acid to prevent evaporation, then tucked it into the pocket of his uniform. He called out wearily, "Next."

"You're done," came Tom's reply, as he began to clear the area of old bandages and empty ointment cases.

The last time John had looked up a line of men had been waiting in the dark and, all the other doctors having long since retired, they should still have been waiting. But Tom was right: nobody was there. "Where have they all gone?"

"I sent them away."

"You did what?"

"I had the orderlies dress the worst of the scrapes and boils. The rest can manage without."

"They can, can they?" John's voice was tight with fury that Tom's quiet, "Yes, sir," served only to stoke. "They needed treatment," he said.

"They needed sleep. As do we."

That Tom had the temerity to argue — it was too bad.

All the heat and frustration of the march — camels sliding in the drifts of sloping sand, the column's progress hampered by the call of rear buglers, a desperately needed break abruptly ended by the signal to remount, the colonel's incessant sneering — and now the disobedience of his orderly, never mind the raw throbbing of his thigh that his time at Jakdul seemed to have worsened, boiled up in John. He'd given up a lot to come to the Sudan and he had learned much since. He was no longer a novice. He was an officer who could not let this undermining of his authority go unchallenged. He had to show Tom, once and for all, which of them was in charge.

"Sergeant," he said, forcing Tom to warily look up.

"Sssh," someone hissed.

Most of the men had already settled down to sleep. "Follow me." John turned and, knowing that Tom had no choice other than to obey, marched off without a backward glance.

Although the soft sand of the dried-up watercourse was comfortable enough for sleeping on, its ridges, baked in by wind and sun, made walking awkward, especially in the dark and especially for somebody like John, whose night vision was poor. He was stumbling so badly over the rough terrain that at several points he needed a hand from the sure-footed Tom, which did nothing to improve his temper.

At last he decided they had put sufficient distance between themselves and the sleeping men. It was time to read Tom the Riot Act and to do it so definitively that he would never again think of questioning John's orders. "Did I not tell you I would see every man who needed me?"

"Yes." Tom's pitted skin always made it difficult for John to read his expression, especially in the dark. "That you did," he said.

"Then why did you send them away?"

"Because —"

"Don't forget, Sergeant, that I am your superior."

A pause before Tom, his gaze level with John's, said, "I sent them away . . . sir . . . because, in my opinion, they did not require treatment from you. Sir."

"In your opinion?"

"Yes, sir. I was of the opinion that their needs could best be met by others, sir." Tom was speaking as softly as he had before and this, along with his dogged stance and his infuriating calm, was almost as much as John could stand.

He went one step closer to his subordinate. "That was not your decision to make."

"Begging your pardon, sir, but I think it was."

"Your medical knowledge is more advanced than a surgeon's, is it?"

"No, sir. But I am your orderly, sir, charged with helping you."

"Helping, yes. Not jumping to conclusions for which you have had no training."

228

"If you say so, sir." The resignation in Tom's voice, the way he looked to left and right, as if seeking to escape, and his air of beaten passivity, further infuriated John. He took one more step, coming up very close as he raised his voice another notch. "You've gone slack, Tom," he said, "from working under the colonel."

He was close enough to see Tom blink and to hear his soft "The colonel's a good man, sir."

"A good man, perhaps, to those he cultivates and flatters. But what does it matter what kind of man he is? He needs to be a good surgeon. And that he is not. His knowledge is so antiquated he's probably never even heard of a fat embolism the like of which killed that poor man in Korti."

"He's a good man in a fight, sir."

"In a fight?" John's voice rose another notch. "Is that all you care about?"

"Well, we are in the army, sir."

The insolence of the man, to suggest that John didn't know, and couldn't learn, what soldiering was. Damn him. And damn his colonel. "Men like the colonel, they're a danger to their patients. And your job —"

"If you'll pardon me interrupting you, sir, my job is to assist you. And this includes making sure that you are fit to treat casualties. Sir."

"Are you insinuating that I might be in any way unfit?" John slapped one hand against his thigh.

The violence of the action against torn skin set off a ricocheting series of sharp shockwaves that made Tom's "No, sir" doubly infuriating and when Tom continued — "I'm not saying you're unfit, sir, but there's fighting

229

to be done" — the pain made him want to slap the man. "All of us old soldiers," Tom was saying, "we get a sense of a battle looming. We can feel it now. It's coming close. That's when you'll be really needed. So you have to have your rest. And, if you'll pardon me again, sir, I can't help noticing that you've not been sleeping well."

John did something that he'd never done before and would never have assumed himself capable of. He raised both hands. They did not seem like his hands. They seemed like a stranger's. He watched them circle Tom's neck. He could feel the warmth of Tom's skin as, still unthinking, he squeezed Tom's neck. As the skin compacted, he began to feel the knotted layers of muscle and cartilage, gland and tendon, vein, artery and bone. It felt so natural that he even visualized the moment when, if he kept squeezing, Tom's trachea would crumple.

"What's going on here?"

A red lamp lit the puce of Tom's scarred face. This, and the sound of Tom's gasping breath, brought John to his senses. He let drop his hands. Stared down at them.

He had almost strangled a man — a man who had done nothing to hurt him but had instead been doing his best to help. He said, "I — I . . ." and could think of nothing else.

The lamp swung in his direction. Seeing him, the sentry saluted. "Is this man bothering you, sir?"

"A minor disagreement," John said.

"Not how it looked, if you don't mind me saying so, sir. Do you want him charged?"

"No, of course not. He — he — was helping me. Demonstrating the art of self-defence."

"Was he indeed?" The sentry turned his lamp to light Tom's face. "Well, keep quiet, will you? The men need their sleep."

They found a place where they could sit, smoke and talk.

"I'm sorry," John said, not for the first time, looking at Tom's dark outline.

Tom shrugged. "It happens, sir, on the eve of battle. The blood gets up." His breathing, at last, was slow and regular.

"You can drop the 'sir'."

"Yes, sir. Thank you, sir. I will."

Was that sarcasm or forgiveness? Glancing across, and seeing Tom's expression blank, John realized he didn't know. He stared up into the darkness.

Without a moon or stars, the night seemed as impenetrable as any night could be. John was shivering not just from cold, although it was very cold, but from the sheer inhospitality of this alien land with its ugly black rocks, its spindly mimosa, its lack of life and its battles foretold. "What are we doing here?" he murmured.

"Following orders." Tom drew on his cigarette, the red glow lighting his face.

"Is that reason enough?"

"We're in the army. It's what we do."

There's dignity in that, John thought, but he wondered what the cost might be for this man. He thought about the only personal detail Tom had ever let slip to him. "What happened to your son?"

"My son?"

"The one you told me about. The one you left."

"How would I know what happened to him? I left, didn't I?" Tom drew on his cigarette again, then pinched the end to extinguish it. He tucked the stub into a pocket. He lay back, stretching out on the sand and gazing up into the darkened silence, broken only by the soft tread of sentries on their rounds and the occasional grunt from animal or man.

Tom's right, John thought. I'm tired. If only I could sleep. He yawned.

"It was a long time ago," Tom said. "I don't much think of him. Haven't done for years." He sounded his usual calm self.

Tom was so self-assured, John thought. It was one of the reasons he liked him so much. He had the knack of living in the moment, without regret. I should do more of that myself, he thought.

"I did go back," he heard Tom say, "once or twice, to see how he was getting on. The last time, he caught sight of me. He was only a nipper but I saw him looking straight and I knew he knew me. He didn't say anything but he saw me. I couldn't think what to do so I went away. Couldn't bring myself to go back after that."

"Must have been hard."

"Hard?" Tom let out his breath. "It was for the best. I was no good for him."

"You were his father."

"His father, yes, but before that a soldier. And after as well. It's what I've always been. The army's as much family as I can stand." Tom's tone was so calm and sure that John envied him the certainty of that belonging, something that he had come to realize he had always yearned for.

"With me and his mother fighting all the time," Tom went on, "William was better off with me out the way."

John felt again how tired he was. He should go and find a blanket and at least try to close his eyes. I will, he thought, even as he heard himself say, "Just before we left Korti, I had a letter from my wife."

"I fetched it from the mailboat."

"She told me something I hadn't known."

"Something you don't like?"

"Something nobody could like."

"Did you write back?"

"I decided not to." He thought about the messages he had drafted. About the things he thought he should say but didn't dare. About the words he had scrawled before crossing them through. And about the relief he had experienced when he had decided that Mary would, without a doubt, have wanted to unwrite her letter almost immediately after she had posted it. It was just like her to act on whim and then regret it. That was why he had given her laudanum: to try to keep her wild spirit at bay. And now this . . .

Much better, he had decided, to pretend he had never received her letter. "I don't know why she wrote to me in the first place."

The guilt he had felt, he told himself, was misplaced. Yes, he had prescribed her laudanum, but never regularly. And, yes, he had taught her how to do some simple dispensing on his behalf — she had so wanted that role — but he had not given her the impression that she could go into the dispensary and help herself.

Why had she not exercised more self-control? That side of her — the fragility that hovered at the edge of her strange high spirits — which he had once cherished, seemed contemptible now. Wasn't her letter, which had masqueraded as confession, actually an accusation that he had introduced her to laudanum, then left her? But he hadn't asked her to depend on it so much that she couldn't do without it. Why did she have to be different? All around him there were men whose wives waited patiently at home and kept the family together while their husbands were fighting for their country. Not Mary: she was selfish. Just as she had always assumed that her barrenness was her heartache and had no effect on him, she hadn't tried to imagine what he and the other men were suffering. If she had, she would never have written that letter.

"Strange," he said, "the many ways in which we fool ourselves. I thought I knew her. And I thought I loved her." He let his sentence hang.

Was this why he had travelled into danger? Because he couldn't face his marriage? If that were true, could he contemplate going back?

He looked at Tom, hoping perhaps that he would make some sense of what he was feeling. But all Tom said was "Doesn't matter what you thought or who you

234

loved. You're in the army now. There's nothing more. Not here. Not now. Whatever your wife wrote to you, you need to set it to one side. No matter what she wants, you'll still be here and she'll still be there. That's army life for you. You have to stop thinking about her and start thinking about the poor blighters in Khartoum."

CHAPTER
TWENTY-TWO

The general was on the roof and, as ever, looking through his beloved telescope but still he managed to register and identify Will by his tread. "Where have you been?" He didn't bother turning round.

Will made his way slowly across the heated roof to the general's side.

"Weeping over that scurvy mongrel of yours, I suppose."

Will bit his dry lips against the stirrings of rage. "Would you like some water, General?"

"If I wanted water, I would get it for myself." The general stepped away from the telescope. "Have a look."

"I already know what's there."

"I said, have a look."

Bending to the eyepiece Will found himself looking directly into an enemy encampment.

"What do you see?"

"Flags. A forest of them."

"And?" The general had tried to train Will to spot what he wanted him to spot, and he liked to know his training had borne fruit.

"The flags are waving in the breeze."

"And?" More impatiently.

"Dust."

"Good. Now turn the telescope in a westerly direction."

Will turned it to face the Mahdi's camp at Omdurman.

"Focus it."

Will moved the cogs as the general had taught him.

"What do you see?"

"More dust."

"Which means?

"That they're on the move?"

"Precisely."

"Are they going to attack?" Will was surprised at how calm he felt. His struggle would be over, Frankie's too: at least they'd go together.

"Not likely," the general said. "There's been far too much coming and going for that. First a caravan of men and animals travelled down the left bank of the White Nile from the direction of Metemma. Now scores of camels and horsemen carrying ammunition are leaving the Dem of the Mahdi and moving north. Which means?"

"I don't know, General." His rush of energy at the thought of the imminence of his end had left Will terribly tired.

"It means Wolseley is close."

"That's good."

"I doubt that. It also means that the Mahdi knows where Wolseley's forces are. The element of surprise has been lost." Muscling Will away from the telescope, the general put his own eye to it. "I hope Wolseley has the good judgement to know how fiercely these fanatics will resist him." He unbent himself to look at Will. "Follow me. There is something I must show you." With that, the general marched resolutely inside.

The top of the stairs. "Hurry up."

Will didn't want to hurry. He didn't want to go down the stairs and out into the blazing sun and a city half dissolved. He didn't want to watch the mad general failing to rally troops who had long since lost all heart. He wanted to stay with Frankie and, if necessary, to die with him. If only it would be over fast.

"Come." The general grabbed Will's shoulder. His bony hand forced the boy down the first step.

With the general weighing on him, Will had no choice but to make the descent, step by dreaded step, his terror seeming almost to consume him. At the bottom, he turned, eyes filled with tears, to look at the general.

The general blinked. "No need for that." His voice was mild. "This won't take long."

Into the unpeopled dusty dusk they went, Will walking slowly behind a general who had all but lost his sting. Even the guards no longer stood up at his approach. They cringed from his whip, but the general had given up trying to chivvy them into the fulfilment of their duties. Now he veered away from the streets where the carcasses of dead animals and humans were lying where they had dropped and made for the river where, at the landing-stage, his last remaining steamer, the provocatively named *Zebehr*, was moored.

Not again, thought Will, wearily, as the general led the way up the gangplank.

Once, armies had followed the general into battle, emperors had sent him precious yellow robes, newspapers had trumpeted his achievements and crowds had ululated at his approach. Now his domain was almost completely reduced to this one steamer, named by him after a notorious slave trader, his empire, which he insisted on revisiting, taking Will with him so he could demonstrate its power — the strength of its bulletproofing, the stroke of its pistons, the speed at which its furnace could be fed, in order that Will might likewise worship it. For what? For the illusion, perhaps, that the general was still in charge.

It was cool inside the steamer. Will collapsed on to one of the hard wooden bunks. As the general resumed his lecture on the workings of the engine, Will let his mind drift. The general's voice grew distant, washing over Will with the vague thought that, in another life and another world, if he had to command a steamer, he'd be fully versed in how to run it.

"Get up," he heard the general saying. And louder: "Get up."

At last. Back to his dog. The only place where Will felt safe. He got out of the bunk.

"Here." The general handed him a screwdriver.

"What's this?"

"Take it."

More of the madness that Will had not the energy to resist. He took the screwdriver.

"Search carefully down there," the general pointed at the lower edge of the bunk's wooden base, "until you locate two screwing points."

Will knelt down by the bunk, conscious that while the general had been droning on, night had fallen. It was dark on the floor. He could see nothing.

"Get yourself lower."

Lower? Will thought. No. He didn't have the energy. He wouldn't. Not to satisfy a crazy general who would never be satisfied.

"Do it." An instruction delivered along with the press of the general's calloused hand against Will's neck. Mad the general might be but he was still capable of wreaking havoc. If he decided to kill Will — which his wild manner suggested was possible — then Frankie would die alone. Will stretched himself out along a planked floor that smelt of dust, engine oil and, strangely, of something sweet.

"Feel along the base."

He let his hand run across the rough surface of the bunk's base, snagging splintered sections until he rubbed across a smoother indentation. "A screw hole," he said.

"Find its pair."

He felt further along. "I've got them both."

"Locate those directly above each."

This Will also did.

"Good. Now unthread all four. Set the screws carefully aside. You will need them later."

240

Having done as instructed, Will removed a panel that the screws had held in place. The sweetness was much stronger, tugging at him. It occurred to him that the general might have hidden something dead inside, a thought he immediately discarded for the smell was nowhere near as unpleasant as the carrion in Khartoum.

"Insert your hand into the cavity."

Gingerly Will did as he was told. His fingers brushed something small. It fell away before he could grasp it.

"Try again, more carefully."

This time his finger alighted on a surface encrusted by a sticky residue. He withdrew his hand. He smelt the finger. A wonderful, unforgettable yet almost forgotten aroma. His stomach cramped, his mind refusing what his tastebuds were telling him. Surely it could not be — it was impossible. A phantom, just like the sight of his father. He licked his finger.

Sweetness exploded. He almost doubled over with the pleasure and pain of it. His mouth watered and then overflowed. He was drooling so copiously it occurred to him to wonder whether a person was capable of drowning in his own saliva. Even as he thought this, he knew for sure that the substance was . . . jam. He shoved back his hand. Too recklessly. The motion caused a pile of tins to collapse away and out of his grasp.

"Here." The scrape of a match. The general must have squirrelled away some precious tallow and a wick. Will could smell its burning sourness, the smoke stinging his eyes as the general lowered the light.

In the feeble yellow flicker, Will saw what he, even after the taste of jam, took as hallucination. The things he'd been dreaming of were real. Tins of potted meat. And jam. And packages of dry biscuit closely wrapped.

The general wasn't mad. He couldn't be. No madman would have had the cunning to save this festival of food, this feast, and leave it intact until the moment when it was most urgently required.

"The light will soon burn out. Before it does, take out two tins of meat, one of jam — one is already open, choose that. And some biscuit. Hand them up to me."

Will's hand was shaking hard.

"Now put back the panel."

Two tins and some biscuit. Not nearly enough for three. Will picked up the first of the four screws.

"Hurry."

It was dark. The general wouldn't catch him. And if he did? Well, he and Frankie were already as good as dead. Surreptitiously Will slid out another tin.

"I said, hurry."

And another, then a third. He tugged at the string with which he had belted his trousers, then shoved the tins down his drawers, along with some biscuits. As fast as he could, he fitted the panel back into place.

"Time to go."

He was terrified the tins would clank or, worse, fall through his trousers. He clambered to his feet.

The general had already turned away. Will adjusted his trousers.

"Come," the general said and, heart banging, his own internal tom-tom, hands hanging down to conceal any bulges, Will followed him down the gangplank. The enemy's drumming started up in accompaniment to Will's heart. Along the river's edge they went, Will's face wreathed in smiles at the thought of opening a tin and giving it to Frankie. Into the palace and up the stairs. Will realized, for the first time, that his fear of the stairs was restricted to the descent. Either that or what he had concealed in his trousers had driven fear away.

All the energy that hunger had drained from him resurged. He wanted to bound up the stairs, take them two at a time, get to Frankie before it was too late. If only the general would dismiss him.

"Here." The general handed him a tin of meat, some biscuit and the whole of the leaking tin of jam. "Dismissed."

"No jam for you, General?"

"Dismissed."

He had got away with it. With food to eat and more where that had come from, he and Frankie would survive at least until the Mahdi attacked. His back to the general, Will walked, as slowly as his racing heart would allow, along the corridor.

He was pursued by the general's voice: "Don't let that dog eat all you stole from me."

CHAPTER
TWENTY-THREE

The grey mist of a winter afternoon was fading as Mary pulled her brown scarf tight and curved in on herself, weaving through the crowd. The musk of close-packed bodies, stagnant water and sewage, and the rancidity of hanging meat, made her want to gag but although she had brought smelling salts, she resisted the urge to take them out.

As the afternoon sank deeper into darkness, the white glare of gas and the red smoke of grease-lit stalls piled with turnips, pickling cabbages and onions. She paid them no heed — she was not here to buy — but that did not stop urchins holding up discoloured potatoes in their grimy palms. They looked at her beseechingly. They were so small and dirty, and so thin. She might have given them something except that, by taking coins from the chatelaine bag hanging from her skirt, she was fearful of attracting pickpockets.

She pressed on, the heels of her boots tapping along the cobbles. So many other sounds as well — cheerful insults, men spitting, women laughing. Such a contrast to the calm, warm tedium of her hushed home, and the plain sobriety of the Salvationists' refuge in which she had been spending increasing amounts of time.

244

She glanced down at the scrap of paper on which a Salvationist had written an address. She knew it was near — but where? To keep circling would be to attract unwanted attention. She needed help.

A woman, shrouded and hunched, was bearing down on her. Clearly expecting Mary to move out of the way, she ploughed straight on. Mary held her ground, so that, at the last minute, the woman had to stop. She seemed not so much annoyed as bemused when Mary thrust up her piece of paper.

The woman glanced down at Mary's white-gloved hand. She frowned. "What's this?"

Mary held the paper higher.

"No good to me, love. Never did learn to read."

Mary read out the address.

"Number ten?" A thought passed visibly over the woman's pasty features. "Do you know what's there?" Before Mary could answer her, the woman's interest drained away. "Suit yourself." With a nod she indicated a narrow opening. "It's halfway along that passage. Beats me, though, why the likes of you . . ." She pushed on, so forcefully that if Mary hadn't given way, she would have been knocked over.

At the mouth of the alleyway, Mary stopped. Ramshackle houses lined both sides of the dark passage. Quiet. And empty. Now that she was so close, what she had planned seemed folly. She thought of turning back. But then: You have come this far, she told herself. You may as well go on.

The alley was narrow and uncobbled and stank of things she would rather not think about. She speeded up and soon found herself outside number ten. No going back. She lifted her gloved fist — there was no knocker — to the door. Even this most tentative pressure caused it to swing open. "Hello?" She stepped into an unlit, foul-smelling hallway. "Hello?"

"Why, hello." A man's voice, thick and soured.

In that moment the bravado that had driven her on deserted her. She was in danger. She must leave. Before it was too late. She turned.

The man, his eyes more acclimatized to the dark than hers, was also much surer and faster. She felt the air displace, his fat grey body flitting past. Then she heard the door bang shut, taking with it the last of the light.

"Please," she said.

"Oh, I will." She could feel his breath hot on her neck. "I will be very pleased."

She shrank back against the wall. "No." She turned her head away from his determined forward press. "You don't understand. I was looking for —"

"I know what you're after." She could feel the soft squash of him pushing into her. "And I would be more than happy to oblige." His thick fingers fumbled at the high buttons of her bodice.

"I beg you." She tried to pull away. "I am not what you think."

"No, you're not. Special bit o' raspberry, aren't you? Quite the toff."

"I am a married woman."

"Doesn't bother me." His nails digging into her cheek, he wrenched her head round so that she had no choice but to look at him. "I like a bit of buttered bun." He had moved in so close that their lips were almost touching.

She wilted under a blast of his stinking breath. His hands, and those iron fingers, wound themselves round her neck.

She was briefly aware of the sagging weight of her body dragging him down with her. Then darkness, more complete than she had ever experienced, closed her down.

A woman's angry voice: "What do you think you're doing?" as she came to.

A smell, damp and foul, and Mary stretched out flat. "Oi. You."

She opened her eyes to see the dark outline of a man framed against a faint yellow glow.

"I asked you a question."

She remembered then. She clamped her eyes tight shut.

"What are you up to?"

She wanted to die.

She felt a movement. "What does it look like I'm up to?" The man was getting to his feet.

"Not without I say so, you don't." The rustle of a skirt. "And not by the front door neither. You'll bring the peelers down on me."

"I wasn't meaning to do it here. But this one's only gone and swooned."

"Swooned. Not likely."

More rustling, a heavy uneven tread and then what sounded like someone kneeling with effort. A strong whiff of oversweet scent. The faint shine of a lamp lit Mary's darkness. Her hair was brushed away from her forehead before Mary heard a catch of breath. Then the woman must have turned her head for when she said, "What a useless mouth you are," her voice was muffled. "She's not one of mine. She's a respectable woman."

"Respectable! Hah. She came in bold as brass, unchaperoned, and turned it on for me."

"Turned it on? Not a woman in Christendom would turn it on for you. Not unless they were well paid." When the woman took hold of Mary's shoulder and shook it, her voice was low and surprisingly gentle: "You're safe to get up, love."

She was sullied. Ashamed.

"Come. I can see you're awake."

And paralysed.

"What did I say?" The man's voice. "She's all pretence, that one."

"Shut your mouth. Be off with you."

"You can't —"

"Out, I said, or I'll fetch someone to make changes to your ugly face — come to think of it, that might be an improvement — afore they chuck you out."

The man cursed, using words that, although Mary might not know them, were unequivocal. They resounded in her head, which hurt. She wondered whether, in falling, she might have cut it. "Bitch, cock-teaser, cunt" — the last of the noxious labels passed over her, along with a toxic brew of spittle and foetid fumes that a blast of chill air soon blew away. She heard the door slam before the woman's cool hand lightly touched her brow. "He's gone."

Her relief was heated by fear. What had he done to her?

"Up you get."

She didn't want to move. Ever.

The rustle of clothes. A tug at her waistband and the soft fumble of fabric parting. Her bag. The woman was opening it.

"You can't stay here. You'll be costing me more trade."

She was too ashamed to open her eyes.

The acrid sting of ammonia bit, the fumes flooding through her mouth and down her throat. She couldn't help but breathe in deeply. She gasped. Another involuntary intake of breath, then another, and she was coughing so hard she was about to choke. She pushed herself up on to her elbows, her chest convulsing as she gasped for air.

"That's what you get for playing dead."

She was bent double with coughing.

"Rise and shine." The woman was behind her now, her arms hooked under Mary's. Grunting with effort, she hauled her to her feet. "Let's get you upstairs."

The upstairs room was soft and rich, with velvet in varying shades of red that covered almost every surface and the walls. A place of soft retreat, Mary thought, as she crumpled into a chair — and, seeing the unmade bed in one corner, something more sinister.

"Let's be looking at you, then," said Rebecca Jarrett. With her thick fair hair, coarse, confident face, and uneven clumsy gait Mary would have recognized Rebecca anywhere.

Embarrassed by her own behaviour — Rebecca would never faint at a man's touch — she was relieved that Rebecca did not seem to know her. "Come on, then." Rebecca stood impatiently, hands on hips.

Mary had no idea what she wanted.

"Lift your skirt."

Instinctively she gathered the lower section of her skirt together and bunched it tight.

Rebecca shrugged. "If you don't want to know where he's been, I'll fetch some water and you can be gone." She made to turn away.

"Wait."

She turned back. "Yes?"

"I do . . ." She couldn't say it. "I do . . ." If anything had happened, a woman like Rebecca would know what she should do. "I do want to know."

"Let's have a look, then."

Mary's hands went to her hem and took hold of it. She was shaking so hard her fingers fumbled and slipped, yet even in her distress she wondered whether it was only fear that she was feeling.

"Here." With effort, Rebecca lowered herself to her knees. She was surprisingly delicate as she raised Mary's skirt. She didn't touch her but took her time inspecting Mary's undergarments, while Mary waited, flushed with shame. Then, at last, Rebecca spoke: "That one's a dirty devil, and a fast mover, but even he

250

couldn't have dug through this lot in the time he had and afterwards set it back to rights." She let the skirt drop. "Far as I can tell you're as neat as you were when you got here." She patted Mary's clothes back into place, then levered herself up, groaning. "I'll fetch that water."

"Here." When Rebecca leaned forward to give Mary the glass, her breath, thick with alcohol, filled Mary's nostrils. "Take it."

It occurred to Mary that Rebecca might just have drunk from this glass. She gave a surreptitious sniff. Sure enough, the faint smell of alcohol seemed to linger there.

Rebecca gave the glass another encouraging thrust. "I made sure to spit in it good and proper so it'd sparkle for your ladyship." She was leaning heavily away from her gammy leg.

Ashamed, Mary could not bring herself to take the glass.

Rebecca threw back her head and laughed. Such an abrasive belly laugh, loud enough to shake windows. It shook the glass she was holding so that, as she pushed it forward, water spilled. If Mary hadn't taken it, she would have been soaked.

As Rebecca continued to laugh, Mary saw herself through the other's eyes. So timid and tousled, sitting gingerly at the edge of thick velvet pile, and holding a glass as if it were a bomb from the Fenian dynamite campaign.

And she had thought to make friends with Rebecca! She could feel a dark blush rising up her throat.

"I keep a clean house here." Rebecca had stopped laughing. "I'm renowned for it." There was no malice in her regard but rather a kind of wry sympathy. "You won't catch nothing from me."

Mary winced.

"Sooner you drink, the sooner you can be gone. Go on, love, take a little water, and then my duty's done."

The water was warm and tasted slightly sour but even one sip brought home to Mary how thirsty she was. She drained the glass and put it down.

"More?"

"No. But thank you." She knew she should go, before Rebecca thought to ask what she was doing there. If she went before any further words were exchanged, that would be the end of it. Once she'd got over her humiliation, she could also look back on what had happened and laugh at her expectation that her fellow feeling for Rebecca — and the possibility that they might become friends — could ever be reciprocated.

She should be grateful to the man. He had stopped her saying the thing that really would have made Rebecca laugh.

She opened her eyes to find Rebecca's gaze boring into her. "I know you, don't I?"

Mary dropped her gaze.

"Course I do. I saw you at that meeting with Mr Stead. You're the one whose husband went with the Camel Corps."

Mary nodded.

"I saw you all right." Rebecca was bringing back to her mind not only the occasion but also its details, "and I saw what you are." She frowned. "So what happened?"

"Happened?"

"Don't play the innocent. If you wasn't under the influence that night, then my uncle's a monkey. Ah," Rebecca held up her strong roughened hands, palms forward, to stop Mary speaking, "no need to say. I've worked it out for myself. Those ladies showed you the light, didn't they, and now you've come to the slums to show it to me?"

A good enough story. More convincing than the real reason for her trip. Mary nodded.

"Funny. All this bother to save me, and I end up saving you."

She should nod again, smile and leave. This she told herself, even as she said, "I didn't come to save you."

"Just as well." Rebecca's voice rose indignantly. "You'd be wasting your time. Those ladies, they're decent enough, but I couldn't be doing with them. My life's my life. My drink's my drink. I'm not for saving." She lapsed into laughter, which seemed to hold more bitterness than amusement.

Mary's heart went out to her: as different as they were in status, their shared difficulty was part of what had driven her here. "They talk about you," she said, "about how close you came to giving up the drink. I told them I was going to persuade you to try again. But that isn't why I came."

She might as well have saved her breath. "I'm a working woman," Rebecca said. "I've got a business to run. You and your make-believe generals and your bogus captains, you're bad for business. You've already cost me one client — a bastard but he had money in his pocket — and since I'm of a mind to keep on falling I'm going to need a bit of silk to cushion me."

Ludicrous for Mary ever to have thought that, by crossing London, she could bridge the gulf between Rebecca's background and hers. When Rebecca looked at Mary all she would ever see was the legion of good women whom Mary had tried and failed to join. By her fainting, and her hesitation over the glass, she had revealed herself. No good could come from denying who she was.

And yet that Rebecca should think she was like the others when she was not, well, she couldn't bear it. She said, again, but softly, "I didn't come to save you."

Rebecca had already turned away to pick up a lamp. "Quite an adventure you've had. Like darkest Africa, weren't it, where that husband of yours has run? A good tale for you to blow on about at your meetings. You can tell them how you near martyred yourself for a sinner so ungrateful she turned you out. It'll thrill them."

"For the last time," Mary's voice was so loud it no longer sounded like hers, "I'm not here to save you."

At last she had Rebecca's attention. "Why did you come, then?" She held up the lamp, lighting Mary's eyes.

The truth — well, part of it — that she had been drawn to Rebecca by the urge to get to know and to learn from her, would sound absurd. She couldn't say it. She sat, tongue-tied, trying to withstand the intensity of Rebecca's gaze, hoping without hope that Rebecca might somehow guess what she wanted and also want to reciprocate. And then, as the silence stretched on, it felt increasingly awkward, and so she was almost relieved when Rebecca threw back her head and laughed again, so heartily that the lamp shook and she almost lost her balance. "Whoops," she said. "Better put this down." Having done so, she turned back to Mary. "Now I understand," she said. "I know what you're after."

CHAPTER
TWENTY-FOUR

When the order came, the column halted and the men sat on their camels waiting for the order to dismount. Time stretched on and no such order arrived. Something going on up front.

Not a word of speculation was exchanged. It was not their business, unless they were told it was.

Mounted on his camel towards the rear of the column, John concentrated on trying not to lick his scorched lips and also not to think. Especially about water. Every bone in his body ached. His hands on the reins were so desiccated they were beginning to resemble claws. His throat was so dry it hurt to swallow. His eyes were gritty, even though he had his goggles on. Still the sun burned so fiercely through his helmet and veil that he had to resist the temptation to throw them off. He felt wretched but, more than that, he felt indescribably exhausted.

Perhaps, now that they had stopped, if he might just rest his eyes . . . Only for a moment.

"Hold up."

Tom, again, shaking him by the shoulder. Damn the man. Could he not desist?

"You sleep, you fall."

John thought about the men who had slipped off their camels, the lucky ones escaping with bruises. He must stay awake. He blinked and shook himself, trying to summon back energy into his body.

At last the bugle cry, "Dismount". Thankfully he dismounted.

"We must be near Abu Klea," Tom said. "They've sent the Hussars ahead to water the horses."

"Lucky beggars," someone muttered, to the general assent of the other men who, on command, lifted waterskins and gulped as much as they could in the prescribed amount of time. They put them away. Out of sight, out of mind.

Time to rest. If they were lucky they might catch a couple of hours' sleep before the midday heat waned and they were ordered to remount.

Suddenly and unexpectedly a fresh bugle call: six short sharp skips, then a long-drawn-out note. It sounded in the far distance, then was repeated over and over again, passing down the column from one regiment to the next, getting louder as it came closer. John had not heard its like before, but the men's reaction left him in no doubt as to its urgency. The whole crowd of them, asleep or awake, were immediately on their feet and looking to their arms, making unnecessary Tom's, "That's the alarm they're sounding."

Up and down the column men were readying their guns. He had only a short sword. He wasn't sure what he was meant to do with it. He could hear word passing from mouth to mouth: "Enemy in sight," and then,

"They're on the hills," and, ominously, "They're commanding the passes." His heart lurched.

He seemed to be alone in this. The men in his close vicinity, far from being fearful, were delighted at this change in fortune. Gone was their sullen apathy. As they continued to check their guns and ammunition, they were smiling and calling out to each other that at last what they had long been praying for, the end of the desert parade and the beginning of the fight, was upon them.

"Save if they run at the sight of us," someone called, which prospect momentarily dimmed the euphoria.

"Here." Tom thrust a waterskin at John.

"I've had my ration."

"Have more. Something tells me you're going to see the action first."

No sooner had John lifted it to his lips than a Hussar galloped up on a small grey pony, a riderless horse beside him. He executed a quick salute. "Hop on, sir. They're asking for you up front."

As he stood on the hilltop among the knot of officers, John could see the wide bleak landscape spread below and beyond. He was having trouble treating his patient, a major from the 19th Hussars, who was behaving as if the wound on his arm was nothing more alarming than a flea bite and John there to stop him delivering his report. Each time John got close enough to treat him, the major danced away.

"We came upon them suddenly," he was saying. "Out of nowhere. Not many of them. They must have been scouts. Ouch." This to John, who was attempting to clean the wound. "Leave it, man, why don't you, and let me finish my report?"

When the officer who had earlier told John to set to nodded, John stepped away.

"Soon as they spotted us, they ran," the major said. "We chased after them — those devils can ride — almost as far as the wells." Standing on the edge of the high ground, the major pointed past the line of black, broken hills to the just visible edges of the broad sandy valley of Abu Klea, with its scattering of yellow grass, mimosa and white-barked gum Arabic trees, whose spreading crowns of spiky olive green leaves provided patchy shade. "I nabbed one of the rascals," he said. "I was about to bring him back for the intelligence, but before I could get a firm hold, a host of others sprang up. By a rough reckoning, there were about two thousand of them — that was when I got this spear thrust. We had to get out of there — and fast. Couldn't hold on to my prisoner, I'm afraid."

"Good work, Major," his general said. "Now kindly stand aside and let the surgeon attend to your arm."

It was only a flesh wound that was easy enough to patch. As John took care to clean it, he had plenty of opportunity to eavesdrop on the officers, who were discussing how best to proceed. They had turned their fieldglasses, and their attention, to the hills beyond. He didn't need a glass to see what they were focusing on: a file of white-clad horsemen progressed slowly across the ridge.

"About fifty of them, would you say?"

"Indeed. But over there — that's where they're massing."

When the officer pointed towards a conical hill, John couldn't at first work out what he was looking at. But when he lowered his gaze he saw the lines of men on foot who, rifles outstretched, were running towards and up the hill.

"Hundreds of them."

"If what we've just encountered is any guide, there are thousands to back them up."

"Disciplined enough, by the look of them." The general lowered his fieldglasses. "Order a detachment of mounted infantry and Blue Jackets to occupy the hill opposite." He pointed to a hill on the other side of the pass. "They are to build a stone wall, reassemble the Gardner and mount it on the wall. From there they can prevent any further descent by the enemy."

A signaller saluted smartly and, tucking his flags under his arm, rode off.

"The rest of the column to advance through that open stretch there."

"We'll be directly in their sights."

"Yes, indeed. In fact . . ." the general pointed to the hill up which the second ranks of running riflemen were climbing ". . . they've already started." Which confirmed what John had suspected: that the puffs of smoke issuing from the hill were the enemy firing.

"Might as well let them waste their ammunition, if that's what they've a mind to do. Tell the men not to reply." The general stood, for a moment, in silence, gazing out as he played absently with his handlebar moustache. "I wonder . . . Should we seize the initiative? Attack now, before they have time to organize?"

"Only three hours of daylight left," one of his officers volunteered.

"True." The general sighed, then drew himself up, a man converted just as his commander, Wolseley, had been converted when he had had to make his decision. The general's thick-set shoulders relaxed, and the sore red peeling of the high forehead where his hair had begun to recede unfurrowed when he barked, "The main to move past the open stretch up that stony slope there." He pointed to the exact spot. "We'll camp on that flat high ground for the night."

"They'll be in a good position to take pot shots at us."

"Can't be helped. And once it's dark, the damage will be limited to blind luck. Nevertheless, a protective zariba to be constructed from available stones. They must build it as high as they can — it will afford us some protection from fire."

"Yes, sir."

"Every man to be issued with a pannikin of lime juice and water. They'll need it tomorrow. A company of each regiment to extend and cover our front. That's all for now." This to a second signaller, who also saluted and rode off.

"Well, gentlemen," the general was smiling. He seemed utterly relaxed as he looked to his staff, who had gathered around him, "we're finally in business."

"If they keep to their positions," one of his officers said, "we'll be sitting ducks."

"Then we'll just have to find a way to lure them out, won't we?" the general said. "Once that's done, we can make short work of them."

Where had Betty got to?

Mary needed to be gone, not because she was late but because waiting made her question her capacity to meet Rebecca after dark and in a public house.

She had made up her mind. Determined not to let in doubt, she stared at the patterned hall carpet until her vision glazed, and she seemed to be staring into the depths of a lush green field. It was one of her more ordered imaginings, a visual metaphor, the like of which she sometimes conjured up when under the influence. The field she seemed to see was divided by a low hedge neatly into two. The first half was plain and regimented: her life with John, which, if she didn't go, she might somehow retain. The second was lush and blurred, the future unknown into which keeping her appointment would lead her.

No. It was too frightening. She couldn't do it. Betty would have to send the driver away. She reached up to take off her hat.

A blast of cold air. Betty was back.

Mary's hat hovered in mid-air.

"I can let the driver go," Betty said. "It won't be no bother."

Mary looked at her maid, and thought: If I don't go, I will have only Betty for company. She lowered her hat. "I will take the cab." She smiled at the hall mirror. When her mirror-self smiled back, she saw herself anew. Not ordinary but different. More worldly and self-assured. Well, her face and hat, anyway.

She tilted the hat, set it at a jaunty angle to suit her face. Slotted in a pin to keep it there. And turned.

Betty, shawled and wrapped against the cold, was standing, like a sentry, by the door.

"Is the hansom waiting?"

"Yes, ma'am, it is."

Betty, Mary saw, was also putting on a hat. "Are you going out?"

"You can't go alone. Not at night."

"I can." She drew herself up." I will. So . . ." She took a deep, cleansing breath, exhaled and swept past Betty.

Notice painted on a Khartoum wall by order of Gordon Pasha.

THEY ARE ON THEIR WAY.

And underneath, in English:

Yes, and when they come all will bow down before the Mahdi, the father of mercy with whom be God's peace.

And underneath in Arabic:

نقسم أن نتخلّى عن هذا العالم لنختار العالم الأخر

We swear to renounce this world and to choose the next.

CHAPTER
TWENTY-FIVE

The general watched as they pushed the prisoner to his knees. He saw the forced bowing of the man's head and the exposing of his neck.

Like the general, the prisoner knew his fate. His fighting was over, their victory won, and they were going to kill him. His eyes, though open, were already staring into darkness.

The sun came out, catching the edge of the long, curved blade. Such a brilliant, blinding blaze of light. The general blinked, and in that moment, the sword swung down, hacking through skin, muscle, sinew and bone until the head was severed from the neck. Down it rolled to the ugly gushing of dark blood.

The general cried out. He was to blame. He sank to his knees. His eyes open, he was looking into darkness. Above him the curved blade was held aloft . . .

The sword had gone. Now the general found himself walking to a bridge. Among the flames, screams and smoke, he saw a boy sitting quietly in its lee. Must be Will, he thought.

"Will." God, in His infinite mercy, had spared the child. "Will."

Head lowered, the boy continued to sit, looking at something in his lap.

"Will." Closing in on the boy, the general saw that, with his sleek black hair and slanted eyes, the boy was clearly Chinese. Not Will but a nameless boy. Son of Wang. A boy the general had come across many years ago.

That horror in his lap.

The boy looked up. "Your fault."

"No." The general was adamant. "I told them. Not a hair on your father's head to be harmed. I gave the order and I gave it clearly. It cannot be my fault."

The boy lifted up the thing. The head. His father's severed head.

Vials are poured on to the earth. Events unfold.

"You killed my father." The boy offered the head to the general. "I am not your son."

The general recoiled from the offering. "I don't want it."

"But you have made him yours."

"Bury him. With honour. I will pay."

"You must take his head," the boy said, "for this is what you did." Blood from the head dripped down on him, staining his small face red. "It's what you do."

As it was, so must it be repeated. The general must relieve the boy of the burden of his father's head.

How, though, to take hold of a head?

Not by the stem, the neck. Too bloodied.

Not by the edge, the nose. Too brittle.

Not by the roundness as you would a bowl.

By the hair, then. That was it. You pick up a head by the hair and you put it into a sack and you take it to your troops as evidence of their great transgression. This was what the general had done, those many years ago in China. He had taken the head and left the boy. And dreamed about it ever afterwards. He thought of it even as he dreamed, fighting his way out so that he could forget the head, which, as he picked it up, had swung round.

He saw a face and he saw that the face was his. His head. His death. And it was close.

Clawing his way out of the dream, the general threw himself across the bed. He pulled out the pot just in time to catch the contents of his stomach. First a small chunk of half-digested food. In its wake glutinous strings of foul-tasting brown phlegm, of which there seemed to be no end. His body was racked by spasms as he vomited up this thickened bile, enough of it, he began to think, to fill the pot. He would not have been surprised if his entrails had followed and, with them, the rest of his Satan body flowing from this mortal shell. There would be mercy in that, he thought, and he willed it on, opening his throat to bring forth what he craved: the end of life, the beginning of glorious immortality in union with his God.

No sooner thought than denied. He lay and retched out nothing. Only God could end this wretchedness on earth, and God was not yet ready to declare His hand.

He got out of bed, shoving the pot out of sight, and went to the window.

The drums were beating. Would they never cease? If only he could stop them. But in this, as in everything, he was impotent. Unlike God, who, all-knowing and all-doing, was omnipotent.

"It's a wearisome life," he told the room, "and I am tired." He marched across and wrenched open the door.

The anteroom was dark, quiet and empty of life, save for one curled figure on the floor: Will, fast asleep, clutching his dog.

The dog gave a low growl. A cunning beast, his warning was soft enough not to wake Will but loud enough to let the general know he was being watched and that this scrutiny would continue until he had gone.

"Growl away," the general told the dog. "As if I care."

The dog bared yellow teeth.

"Not scared," the general said, and shivered. This dratted climate. So cold at night. He picked up the blanket that the boy, in his uneasy sleep, had discarded and, still ignoring the growling dog, laid it gently over Will.

The boy was frowning but his colour had improved. By sneaking out, almost daily, to the steamer, he was getting more food. As was his dog. Through his telescope the general would watch the two of them making a shifty dash for it in their pilfering missions. What an innocent the boy was, even as he stole.

He felt his heart swell with love and regret. Looking down, he silently repeated to himself the promise he had made: unlike his desertion of that Chinese boy, he would stand by Will. "I'll make sure you don't suffer." His eyes welled with tears that, as he turned, he blinked roughly away.

In the darkness and past columns that held up the arching roof, he walked. Not a soul in sight. If the enemy came — as they were bound to do, and soon, before Wolseley's troops could fight their way through — they would meet little opposition.

If only they would come, the general thought, and end this vale of tears.

He went to the edge of the balcony to stare out at the moonless darkness. The banging of the tom-tom, so constant that mostly he cut it out, came at him, swelling through the night. The beat of life, he thought. Of their power and resistance. And the end of him.

CHAPTER
TWENTY-SIX

If only the noise of the Dervish drums had been regular, John might have been able to incorporate, and ignore, the sound. But the beat kept changing, swelling as the enemy neared, softening as they moved away, only to blare loudly as a new section shifted position.

It would be easier in the light. Then, at least, they would be able to see from which direction danger lay. Unlike in this intense darkness, with gunfire sparking off hills and bullets cutting through the air in the search for flesh.

A stone sangar served as a hospital not far from the red flag of the command post. Beyond that were the three walls of the makeshift zariba behind which almost the entire Camel Corps had bedded down. For lack of stones, the walls were no more than thigh high and manned by a double row of sentries who, to avoid being picked off, had to maintain an almost permanent crouch. At least the camels, hobbled in the pits that served both as pens and the fourth wall of the redoubt, had stopped protesting and let most of the men, trusting in their sentries, sleep.

"Hold the light closer," John said.

He was crouched on the sand, trying to dig out a bullet from a man's bloodied chest.

"Closer." He inserted the pointed end of a bullet extractor into the open wound and probed as carefully as he could. He was alert to the ringing that soon sounded: his instrument had made contact with the metal bullet. He manipulated the scissor handles to close them around the bullet and then to pull it out. Another ping, this one followed by an angry "Put out that light."

The lamp was snuffed so suddenly that John could not stop himself jerking back. The pinging was louder now, and it was all around. It hadn't been the sound of an electrical circuit closing that he had heard, but the strike of bullets against the stone boulders that made up the walls of the sangar. Fear flooded him — was this it? — as Tom warned, "He's going."

His patient was haemorrhaging. In pulling back so suddenly, he must have enlarged the opening of the wound. He could feel the sticky warmth running down his own leg while the metallic smell of fresh blood filled the air. He had urgently to close the tear. But how, if he couldn't see? He groped for the lamp to light it with matches he did not possess. At least the enemy had stopped firing.

Tom's calm voice. "You need to compress the opening."

Of course. He must feel down and compress the wound. "That's right." Tom again. "When you make contact, hold firm." John touched the man's chest. The opening, clotted by the stickiness of welling blood, had enlarged. "Help me." There had been no need to say it:

Tom's hand had already joined his. To no avail. A wound the size of two men's palms would never hold, especially when they couldn't see well enough to pinch the skin together. The patient, John thought, would soon be lost and, sure enough, they heard gurgling: the man was choking on his own blood, a process that was at least mercifully short. One last great sigh and "He's gone." Tom moved away.

The colonel had been right. The man had been too badly injured to think of saving. John shouldn't have interfered.

Tom was fumbling with the medical supplies. "Here." He handed something to John. It was soft and pliable. Lint: "To mop up the blood on you. You wouldn't want to scare the men."

The drums sounded relentlessly and John stood in the darkness wiping blood from his hands.

"He was a goner anyway," Tom said.

"I pulled out too quickly."

"At least you tried."

Perhaps, John thought, but a more competent surgeon, or a more courageous one, might have given the boy a better chance.

"It happens in the field. Just like the colonel said."

If I didn't do something wrong, John thought, why is Tom trying to console me? He could hear the drums, closer now.

"We can only do our best," Tom said.

Handing back the bloodied lint, John couldn't help wondering if, when battle commenced, his best would be good enough.

When the door to the public house opened, a blast of chill air set the dirty lace of low-lying cigar smoke a-dancing. Then, *bang*, the door shut, and the flames of the open fire flared and died down.

The banging no longer troubled Mary. Less easy to ignore was the hostility. "Give them time," Rebecca had said, and Mary had, but still her every glance was met by a glare. Although perhaps things were improving: a woman, her heavy fringed shawl mud brown to match her dirty dress, hoisted a pot of ale and said, "Good health," to Mary. Mary lifted her untouched glass of gin.

The woman was toasting someone behind Mary. Now she bent close to her equally dishevelled companion to whisper in her ear. They sat up, looked straight at Mary and laughed.

Mary diverted her glass to her mouth, trying not to cough as the liquid burned her throat. Beside her, Rebecca drained the dregs of ale and slammed her pot down on the wobbly wooden table. Her expression was grim, a match, Mary thought, for the unpleasantness of this place, with its filthy walls on which were arrayed dark portraits of stiff politicians.

She had made a mistake, not by coming for laudanum, which she had secured, but in thinking that she and Rebecca could ever make common purpose. In this environment, which was Rebecca's own, Mary saw the other for what she really was: a hard, unlikeable drunk.

Rebecca lifted her empty pot and tried to drink from it. "Oh." She was surprised to find it empty.

What she would do next was drearily predictable. Grumbling, she would haul herself up and then, leaning heavily on her one good leg, limp over to the bar and buy herself another. This time, Mary had decided not to stay and witness the routine. When Rebecca got up, so would she. When Rebecca went to the bar, Mary would leave.

"Here." Rebecca thrust out the pot.

"No, thank you." Mary shook her head.

"I weren't giving it to you." Rebecca gave the pot another forward push. "Buy me another. It's the least you can do."

How could Mary go to the bar? "I can't," she said.

Rebecca raised her voice: "Too grand to fetch a drink?" She was drunk and without restraint. "Here." She was practically shouting as, with the back of one large hand, she swiped the pot, flicking it across the table so hard that, had Mary not caught it, it would have smashed to the floor.

Rebecca was about to create a scene that Mary, the outsider, could ill afford. Pot in hand, she got up. It didn't feel so bad. Little bells of laudanum had begun to sound their wonderful warm tune. She would manage. She had to.

She moved through the crowd.

None of the drinkers seemed to be looking at her — or, at least, she never caught them looking — but they kept shifting in her way, forcing her to change her route to avoid bumping into them. And when she reached the bar the publican, whose potbelly was half supported by the counter and half pouring over it, took no notice of her. His red nose was bulbous, and when he yawned he shifted into shadow and she seemed to see a set of horns sticking through his greasy hair. A laudanum invention she was determined to ignore. In the manner of his other customers, she slapped down coins. That did the trick. He ambled over, his huge paw gathering up her money before he pumped the pot full of ale.

As she took it up there came another loud bang. The door swung open to admit a man who stood, theatrically, on the threshold: "The Alleluia crowd's on its way."

"Who cares?" someone muttered, while most did not even look up.

Undismayed, the man used his bulk to prop open the door.

"For pity's sake, close the door."

He opened his arms wide. "And the Skeleton Army's agatherin'. There's going to be a hammerin'."

That got the response — cheers followed by commotion — the man had been expecting. Drinkers headed for the door, so many of them that Mary had to pull back against the bar or else be swept along. She searched the crowd for Rebecca. At first, she spotted her still seated, staring down, but as the stampede accelerated, Rebecca was hidden from view, and when next the space had cleared, her seat was empty.

Mary couldn't stay alone in a public house. She stepped into the wake of the departing drinkers and found herself pulled along and eventually catapulted out.

A cacophony of sounds greeted her, accompanied by a sight so unexpected that Mary might have mistaken it for a hallucination, but jubilant cheering told her that the crowd could see what she was seeing.

The dark was lit by flares and shaken by the raucous shouting of a band of rough men, who had formed a line in front of the crowd. They were holding up placards, which, as the crowd pressed forward, they hoisted high. Laudanum had made Mary brave. She pushed into the centre of the crowd and saw skulls and crossbones on the banners with — surely she must be hallucinating? — what looked like pictures of monkeys and rats.

"Rats?"

She must have spoken her thought, because "The Skeletons are partial to rats," someone said.

"Being rats themselves," this from another member of the crowd, which might have provoked an argument except that a cry of "Here comes the Alleluias," turned every head to the left and towards a figure who was moving down the centre of the cobbled road.

All Mary could see at first was a prancing shadow, but as it came closer, it gained definition, and then turned into a flesh-and-blood woman, whose wild hair was interlaced with red, yellow and blue streamers that blew up behind her. Her face was ecstatic as she banged a tambourine.

The cry "It's Happy Eliza Haynes!" triggered a round of applause. The woman grinned and shook her tambourine harder, drawing a louder cheer. Behind her marched ordered lines of others, more soberly dressed in Salvation Army uniforms, also banging tambourines, some of them blaring trumpets, creating such a din that they caused doors they passed to open, the occupants of houses flooding out, some joining to dance behind the procession.

What a sight. Mary had never seen its like — and would not have done if she had played safe and stayed at home. Now, surrounded by the cheerful crowd and no longer conspicuous, she was enjoying herself. So much so that the procession was almost upon her before it occurred to her that some among their number might recognize her.

The crowd was pressing in.

She didn't want to leave. It's dark, she told herself. I won't be seen. And, besides, unlike the ladies of the refuges, these were rough people, the foot soldiers of General Booth's army. None of them would know her.

"Give us a song, Eliza," someone called.

The woman began to sing, loud and tuneless:

"March on, salvation soldiers
March forward to the fight,
With Jesus, as our leader,
We'll put the foe to flight."

The line of placard-holding men took one militarily precise step forward and also began to sing. Same tune, different words, their off-key male voices rising into the thickened darkness:

277

"March on, you skeleton army,
And put this lot to flight.
With beef and beer and bacca,
We'll lighten up the night."

The crowd cheered.

The woman was undaunted. Streamers flying, feet high-kicking, she used a Skeleton pause to continue:

"In spite of men and devils,
We'll raise our banner high,
For the day of victory's coming,
It's coming by and by."

The rest of her group, who had caught up with her and had arranged themselves to face the line of men, banged drums and tambourines to drown a bawdy riposte:

"Jesus was a bastard,
We devils know this well.
So we'll drink ourselves quite happy,
And you cunts can go to hell."

Another jubilant cheer as the men pushed forward again, and behind them the crowd, so that the Salvationists, surrounded on three sides, could only back away.

A shout, "They've tarred the walls!" and Mary could see how the members of the Salvation Army were trying, in most cases hopelessly, not to be pushed

278

against dark, sticky brick. The Skeletons moved a pace closer. If the Salvationists backed any further, they would be trapped.

The flickering firelight lit their panic. They were good people, intent on good work. It shouldn't have been funny. Yet there was something humorous about those faces yellowed by flare and fright, those lips and chins juddering.

A shout, "Take aim," and as one the crowd, Mary with them, stepped quickly back. Now she could see the arms of the Skeletons lifted until at "Fire!" they launched their missiles, which flew and landed just short of the Salvationists in a spectacular burst of blue.

"Dyed eggs," someone called.

"And there'll be worse to follow."

"If I was them Alleluias, I'd be off."

That last remark was reinforced by a shout: "Watch yourselves, they're going again!"

Sure enough, the Skeleton Army now made a run at the Salvationists, stopping in a line just in front of them to throw a fresh batch of missiles that sprayed blue. The tambourines, some of which had been held up as shields, were dripping. The Salvationists faltered.

"Run!"

The men and women of the Salvation Army were trying to regroup.

The crowd took up the cry, "Run!" and sent it out as a drumbeat, "Run! Run!"

Mary joined in: "Run! Run! Run!" The spirit was moving in her — now, finally, she understood what it felt like — a euphoria that had gripped her and now gave her mad strength. "*Run, run, run, run!*"

As the crowd parted to let out the Salvationists, they looked as if running was what they were going to do but one of their number pushed through their ranks and stepped out.

"*Run, run, run, run!*" shouted the crowd. The man did not run. Despite the blue paint on his thin brown hair and high forehead, he stood motionless before the baying crowd.

"Run!" someone yelled but was shushed. As one, the crowd had begun to soften. Once, and then once again, as the man began to sing:

"*A mighty fortress is our God,
A bulwark never failing . . .*"

The crowd's collective voice was fading.

"*Our helper He, amid the flood.*"

All was quiet now, save for that one lonely, lilting,

"*Of mortal ills prevailing.*"

So much longing, not just in the words but in the purity of their delivery. It drew from the crowd a deep sigh and a shame-faced inching back. They might even, Mary thought, have turned on the Skeletons, and chased them off. Except the Skeletons had, among their number, a man of equally quick reactions and courage.

He now stepped in front of his gang. He did not, however, sing. He swung his arm . . .

"For still our ancient foe
Doth seek to work us woe,"

. . . round and round until, at last, he let his missile fly. Up it shot, a dark thing in the night, crossing the space between the two groups to land on the singer's head.

No egg this. The singer shrieked. It was a rat. He jerked his head and flailed his arms, trying to flick it off. Without effect. It was decomposed enough for parts to stick to his skin. It must, as someone called out, "stink something terrible", which comment, rippling through the crowd, caught hold and grew, as more Skeletons copied their leader. Soon the air was thick with flying rats that coasted over the Salvationists and splattered down as a fresh bellowing of "Run!" fed their panic, so that first one, and then the next — "Run, run!" — turned and ran, feet slapping against the wet cobbles. *"Run run run!"*

"Watch them go."

"Run! Run! Run! Run!"

Someone sniggered and someone else joined in, which was enough to set the whole crowd laughing, Mary as well, and the more she laughed, the more her laughter fed itself. She grabbed hold of a woman who was also laughing helplessly but seemed not to mind being used as a support. Laughing, gasping for air, Mary felt a different spirit burst from somewhere deep inside her. It annihilated the stay-at-home miserable

Mary and replaced her with this wild, ecstatic thing. It was as if she — no, it wasn't her, it was something over which she had no control — had thrown away the months of loneliness and despair, and brought back the first time she had been in bed with John, when an energy the like of which she had never experienced had made her shake and cry out.

Which was when she caught sight of Rebecca.

Rebecca wasn't laughing. She was looking at the retreating Salvation Army, with less amusement than great pain.

Mary no longer felt like laughing. She felt, in fact . . . She shook herself and, as the fog cleared, all she could see was Rebecca's stern gaze boring into her.

"We all have a good laugh at their expense," Rebecca said, "but it isn't really funny."

They had gone back inside and, with the gaslight flickering across strands of her blonde hair, Rebecca looked almost beautiful. "That's why we laugh," she was saying, "because it isn't funny." She picked up her pot. "Same as why we drink. Because if we don't, we can't get on." She set it down again. "But drinking's what stops us getting on."

Here was evident in Rebecca a sensibility Mary had already guessed at.

"The publicans are the ones who put the Skeletons up to their tricks," Rebecca was saying. "If salvation means saying no to drink, then those bastards will do anything they can to stop salvation."

Flushing at the memory of herself among the baying mob, Mary thought of the lone singer, emboldened by his beliefs. What had she become that she could laugh at such purity? Yet she couldn't help thinking that it had been fun.

"My father was a tradesman," Rebecca said, "a good enough worker but he suffered from pains in his legs. He took to Battley's drops and then to drink. Drank himself into the grave. Left seven of us behind." She took a deep draught of ale. "I was the last, sent into service. I didn't see much of my mother after that. She said I was wild." She looked away suddenly, as if she couldn't bear the thought.

"The man I went with," her voice had dropped, "he promised me the earth. When I couldn't hide my condition, I was turned out of my place. He put me in a room in Manchester, said I must work my way." She set the pot down again. "What chance did I have of resisting?"

It was a story similar to others Mary had heard at the refuge but from Rebecca's mouth it seemed to carry extra weight.

"Before I could so much as draw breath," Rebecca went on, "I had the two children. It was too late, then. The trade I'd fallen into was my only way of making money."

"I'm sorry."

Rebecca sighed. "My hips was always full of disease. When I was sent to the infirmary, he took the children. Said I wasn't a fit mother. It was him they were with when one of them, the youngest, died." She wiped the back of her hand across her nose. "I never saw the other. They were both gone." She looked suddenly at Mary. "What are you crying for?"

Mary realized her cheeks were wet. "I'm sorry," she said again.

"For what?"

"For you." As soon as the words were out of her mouth, she regretted them.

"It's easy to be sorry for the lower orders." Rebecca — how quickly she could turn — picked up her pot and drank it to the last drop. She slammed it down. "Your turn. What makes a lady consort with the likes of me?"

Mary swallowed. "You know."

"I know what you were after. The black drops. Those you got. But what I want to know is why."

What could Mary say? That she was lonely? That her life was empty? That she had come to Rebecca for friendship? How, in the face of Rebecca's tale, could she give voice to any of these thoughts?

"Come on, Miss High and Mighty." Rebecca took hold of Mary's head and wrenched it towards her. "Let's have your story." Her strong fingers prodded deep in Mary's jaw.

"I don't have a story," Mary said. "You're hurting me."

Rebecca let go, her fierce interest draining away. "You make me laugh." She wasn't even smiling. "I need another drink." She picked up her pot.

If only she would go and get herself one, Mary would be free.

284

"Money." Rebecca stretched out an open hand. "You owe me."

Mary undid the strings of her pouch.

"Hurry."

Hurry was what she should do: pay Rebecca and run.

An image of those rotten-toothed, open mouths and the jeering "Run, run, run!" returned, the crowd chasing away the thing that had moved them. And she among them. How could she have sunk so low?

"Hurry, I said."

She lifted her hand from the bag. Then she stopped. With the laudanum working inside her, she looked Rebecca in the eye.

For the third time that night the order to stand down was passed along and for the third time the crouching men laid their weapons and their weary bodies on the ground, and settled back to sleep. John knew he should join them, but his nervous energy from the last abrupt awakening — a result, it turned out, of someone yelling in a nightmare — was still coursing through him. He pulled tighter the greatcoat Tom had magicked from nowhere, and turned on to one side. Sharp stones dug into him. He turned back to get away from them. The coat parted, letting in the wind. He tugged at it, trying to free it. "For pity's sake," someone hissed, "settle yourself."

He forced himself into an artificial stillness. If he concentrated on keeping his breath soft and regular, he thought, and on being very quiet, the other men would fall back to sleep, after which he might find a more comfortable position. He lay on his back, trying to keep still. But the muscles in both legs seemed to have developed a life of their own. As soon as he had relaxed sufficiently to close his eyes, a pulse would jump and strain until it was all he could do to stop himself kicking out.

It was no good. He'd not be able to sleep unless he could stretch his legs. Up he clambered. When the man closest to him muttered, "Keep low, you bastard, or they'll use you as a target and end up hitting me," he lowered himself back down.

He crawled through the lines of sleeping men — what a relief simply to be on the move — and then, in a half-crouch, headed for the boundary of the zariba where he could see the line of sentries, as motionless as dark clay. As he approached, one swung a lamp, shaded from sight of those beyond the zariba by a piece of material, towards him. The sentry's face was ghostly in the faint yellow light. Having inspected John, he lowered the lamp. Without a word, he shifted to one side.

By the zariba wall, John could hear the soft breathing of the line of sentries. He stayed crouching as he stared out at the beyond. Although there was no moon, not all the hills were dark: on the crest of one, fires were blazing around which, and in accompaniment to the drums, the blackened shadows of a group of Dervishes could be seen moving to and fro.

"Poor devils," someone muttered.

"They've no idea how hard we're going to hit them," another responded.

A murmured agreement fed John's growing admiration. Not only were the men apparently immune to fear, they also seemed to share an almost universal pity for the men they were about to kill. "There's no pride in annihilating an enemy with the odds so stacked against them," was how Tom had voiced it. How wonderful to be included in their number, John thought. All he had to do now was learn to put aside his own fear.

A rippling movement along the line: the new guard coming to relieve the old. John watched the careful synchronicity of one shadow slipping into the night as another took his place without the need to exchange a word. In that moment he understood how a man like Tom could have chosen the army over his son: here, among the rules and regulations, pettiness and courage, a man's better self could flourish.

"You, too, sir," a departing sentry said. "You should also rest."

John thought that now he had stretched the agitation out of his legs he might be able to.

Mary slipped quietly into the house, lit a candle and placed it on the shelf by the mirror. She took off her hat and coat, then gazed at herself in the flickering light.

Not many hours had passed since last she had stood there. Now everything was different.

She had done things she had not thought herself capable of doing. She had braved an unfamiliar and dangerous part of the city, negotiated the purchase of a considerable amount of laudanum and then, on the spur of the moment, she had made a proposal that Rebecca had quickly accepted.

Now all she need do was find a place of refuge and some Salvationists to help. No wonder she was smiling. She was imagining a future that, until recently, had seemed impossible. She saw a coach pull up outside the gate. She saw the door open. She saw a man — her husband, John — stepping down. And she saw herself running down the path, passing through the gate and throwing herself into John's arms. She saw his strong hands stroking her dark hair. She saw him breathing in the scent of her. And she saw that what had happened in his absence would never need to be talked about or even known. For what she saw was that everything was going to be all right.

She smiled again. She curtsied and her mirror self curtsied back. "Good," she said, and saw herself say it. She lifted the candle and went to bed.

There's a breathless hush in the Close to-night
Ten to make and the match to win
A bumping pitch and a blinding light,
An hour to play, and the last man in.

And it's not for the sake of a ribboned coat,
Or the selfish hope of a season's fame,
But his captain's hand on his shoulder smote,
"Play up! Play up! And play the game!"

Henry Newbolt: "Vitai Lampada"

CHAPTER
TWENTY-SEVEN

The sand of the desert is sodden red . . .

The sun, as it rose, was a great ball of fire that reddened the desert. By then the men had been lying in formation for hours and the blush that polished their pale skins seemed like an augury. Not that they were looking at each other. Their gazes were fixed on the hills beyond, where the faces that looked back were too dark to be affected by the sun. Bullets, like a plague of mosquitoes, rained down on the men who, crouching lower, pulled in their heads.

Time passed slowly. One hour moved on to the next. The sun yellowed and brightened and, by 9 a.m., was burning white. Still the men waited, and would have waited on and on, a shared litany passing through their minds: *If it is going to be, then so be it,* with its partner, *If it is going to happen, let it happen now.*

At last, orders were passed quietly from man to man. Blue Jackets who had, from their high vantage point, been cranking the handle of the Gardner for hours were brought down, and flanking parties called in. Bugles sounded, and the square was formed. The Mounted Infantry, Foot Guards and Royal Marine Light Infantry, with the guns between them, were to lead, while the Heavies and the Sussex, the navy's Gardner between them, occupied the rear, with two contingents of the 19th Hussars to left and right. Since the enemy would not come to the army, the army would go to the enemy.

Here was a moment so oft imagined that John could almost believe he had already inhabited it. How different in reality. What he could never have predicted was the intensity of the silence and this despite a hail of bullets that fizzed and ftted through the ranks, dropping men and especially the central core of officers, with the red flag that marked them out for the enemy. The men neither flinched nor drew back. It was almost, he thought, as if they were straining forward, waiting for the moment when their commanders would unleash them.

Everything was so clear — not what would come to pass, not that at all, but what had gone. As he waited for the moment of his testing, John thought about Mary. Not as he habitually thought of her — discontented and demanding — but as that other, spirited Mary, the wild country girl he had first encountered, whose life force he had taken to himself. Now, at this moment of truth, his anger over her weakness seemed unimportant, as did the fact that he had not acknowledged what she had written to him. For here, among men about to march into the blare of day with murderous intent, Mary seemed well matched with the man he had discovered he could become.

A bugle call. The men got up. Another call, and the square began slowly to move off. John was at its centre, with the clump of camels, camel drovers, orderlies and other doctors, all protected by the square. He had thought he would be scared. He wasn't. He felt icy calm.

Was this just a different degree of fear, he wondered, one so fierce it threw up different symptoms? He lifted his hands and, holding them up in front of him, he saw that they were as steady as the faces of the men surrounding him. Granite to match the ring of hills from which the enemy kept pouring down fire.

As the square inched forward gunfire rained down and men dropped. Over rocks and rutted sand went the square, its progress impeded by the need to pick up casualties and close the rear. Still the men looked forward, and in their expressions John could see only eagerness and serious intent. Camels groaned, bugles blew, orders were yelled, as lines of Arabs raced across the yellow hills, their bullets flying so that no sooner was one casualty conveyed than the bearers must race across the square to catch the next while his comrades closed the gaps created by each loss. On and on, a vast, clumsy conglomeration of man and beast, an age, a lifetime passing, as they set their lure to tempt the enemy into charging. And when this happened, as inevitably it would, the square would halt, its front ranks stretching out, rifles at the ready, while to their back two other lines, one kneeling, the second standing, and all of them unmoving and unfiring (that was the key, Tom had told John, not to shoot too soon) until the enemy was close enough for both lines to deliver their first, and most deadly, barrage.

292

This had been practised, refined and played out in countless other countries and countless other wars. The Dervishes might draw their swords and flash their spears but they would be no match for the deadly blazing of the Gardner and the discipline of the English square, which soon would decimate the enemy's front line, the better to create a barrier of dead and dying to those who dared to follow. "Poor buggers." The same refrain passed through the square as white-clad figures swarmed over nearby hills, tracking and firing on them.

John swallowed. He was suddenly very thirsty. He chewed the inside of his cheek as if there might be moisture there. He was not alone in this. Men's jaws moved silently as they marched on through a landscape that seemed to twist and to curl in the shimmering heat. And, as they marched, the hills seethed with running men, who, despite the skill of the skirmishers at front and flank, continued to pour down fire.

Tending the wounded as fast as he could, John saw the colonel working even more furiously, his bloodied hand occasionally straying to his short sword as if ready at any moment to wield it.

"Over there." When an injured man, whose position on a camel gave a better view, pointed to the left flank, heads turned to see what he was gesturing at. There, above the spikes of dry grass that had managed somehow to hold on in this waterless desolation, a series of coloured flags had been planted on poles. "Just another burial ground," an officer called, for they had passed many on their march, and everyone knew the enemy was on the right.

On they went, and as they did, something about those flags kept drawing John's eye. What was it? They seemed innocent enough, waving gently in the wind . . . It dawned on him then what was wrong: there was no wind. The sudden upthrust of a forest of similar flags confirmed it. This was no burial ground: it was the massing station for the enemy.

At that moment, everything changed.

The very earth seemed to rupture to unleash a horde of enemy cavalry from the ravine. Phalanxes of them and, at the head of each, banners flying. No sooner sighted than these horsemen were bearing down on the square. As buglers and officers rallied their men, skirmishers who'd been out of the square, doing reconnaissance, sprinted for it, tripping and being pulled up by their comrades, the wounded half carried, half dragged in, while the enemy continued to race towards them, light raging against the blades of swords sharp enough to cut the air into a vast reflective prism, so brilliant it could blind, the urgent rallying call of the British troops drowned by the swordsmen's cries as their dark knotted hair flew up behind them.

"Stand fast," the bugles called and, their guns at the ready, the front row of men dropped while the others took aim above their heads. Still the enemy came on, swords lifted to strike down a running skirmisher, who, blood pouring from his middle, continued running until he crumpled, soon to be lost from sight by the stirring up of dust, the buglers' "stand fast" competing with the thunder of hoofs, as John stood mesmerized by the wild men behind their green flags and their black

294

flags, and by the lines of soldiers calmly waiting for them to come into range. "They're rabble. They're going to be cut down," Tom bellowed.

A frieze: it might have been a painting rather than the moment before a slaughter. Officers, swords in the air, poised to drop them as the signal to open fire. Men narrowed their eyes, their pity mixed now with contempt for the savages who were riding so furiously to their death. Their concentration was almost palpable. John could feel it surging through him, along with something he had not expected. He was about to be in battle, and he wasn't scared. He was excited. His blood pumped, but his breath was calm and his hands steady. His heart was racing and his vision clear in that moment of suspension. Soon, he thought, soon.

And then the unthinkable occurred. The riders wheeled to the left. No rabble this: lines in perfect formation turned and vanished into a gully that no one in the square had spotted.

The world quiet, the men of the square still expecting the sudden disappearance to be just as suddenly undone. Seconds ticking by. Each man checked his neighbour: was it possible that they had collectively hallucinated a murderously moving mirage? But, no, at that moment the riders reappeared. They wheeled into ordered lines and charged — how could this have happened? — at the left rear of the square. The shout went up, "They know what they're doing," as battle was joined, officers' swords striking down along with the bugled order to fire unleashing a barrage of bullets, so many that they seemed to solidify the air.

Martinis crackled, the Gardner thundered, and the field guns flashed shells into the fast-sweeping forest of shining spear blades. Still the enemy cries of *"Allah Akbar"* competed with the sound of officers roaring, "Aim lower, men. Aim lower," as horses juddered, reared and tumbled, their riders flying over their heads and landing, one against another. Still the square kept firing, men cursing and throwing down weapons that jammed, orderlies racing to the centre for more guns and ammunition, and still the riders came on, and behind them a dense mass of spearmen, running faster surely than any man could run, scrambling over the growing heaps of their fallen comrades, and they, in turn, falling and, in turn, replaced by others until the first survivors had reached the wall of bayonets when swords and spears began to clash, and still more of them were coming. "How many of the bastards are there?" someone shouted as, in one corner of the square, an officer, his snow-white shirt sleeves elegantly tucked over his elbow, walked forward calmly.

John could not tear his eyes off the man who was firing a double-barrelled shotgun at the onrush, dropping men as if they were big game, and at the same time moving on until he had walked through and out of the square. A voice sounded over the din: "Where the devil does he think he's going?" as the officer turned, gestured languidly to his men and, when they didn't respond, gestured again. He must have been shouting at them as well, something that only they could hear, but they obeyed, trundling out their Gardner as "They're breaking the square," the cry coming too late.

Already enemy lines were pouring through the space created, the 4th and 5th Dragoons wheeling left-face to cover the men outside the square as they dashed back in. By now the desert was already sodden red.

Red with the wreck of a square that broke . . .

The officer speared and his gun stopped working.

The Gatling's jammed and the colonel dead,
And the regiment blind with dust and smoke . . .

No time for the men to mourn their brave and foolish colonel for, out of the fury of dust and smoke, came more riders to breach the square, so many of them caving in its corners. John found himself half lifted off his feet in the crush and pushed back against the camels. All around him, men fought, slicing, stabbing and thrusting to repel the fury that was bringing with it so much death. And still more kept rushing in.

Time slowed. A new rider was making straight for John. Fast and furiously he rode. Out of the corner of his eye, John saw his colonel plunge his short sword into a man's chest and twist it. He saw Tom firing, point-blank, at another. He saw swords clash and men fall. He heard the roar of musketry. And all he could think to do was to stand and receive his fate, his death, which, without knowing it, he had always expected.

He watched the rider almost with dispassion. He registered him holding a black banner and steering his horse with his other hand, his feet spurring on his mount, black robes streaming behind. The man was almost upon him. How easy this had turned out to be.

A shot, one among the blast of gunfire, yet John heard this separate, crucial shot. The horse reared. Its hoofs came within inches of John's face, blood spurting from its neck as it tried to slam on through the air. It skidded past John. He turned to watch it slither to a halt. He was in time to see its rider leap off and plant his banner before, sword in hand, he began to whirl. Round and round he went, faster and faster, cutting down first the man who ran at him, and then the man who came after, before slicing through the leather strap of a cacolet, which fell, bringing with it its injured occupant. The sword upheld, he was going to kill the casualty, the horror of this realization accompanied by a shout — "Get down" — an order John had no time to obey for his feet were knocked from under him. He fell, sprawling, as a fusillade of bullets passed over his head. So loud was the volley it deafened him. In merciful silence he watched the body spin and judder under the hail of bullets from the line of soldiers who had turned, as one, to fire at him. And then it was over. And John lying there.

A hand thrust down. He took it. Tom hauled him to his feet. All around swords flashed, guns fired, men's mouths contorted to issue orders above a din that John could no longer hear. Tom gesticulated towards the knot of camels and, of course, Tom was right: John must get to work. He walked as if in a dream, men falling, which, in his soundless world, John found normal, natural and not to be remarked on. He bent down, calmly, to apply his skills to the fallen, walking about the square and, with a casual flick, indicating to the bearers those who had a chance of survival and should therefore be carried to the medical station, and a thumbs-down to those who were already too far gone, the division into the living and dying easily accomplished. His hearing came back, first in short bursts, and then prolonged, although the noise had muted now: not his ears, but a slowdown in the action for the enemy was defeated, those who could were riding away as, in the ragged square, hands and voices were raised to cheer the victory that had cost both sides so dear.

The river of death has brimmed his banks,
And England's far, and Honour a name,
But the voice of a schoolboy rallies the ranks:
"Play up! play up! and play the game!"

Henry Newbolt: "Vitai Lampada"

From our correspondent

The battle of Abu Klea is won. Britain's honour has been preserved. The main bulk of the Camel Corps has moved on to Metemma where it will join with General Gordon's steamers in the relief of Khartoum. A small force has been left behind to bury the dead, tend the wounded and de-commission the enemy arms that litter the battlefield.

Our troops fought as only Englishmen can. By the time the battle was over nine valiant officers and 86 men lay dead beside the stiffening carcasses of their camels. Yet this loss was as nothing compared to the enemy's.

Thousands fell. So intense had been the barrage of our rifles that several heaps of bodies were still smouldering some hours after the square had moved on.

Our men did what England demanded. They held the line even after their square had been breached. The whole country will be grateful for their endeavour and their sacrifice. Yet this correspondent cannot but also pay tribute to the enemy. Never has the British army faced an opponent so determined or so brave. On they kept coming against deadly salvoes, without a thought for themselves. As we mourn our dead, we think also of their families, and their loved ones, who must only now be receiving news of the deadly consequence of their engagement with the British square.

The Times, 21 Feb., 1885

CHAPTER
TWENTY-EIGHT

A sound unlike any Will had ever heard rose up. It was unbearable. Will cut it from his ears.

"What is that dreadful racket?"

Seated on the floor in the general's room, Will threw a ball for Frankie.

"Go and find out what's going on."

Will watched as Frankie, so much stronger now, ran to retrieve the ball and then, ball in mouth, came back to stand expectantly.

"Hurry," the general said.

Will wrestled the soggy ball from his dog.

"Go and see." The general's tone was menacing. "Now."

Wearily, Will got up. "Come on, Frankie." He clicked his fingers.

The door to the general's suite burst open to admit one of the palace guards.

"Knock," the general shouted.

"Come." The guard beckoned to the general. "Come."

"That's it." The general threw up his arms. "I give up."

"Come."

"Knock." The general rapped his knuckles on the table. "Like this." He rapped again. "Knock."

The guard made a fist with his hand and then, in imitation of the general, he rapped on the open door.

The general sighed. "Yes. What is it?"

"Come."

Outside a crowd of soldiers and palace guards, servants and ordinary inhabitants were talking furiously to each other above the drumming of tom-toms which, Will realized, were much louder than usual. "Stay." He held tight to Frankie.

The general stared down at the crowd. "What is it?" Getting no response, he strode down the steps. "What is it?" When everyone just carried on jabbering and gesticulating, he removed his gun from holster and fired it in the air.

The crowd turned as one to look.

"*What* is going on?"

There was a muttering before a man crept reluctantly from the midst of the crowd to stand before the general.

"Who is this?"

A soldier stepped up beside the man. "He is a man. He is gone out the gate."

"If I've told you people once," the general said, "I've told you a hundred times. If you leave, you cannot come back."

The man looked at the general.

"Tell him so," the general ordered the soldier.

The soldier turned and said something to the man, who shrugged and made as if to turn away.

"Wait," the general said.

The soldier put a hand on the man's shoulder.

"He might as well share with us what he has to say."

The soldier transmitted his words to the man, who nodded and spoke at length, with many gesticulations in the direction of the Mahdi's camp. As he spoke, the soldier's expression grew increasingly grave while the crowd once more began to mutter.

"Silence." The general stamped his foot. "What has he to say?"

"This man he say that the Mahdi he has won a great victory. The drums, they speak of it. He say your Wolseley, he is dead."

Will reached down to pick up Frankie. "Nonsense," he heard the general say. "If it's true that Wolseley is dead, this cannot be the Mahdi's doing. Wolseley is far away, in Korti."

The soldier said something to the man, who replied. "He say it is the men of Wolseley," the soldier said. "They is the one who dead."

"Are," the general said. "They *are* the ones who *are* dead. But I don't believe it. Listen . . ."

Nobody in the crowd was listening to the general. They had turned to each other and, against the rising sound of the tom-tom and of gunfire from across the river, had begun to argue among themselves.

"Can't you hear?" the general tried to out-shout them. "Can't you hear the sound that runs below the tom-tom and the gun?" No effect. He raised his gun and fired another shot. When this had no effect on the crowd, he widened his stance. He lowered the gun to aim it directly at the crowd. His skin was sallow, the area below his eyes dark and lined, and his hair had gone completely grey. Only his voice was as strong as it had ever been and he used it to bellow, "Stand fast and listen."

For a moment the crowd did stand fast and they did listen, and they must have been able to hear, as Will could, the sound that the general's sharp ears had picked up. At first it sounded like a wind playing under the celebration, but the more they concentrated, the more they came to realize that this was no wind. It was voices. Women's voices. And they were keening.

"Listen to that. The Mahdi has forbidden mourning in his encampment and yet they are crying out in grief. For those downtrodden women to disobey the Mahdi, some terrible fate must have befallen their men."

"Has fallen you," the soldier said. "The English square, this man he say it is broken."

The general blanched.

"The English square, you say to us, cannot defeated be. But it broken."

"While it may be true that Wolseley has taken casualties," the general drew himself up, "listen to those cries. The Mahdi's losses must have been much worse than ours." He looked to the soldier. "Tell them."

The soldier shook his head. "It over."

"I said, tell them." The general aimed his gun directly at the soldier's head. "That is an order. Do it, or take the consequences."

For a moment, the soldier just looked at him, as if he were going to disobey. The general cocked his gun. The soldier turned away and spoke to the crowd for a long time. For a long time they listened. When finally he stopped speaking, the crowd turned in on itself. Many voices were raised in argument, on and on, as the general waited. At last an old man, who, by the manner in which the crowd respectfully let him through, must have been be a senior member of the *ulama*, stepped up. He turned to the now silent crowd and he, in turn, spoke at such length that the general lost patience. "What is he saying?"

The soldier ignored the general.

"I asked you a question, soldier."

The old man nodded at the soldier.

"He say," the soldier said, "we is . . . we *are* disbelieving of what you say. He say we go."

"The civilians, yes. I have permitted that."

"He say we soldiers, we also must go."

"If you do, you will be killed. Or, worse, enslaved."

"He say as true believers we are protected."

"He must be a Mahdist spy. Have you not heard how the enemy speak of you? They call you Turks, dogs and infidels. They say you have driven Islam into disrepute. Do you not know that the Mahdi urges his followers to rid their land of your scourge? Translate that."

The soldier shook his head. "We stay, they kills us."

"If you stay, you have a chance. Wolseley's troops are on the way."

"The river falls."

"Our defences are strong."

The soldier shrugged in such hopeless disbelief that a titter ran through the crowd.

The general narrowed his blue eyes. "By fiat of the English government and the Khedive Tewfiq, I am your commander. I command you to stay."

The soldier shook his head. "Your English time it gone, old man."

"Tell them," Gordon pointed at the line of other soldiers, "that this is my order and that I will not be disobeyed."

The soldier shrugged.

"Tell them."

"They know what you say." The soldier had already half turned away. "We go."

"Stop."

The line of soldiers, including their spokesman, began to move off — "Stop! I order you!" — the crowd preparing to follow them. "Or I will shoot."

Was Will the only one to hear these words? Or was he the only one to take them seriously? Still clutching his dog, he started forward.

The general had already raised his gun. Now he aimed it at the soldier. As Will yelled, "No!" the general shot the soldier in the head. The man fell. The crowd screamed and scattered.

Calmly the general took aim at another of his troops. "Will you be next? Will you?"

Through the darkened palace the general roamed. Each door he passed he opened to poke in his head: "Will?" The general had not seen hide nor hair of the dratted boy since he'd vanished during that unfortunate incident with the soldier.

It was over. Peace had been restored. Will could come out.

"Will?"

Where could he have got to?

The general opened the next door in the sequence. "Will?" When he met once more with silence, he closed it. But just as he was about to resume his search, he heard something. He stopped and waited. It came again: the sound of scuffling and someone — it could only be Will — whispering.

Whose room had this once been? the general wondered. And then he remembered. Stewart had lodged here on their arrival. Poor Stewart. He'd been a good officer, the best, and yet they had killed him like a dog.

Strange that Will had chosen to hide in Stewart's room. He had hitherto displayed a tendency to avoid it. Perhaps it wasn't Will. Carefully the general turned the knob and pushed the door again. A movement. He was right, somebody there. He could smell that noxious dog.

"Will?" The general stepped into the darkened room. "I can hear you breathing." He took another pace forward. The breathing was coming from below the desk. "Will?"

"Go away." Will's voice was thick with tears.

"I'm a general," the general said. "I cannot have a mutiny."

"Go away."

"You have no right to evict me. I am the governor general of Sudan. This is my palace. This is my room."

"It's Stewart's."

"It was. But they killed Stewart. They would have killed those soldiers as soon as they stepped out of my protection."

"You don't know that."

"Yes, I do." The general took another step.

"Come any closer and I — I'll — I'll set Frankie on you."

The general stopped. "We have to stand fast and await Wolseley's army."

"You should have let them take their chances."

"How could I stand aside as they abandoned their posts?" the general said. "If I had let them go . . ." Why was he justifying himself to this callow boy? "If I had let them go it would mean that my every decision — in coming here with Stewart, in fighting for the preservation of everything I believe — it would mean that all of this was wasted. I couldn't allow that."

"I don't care what you say," Will said. "Only go away."

CHAPTER
TWENTY-NINE

Behind their barrier of biscuit boxes and saddles, one thought — *If only the man would stop groaning* — seized hold of the soldiers and would not let go. *If only he would stop groaning.*

He was out there in the dark, among the dead, and when he wasn't groaning, they could hear him praying to his God. If only he would stop.

If only men were like camels. Like the one beside John that had been hit by a ricochet. Blood was trickling down a neck that dropped lower with each passing moment and was crinkled. A sure sign of the animal's impending death. Yet, apart from the occasional shiver, the camel made no sound. Not like the groaning man. If only he would stop.

The sliver of the crescent moon had already risen high.

The rest of the corps must surely have reached the Nile by now, and begun to slake their desperate thirst. The men who'd stayed behind had blackened lips and their throats were sandpapered by lack of liquid. They tried not to think how glorious it would be to have water and to repress the unspoken *What if they forget us?* Nonsense. They knew they would not be forgotten, but they also knew that each stretch of this godforsaken land, however short, had to be hard fought for and hard won. Even if the main column reached the river without another fight, their relief would be ordered to wait until morning before risking a return.

In the meantime: if only the man would stop groaning.

A tin of meat passed from hand to hand. Only the one. It was too dry and they too dry to eat.

"I'd murder for a beer," someone said.

"I'll murder you if you say that word again."

Out in no man's land, the man groaned.

"Where is the bastard?"

"Cover me. I'm going to look." A soldier poked his head above the barrier that separated their group from the long stretch of dead. In the distance the blackened outline of the hills stood witness to dark heaps of Arab dead. Wraiths flitted through the darkness. "They're carrying off the bodies."

The man groaned.

"Why don't they carry him off as well?"

"They don't dare." The soldier lowered himself again. "He's too close."

They sat, lined up in silence, trying not to think of the things they had that day seen, and the things they had helped do. Images from the battle, the spewing blood and twisted guts, its sheer ferocity, kept hitting John. He pushed them away. He had patients to attend to. He must not think of it. Beside him, the camel rolled over and, still without a sound, died. Soon its body would start to cool. He edged away from it.

"By daylight," someone said, "they'll be back for us."

By daylight. Hours away. Hours of numbing cold, without water. And still the man groaned.

Inside their enclosure one of the wounded muttered something. John felt for his faint pulse. He touched a burning forehead. The man would not long be with them. "Are you in pain?" The man moved his head but whether he was saying yea or nay, or just moving in his fever, John could not tell. He was going to die. No need to be in pain. John injected him with another dose of morphine.

Out in the darkness, just beyond their barrier, a man groaned.

When the thing they'd been waiting for — first light — came, they half wished it had not. Now the fields of enemy dead, despite the number carried off in the night, stretched as far as the eye could see. Waxen corpses smeared with blood. Mouths open in the rictus grin of death. The litter of severed limbs and discarded weapons, broken banner staves, spears and hatchets, swords, knives and guns in their thousands that, when reinforcements came, the men would be ordered to destroy. In the meantime all they could do was sit, wait and try not to think of water.

The early-morning light was milky, their faces dulled and dark, while the sorry sagging skin of the dead camel had turned a dreary beige. The men were freezing. They slapped their hands and moved their ankles to get more feeling into their extremities.

Not far from them, as if responding to this sign of life, the man groaned.

"That's it." One of the soldiers reached for his gun. "I'm going to shoot the bastard."

"They'll shoot you if you try."

"There's no one out there any more."

And it was true: the land that stretched as far as the eye could see had been given over to the dead.

"You never know with them."

Heads nodded.

"They're brave," someone said. "You have to give them that."

More nodding as the soldier put down his gun. Just outside the enclosure the man groaned.

All night John had thought about this moment and all night he had resisted it. All night, he had argued with himself. Now he opened the first-aid tin. He took out a syringe. He loaded it carefully with morphine, tapping it to get rid of the air. He put it back inside the tin and levered himself up.

"You're not going." This from Tom.

"I must." He was a doctor. He had come to war to help the injured. He had done precious little during the battles they had endured, other than make himself a burden for the real fighting men. But now he knew there was something he could do. That he should do.

"He is a man like us."

"I never said he wasn't," was Tom's reply. "But he's not one of ours."

"He is still a man."

"Not our responsibility."

"I have made him mine." His voice was firm and clear, he noted, and he liked it in himself. Ministering to the injured was his terrain, not Tom's. He was a doctor who had taken a doctor's oath. If he turned his back on a patient he might be able to save, even if that patient was an enemy soldier, he would not be able to live with himself.

"I know what I'm doing," he said.

"You do, do you?" He saw Tom's brown eyes, calm, and Tom's pockmarked face, and he saw Tom frown.

"You can't stop me."

"I can see that." Tom sighed and levered himself up reluctantly. "Come on, then."

"You need not come with me."

Another sigh. "If you must, then so must I. It's what they pay me to do." Tom bent down to pick up his gun.

The men who had sat silently through this encounter began to move, going to the edges of their makeshift barrier, and propping themselves beside it, guns at the ready.

"Where do you think?" Tom asked of the soldier who had previously located the injured man.

"There. East-north-east."

Tom nodded.

"Looks clear."

"Let's go, then." Tom hauled himself over the barrier and waited for John to do the same. "Follow me," he said. "Try not to make too much of a target of yourself, will you?"

At a crawl, John followed Tom across the ruts that separated their temporary sanctuary from the mountain of the dead. A sweet, noxious smell filled the air. He felt strangely detached as he registered the soft scuffle of their knees sliding forward, the tin as it scraped against the grit, his breath and Tom's and, oddly, the low call of a bird he could not see and could not believe was really there. A dusty yellow sandfly jumped on to his hand. It flicked itself off, soon to be replaced by another. Looking round, he saw that the ground was teeming with its like.

"The dead call their own companions," Tom said.

On in single file they continued. Behind them, they were conscious of their comrades keeping watch. John's breath resounded, loud enough, he thought, to summon a horde of enemy, yet no enemy came. Not far, but it felt like a marathon. At last they reached the man.

He was lying by a mound of bodies over which flies were crawling. He was on his front and looked as dead as the others, except that as they approached he twitched and groaned. Tom held up a hand. John waited as Tom circled the groaning man, checking those that surrounded him, pulling out guns and swords and shuffling them out of the way. When he was finally satisfied, he nodded and they made their approach.

"We've come to help you," John told the man, who did not speak their language.

He groaned. When John touched him he went very still. A cursory inspection yielded nothing. "We'll have to turn him over."

Tom nodded. "You pull from the back, I'll roll from the front."

John took hold of the man's shoulders and, as they began gently to edge him on to his back, he could see the wound high on the man's chest from which spread a dark stain of blood. He had survived because the wound was so high.

"Watch yourself." Tom's voice was quiet.

In the life that remained to him, John would always remember the calm in Tom's voice. And he would remember a knife slashing up, and the blast of air that, later, when he reconstructed the occasion, he realized must have been Tom pushing him out of the way. Two other things he would remember: the look of surprise in Tom's expression and the sound — a gentle *oof* — he made as, clutching the knife that was now embedded in his stomach, he slowly, slowly, crumpled in on himself.

Mary's skin, the flesh of her lips, the tips of her fingers and thumbs seemed to jump and jangle while her breath banged in her throat. Not long to go. She forced herself to sit still and look at the accounts.

What she saw there strengthened her resolve. She had made an appalling mess of John's formerly meticulous columns. She had totted them up incorrectly, only later to scratch out her mistakes so that blobs of ink splattered the pages.

The fury that shot needles through her nerve ends made her want to rend the book in two. She clenched her fists. If she destroyed it, John would be bound to ask why.

She would repair the book or, if it wasn't reparable, rewrite it. Not now. On her return.

316

And if she didn't come back? Well, she told herself, the chaos of the accounts would pale into insignificance.

And if he didn't? Ditto. She slammed the book shut.

The clock ticked. Only five minutes had passed since last she had regarded it, despite its endless ticking. She got up so hurriedly that her chair fell away. When she picked it up and put it back she pressed on the frame hard enough to buckle its legs.

What did it matter? It was only a chair.

She tapped her right foot.

Tap.

The sound outraced the clock . . . tap . . . tap . . . tap . . . but couldn't make the time go faster. She forced the foot into stillness.

She should go. Now. Before she changed her mind.

But if she did, she'd be there before Rebecca.

She knew the nice ladies well enough to be certain that, in Rebecca's absence, they would focus their attention on her. If they did, even they might guess how badly things lay with her. That she couldn't bear.

What to do, though, with the time remaining?

Her case was packed — not much in the way of clothing: she could always send for more.

She had made a list for Betty and there it lay beside the accounts. She thought to check it through.

But no: that would entrap her at the desk.

She could leave the library. Yes. That was what she would do.

Out she strode and into the drawing room.

There another clock ticked. And ticked. Odd how she had not previously realized that, in every one of her rooms, the slow passing of time was such a feature. Another thing for her to change . . . if . . . when she returned.

The canary. She must say goodbye to it.

Not that the bird seemed to know who she was. Or to care.

She went to the cage.

The bird was on its perch. As she neared, it shivered. It was frightened of her. Not that she had ever done it any harm. But perhaps, she thought, birds could sense intention.

She did not put her hand inside the cage. She did not want to frighten it more.

"Sing," she told it. "Sing."

The bird sat, crestfallen, on its perch.

Perhaps it was hungry. She pulled the drawer at the cage's base, took out some seed, filled its little plate. Overfilled it. The seed scattered. She reached down to pick it up, which was when she heard the door opening.

"Yes?" She shoved the seed into her skirt pocket.

"The driver's here."

At last. She looked at the clock and saw she could go.

"If you wouldn't mind carrying my case out." She followed Betty to the hall but not outside. "I'll only be a moment."

With Betty out of the way, she went to John's dispensary. Walking in, she felt its chill. She saw the mess she had made, which Betty, on her instructions, had not cleared. Another thing for Mary to do. On her return.

She went to the drawer into which she had put her supplies. There they were.

Rebecca had been generous.

Since that night she had tried to keep away from the laudanum. But the less she took the more she wanted to take so she had mixed a small batch from which she had sipped when the urge had overpowered her. Now she placed a cloth on the counter, took out the bottles, with the spare opium, and put them on it.

So poisonous, she thought.

She pulled up the four corners of the cloth and tied them together. She picked up the makeshift package and immediately put it down.

If John had received her letter, the first thing he would do on his return was check how much opium remained. If she threw it all away, he would know how profligate she had been. And even if he hadn't had the letter, he was bound one day to require laudanum. When that day came, he would want to know what had happened to his stock.

She would not have him questioning her. For this reason, and for this reason alone, she must keep back some laudanum.

The knot was tight. As she fumbled with clumsy fingers, she heard footsteps. "I won't be long," she called. "Wait for me outside."

At last she had the knot undone. Some of the laudanum she would, on her return, transfer to John's original containers. The rest she would now throw away. But how much had there been?

She couldn't remember.

Her heart was thumping. How much to keep and how much to throw away?

To keep or throw away?

So poisonous, she thought.

She wanted to cry out. She twisted the stopper from one of the bottles. She raised the bottle to her lips.

So poisonous.

Every cell in her body, every fibre of her being, crying out for it.

So beautiful.

Every breath willing it in.

So bad.

She forced down her hand.

She was shaking but she was determined. She opened the drawer and put back a few bottles. She left some opium as well. Then, retying her bundle, she took the rest outside and threw it away.

They carried Tom in a cacolet, John riding by his side. For almost the entire duration of the journey, he did not take his eyes off Tom, but when at last the first grey streaks of river glimmered through the green that lined its banks, his attention was drawn inexorably to the water. It was the obsession that tussled with the prayers he silently issued up. *Please, God, please, God, let Tom survive*. Then the river beckoned and his every fibre was concentrated on getting there as quickly as he could.

Tom sensed his eagerness. "Go." A word mumbled through swollen lips.

The colonel was there to supervise the unloading. "Tom's right. Go and get something to drink. You'll be no good to anybody until you do."

Afterwards John had no memory of making his camel kneel, or clambering down, or leading the animal to the river. The only image he retained was the line of men waiting to refill their water containers who, at his approach, moved out of his way. Their faces reared up, huge and distorted. They know, he thought, as he stumbled forwards. They know what I have done. And still the base urge to drink drove him until he threw himself down, an animal, sprawled, his head in the river as he drank and drank and drank.

It took an age for his mouth to yield and for the swelling of his tongue to subside. Then at last he was done. He got up. And would have toppled over if not for the quick reflexes of a private who caught and held him until he had his balance back.

"Like being drunk, sir, isn't it?" The private grinned.

Where had he heard a comment like that? Oh, yes, at Jakdul, after Tom had given him water. And here he was, drinking himself to satiation, without a thought for Tom.

"Look to my camel." He staggered up the bank in search of Tom.

The medical station, canvas sheets strung up between trees, was near the river beside the red-flagged command post. As he walked along the lines of beds, John was conscious of a strange sound: it was a panted bass rumble that rose in the dryness, then oppressively hovered. It took him a moment to realize that he was hearing the collective breathing, turning and groaning of the wounded. Strange that he had not previously registered its like. He must always before have filtered out the sound, but now that he was there, among the sick, not as a doctor but as a friend, he could not.

"Can I help you, sir?" said a private he vaguely recognized.

"I'm looking for Tom Jenkins."

"Ah, Tom. The colonel sends his compliments, sir. He asks," the army expression for an order, "that you have a word with him before you look in on Sergeant Jenkins."

"Where is the colonel?"

"Over there, sir." The soldier pointed to the edge of the sprawling encampment of the wounded.

Finding the colonel, John simultaneously found Tom, for the colonel was leaning over him. The two were talking, but so quietly that although John could make out the patter of sentences, he couldn't hear what was said. Such obvious intimacy — John experienced a curious pang — before the colonel straightened up. "Ah, there you are."

John had his first view of Tom. He was lying motionless and pale, the pits in his skin making darkened craters against the wrinkled white. They had redressed his wound, but fresh blood was already beginning to ooze. His eyes were closed. He didn't seem to know that John was there.

"How is he?"

The colonel shrugged.

"You won't mind, sir, if I examine him?"

"Yes, Major, I do mind. He is my patient."

"While I was recovering from the journey, surely."

"No. He is my patient. Without reference to you. Tom is a good man. He doesn't deserve to be meddled with."

"I don't meddle."

"Really?" The colonel looked coolly at John. "Well, then, don't do so with him. He is beyond saving and has seen enough of death to know this. Leave him be. That is an order. Do you understand?"

John nodded.

When the colonel said, "It's what Tom wants," he sounded as if he was trying to be kind and, hearing that, John thought that he must already have learned how Tom had come about his injury.

He could not let the colonel believe he had wanted Tom hurt. He must defend himself. "It wasn't what you —"

The colonel used an upheld hand to stop him. "I'm a surgeon," he said, "not a priest. You may sit with my patient but, if you take my advice, you'll not be gracing him with your confession. This is his dying, not yours." With that the colonel marched away.

John sat on a shooting stick and watched the slow rise and fall of Tom's chest. The colonel was right. The wound was far too deep, the blood loss too severe. Tom was going to die. He shut his eyes, dropped his head and sat. He was filled with terrible regret. If only, he thought, if only . . .

For an age he sat unmoving and unaware. Men might have been discharged and others might have died, but he would not have noticed. He sat and sat as the light of day began to fade. Vaguely he was aware of a commotion outside, a sound that he ignored, but when at last a ragged cheer passed from bed to bed, he looked up.

"Gordon's steamers have been sighted," he heard. "As soon as they've cut enough wood and recrewed, they're off to Khartoum."

The thing they had been working for, waiting for, dying for. Even the cheers that greeted this news seemed hollow.

Tom's eyes opened. John started forward. Tom's expression contorted, and his fists clenched. John could hear his sharp intake of breath. A spasm of pain. His entrails had begun to fester. A terrible way to die, John thought. "Is there anything I can do for you?"

Tom grimaced.

"You need morphine." John began to rise.

"When I want it," Tom winced, "I'll ask for it. Sit."

John did so. For a long time Tom's eyes remained closed. By the regularity of his breathing, John thought he might have sunk into unconsciousness.

"Remember?" With a great effort, Tom unclenched his jaw. "About my son?"

"Yes, I remember."

"I told . . . I never thought of him. A lie." Tom gasped as a fresh spasm of pain rolled through him. "Not a day goes by when I don't think of him. About where he's got to . . . how I left him . . . never should have." He breathed in, and the exhalation, when eventually it came, convulsed his whole body. "Some things," he whispered, "can't undo."

"I know." John leaned forward. "Just like I —"

"Shut your trap."

So much fury in those words that it almost knocked John over.

"You know?" Tom used his elbows to push himself halfway up. His eyes, John saw, were blazing red, his fury seeming to fuel whole sentences. "Don't say you know until you really do." He collapsed. Out of his twisted mouth there issued an unearthly groan that ricocheted against the canvas and out, and John seemed to see the sound crossing the blood-soaked desert to bury itself among the thousands of the unburied that lay scattered in the sand.

"I can't," Tom said. "I can't." His face was contorted.

Suddenly it came to John what he must do. "I'll find your son," he said.

No answer.

"Did you hear me? I'll find your son."

A fresh paroxysm of pain shuddered visibly through Tom.

"Did you hear me?"

Tom lifted his head, but not to answer John. Instead he called out, "Time."

That one word, directed not at John but at the colonel, who came hurrying over. "Ready?"

"Finish it."

"Are you sure?"

Tom nodded.

The colonel turned to an orderly and, from the man's upstretched basin, took a syringe. When he tapped to clear it, John saw how much liquid it contained. "You . . ."

"For pity's sake," the colonel snapped, "learn when to keep quiet." Then, in a soft voice, to Tom: "You're a good soldier."

"And you're a bastard, sir."

The colonel smiled. "Time to go. I mean you, Major Clarke."

John felt as if the ground had melted, but when he forced himself upright his feet did not sink into it.

Nothing he could say. Nothing he could do. He was not required. He turned away.

"Oh — and, Major?"

He looked back.

"They're going to want a surgeon for the ride to Khartoum," the colonel said. "I'll put in a word for you."

PART FIVE

CHAPTER
THIRTY

The edge of the long, curved blade caught the sun. Such a brilliant blaze of light, it almost blinded him. "No," he cried loudly, but not loudly enough to stop the downward slashing of a sword that soon would hack through skin and flesh, muscle, sinew and bone. Even so: "Stop," he cried.

The swordsman turned to look at him and smiled. "Gordon."

Gordon said, "Wake up," as, once again, he hefted his sword. Its hard edge caught the sun.

"No," he said.

A gentle hand was shaking him and her voice: "Wake up, William."

William Stead opened his eyes to find his wife by his bed. She was in her dressing gown and was carrying a candle. He must have been shouting for some considerable time. "I'm sorry, my dear."

"There is no need for that."

"I had the most dreadful dream."

"Gordon again?"

He nodded. The same dream he'd had for weeks.

"I'll warm some milk for you."

He fought his way out of the tangled sheets and sat up. She was halfway to the door.

"Did I do wrong?"

"How so?"

"In persuading Gordon."

Her expression was inscrutable.

"It was my doing."

He'd been so proud of the manner in which his interview with Gordon had been taken up by all the other newspapers, pushing the government to action. Few journalists could ever boast of that.

And yet: "By sending him to the Sudan, did I do wrong?"

"You didn't send him."

"I laid the ground ready for the nation to send him, and I did it deliberately. I thought he was the only man who stood a chance of freeing the Sudan from the Mahdi's oppression."

"And was he not?"

"But what if they are right? What if Gordon was not in a balanced state of mind? What if they were better judges of character?"

"It is not for us to judge another."

"Did I, in the name of virtue, send Gordon to his death?"

"It is for God," his wife said. "You, my dear, no matter how talented, are not God."

CHAPTER
THIRTY-ONE

He had spent the night pacing his rooms while he smoked, smoking while he paced his rooms. Suddenly something seemed to change. In that moment, the general knew that the time he had been anticipating for so long was upon him.

He went to the window. Dark. And quiet, the air so thick with silence that he could barely catch a breath.

He had heard shouting, earlier, from their encampment. He could picture that showman, the Mahdi, on his white camel as, before him, the legions of his countless faithful would have gathered. The hum of their repetition, *We swear to renounce this world and to choose the next*, rising up as their swords were also raised, *Allahu Akbar*, their battle cry, *Allahu Akbar*, crossing over the river and into Khartoum, *God is Great, God is Great*, the doom pronounced on his city and on himself.

And now, in this hour before dawn, the general stood at the window and agreed with them that God was Great. And then he thought of what would soon come sweeping through his streets to deliver him to God.

Not yet. It was still too dark. Only at first light would they cross the point on the White Nile where the

331

floodwater had retreated, leaving only earth and silt. They would creep forward on their bellies through the mud, past the sentinels on the southern fringe, whose slack fingers would long since have slipped off their Remingtons. And when there were enough of them, they would raise their bodies and their voices, and they would cry out to their God, "*Allahu Akbar, Allahu Akbar*," and the killing would commence.

"'And I looked'," he said, "'and behold a pale horse: and his name that sat on him was Death.'"

He dressed carefully, putting on one white uniform he had had cleaned and pressed for this moment. He stood in front of a tarnished glass to regard his earthly body. He parted hair that had turned almost white during the last phase of his waiting. He smoothed a moustache that, he saw, could do with a trim. He tried to smile, but his lips made an unsmiling thin pink line.

He stepped away so as to look at the whole. He saw how the reflection of his clear blue eyes, his most remarkable feature, which he had used all his life to good effect, gazed coolly back. He nodded, this grey old man on the brink of death. "And hell followed with him," he said as, having unlocked his door, he left the room.

There had been a time when he would have shouted and even fired a shot to raise the alarm. That time was gone. Let them sleep, the palace guards who no longer guarded, the slaves he had not been able to free, the soldiers who frowned when he approached, the women who dreamed uneasily of their men, the men who would be unable to protect their families, and their children slumbering on the brink of their disaster. Let them — save the spies and traitors who would even now be creeping through the streets to undo his last defences — let them all sleep.

Up he went to the roof. His last moment there as well. And there he stood, as he had done for many months. Not a sound to be heard. Not even drumming. Which told him what he already knew. His time had almost come.

Too dark to use the telescope, to see what had been long anticipated. Dense masses, a forest, of men, waiting for the signal to begin the crossing.

The start of the Mahdi's reign. The end of Gordon's.

Had he always known it would come to this?

He could not have known, for such knowing belonged to God. Yet he had suspected it. From his first tour of duty, in fact, when he had seen the lengths to which this country could drive a man. When he had stopped the traffic of slaves down the Nile — he was lauded for it in London — only to discover that the privation of slaves, now driven north through the desert, grew worse with each passing day. And when he had returned to witness just how thoroughly the Egyptian tax collectors and the Egyptian soldiers had plundered the country and persecuted its people, he should have known that the only possible victory was the Mahdi's.

Stewart had recognized this truth. And yet poor Stewart, a brave soldier to the last, had stood by his general, had done his best to do his bidding. And had died for it.

But Stewart had been a military man.

Not like Will. Will was an innocent.

It was his fault Will was going to die.

The general had always known the desperation of Will's predicament, and he had played on it. From the first moment when he had wrestled with the pride and vanity that had driven him to Khartoum, he had made a secret pact with himself. He had resolved that he would make the trip only if he succeeded in persuading the reluctant Will to go with him. After that, he had used every weapon to hand to coax Will into coming.

That was his greatest sin.

A sin of love, he thought.

"The wages of sin is death," he said.

It was time. He was going to have to do now what he had promised Will he would do.

"But the gift of God is eternal life through Jesus Christ our Lord."

The dog was dreaming.

Of another time.

A time before Will.

Before he had had a name.

Before his name was Frankie.

Before the hunger.

His paws twitched. He was dreaming that he was running. Not in joy — his life had never contained much joy — but running in this dream of life. Panting in the effort to get away from the thing that was pursuing him. The thing he could smell.

It smelt sweet. He slowed. Perhaps it was something to eat. He stopped and moved his snout around, sniffing out the source of the wonderful aroma. But as he drew closer to it it was no longer so sweet.

It was rotten.

He needed to get away.

Too late.

It poured its vapour into him and his dream was ended.

There. The dog disposed of. The general straightened up to look down on the sleeping Will.

In his innocence the boy looked so very young. For the last time the general took in the sight of his dear sandy, tousled hair, and his smooth, clear skin. He thought back then to his first sight of the boy. As hungry and desperate as Will had been, the general had seen something special in him. Will had not grabbed what he had been offered. He had waited to check that it was freely given. Beneath the dirt and the fear, the general had seen the blazing light of goodness shine.

He had always known that he himself did not possess such goodness. That was why he had needed to bring Will with him. That, and because he could not bear the prospect of their parting. His faith was confirmed: despite all the privations he had suffered, Will had held on to his purity.

Perhaps his love for the dog had sustained him. Just as the general's love for the boy had kept him going.

And now, he thought, the time had come. He must fulfil his promise.

"Sleep," he told the sleeping Will. "For, behold, the hour is soon at hand."

He uncorked a stopper and put it carefully on the floor. He laid a cloth over the open mouth of the bottle and upended it. He watched in the candlelight as the liquid soaked the cloth, turning it from white to dirty grey. He took the cloth away but then — better to be safe than sorry — he put it back and, once again, he soaked the cloth, all the time careful to keep his mouth closed, his breathing shallow and to hold the cloth at a safe distance from himself. Then, at last, enough. He set the bottle on the desk below which Will was sleeping. He recorked it. He took up the cloth.

His heart was heavy — that it had come to this.

"Oh, my Father," the pain welled, "if it be possible, let this cup pass away from me."

He looked up to the heavens.

No answer.

Nor had he expected one.

He knelt down.

The boy was still clutching his insensate dog. At least they will be together, he thought. And then saying, "Not as I will, but as thou wilt," he covered the boy's mouth and nose with the cloth and held it there until Will went limp.

There. He was tired. It was as he had promised. So very tired. Only one more thing to do and then he would go to bed.

CHAPTER
THIRTY-TWO

In the cell they had given her as a bedroom all Mary could think was: If only I could sleep. The thought held her in its grip. If only I could sleep.

She sat on a hard-backed chair and looked at the iron bed with its thin mattress. It will do, she told herself. Lie down. Lie down.

How could she lie down when she couldn't bear to sit?

The siren laudanum in John's dispensary was calling. Though her mind resisted it, every fibre in her body ached to respond. Not for the first time she found herself on her feet, determined to leave this awful room and go downstairs, then home.

But she could not go.

She would not go.

Over to the window. Dark. It seemed always to be dark. She turned to look at the bed. So plain. And there, above the headboard, a large wooden cross. It was meant to comfort her but when she looked at it all she felt was pain.

Jesus had been racked with pain. But she was not like Him. She was without His strength. His love. His faith.

This was the aching loss that kept rising in her. Worse than her nose and eyes, running so incessantly that they had turned her skin raw. Worse than the cramps, so painful they squeezed out her gasps of air. Worse than the thin running out of the little food she could bear to swallow. All of these bodily symptoms she could tolerate for she knew that, once the drug had left her system, they would cease. What she could not bear was the grief that welled, the crest of anger on which it rode, and the hopelessness it induced. She was possessed by feelings that she would once not have allowed in. They attacked her now with terrible ferocity. Heightened by the drug's horrifying withdrawal, she knew that they were an integral part of her, her familiars, of which she would never be rid.

A cross too far. And she knew, without doubt, that all she had to do was leave this room, this house, this area, and go home, step into John's dispensary, take one glorious sip of laudanum and the unbearable feelings would dissolve.

"No." She launched herself on to the bed. Face down, she spread her arms to grip its iron frame. "No." She forced herself to hold tight. For life itself.

"Mrs Clarke."

They were calling her.

"Mrs Clarke."

She had finally managed to sleep and they had come to wake her. Go away, she thought, keeping her eyes tight shut.

"Mrs Clarke."

338

Two of them. Tweedledum and Tweedledee.

"Mary."

Did they not know how ill she was?

"Mrs Clarke." A hand on her shoulder, shaking her.

She must not let them pull her out of sleep's dark web.

"Wake up."

Nor let them distract her.

"Please, Mrs Clarke. It is important."

John, she thought suddenly. She opened her eyes. "Has something happened to John?"

"John?"

"My husband."

"We have had no news of Dr Clarke," the fat one said, her thin companion nodding to confirm it.

She looked to the window. Still dark, she saw.

"It's Rebecca," the fat one said.

"She is asking to be let go. We need your help."

"She has been calling for you."

"We know you have been unwell. We didn't wake you lightly. But we fear for Rebecca's soul."

"It is our sad experience that one failure can be tolerated. After two such failures — and this is Rebecca's second time here — we lose these poor, suffering women for ever."

"And, besides, your colour is much improved."

It was true: she did feel better. Sleep had loosened laudanum's grip.

For the first time she could imagine that she might soon be free of the drug, and also unafraid. This she thought at the same time as she knew that, even though the thing she most feared was waiting for her downstairs, she would have to go and meet it.

CHAPTER
THIRTY-THREE

Night glimmered darkly in the sky. Soon it would be dawn. The general's last. This he had known on the previous day as he had watched the crossing of enemy boats. He had taken especial note of one. It was small, ferrying four long-robed Arabs — the Mahdi and his three *khalifas* — to bring on the attack.

Babylon had been taken from the Euphrates, and through the rising of the Tigris, Nineveh's end had come. Now the falling of the Nile would be the undoing of Khartoum. He drew himself up. He'd never been a big man but at that moment he felt himself big, his feet planted solidly, his arms still muscular, despite the loss of fat, his white hair lending him the appearance not of frailty but of steel. He buckled on his sword and slotted his revolver into its holster. He was on his way to God. Not as a lamb but as what he had always been: a soldier. For the last time, he left his room.

He glanced down as he emerged, some unthinking part of himself expecting to catch sight of the familiar crumpled figure and his mangy dog. Foolish: both were gone, and by his hand.

Out he strode and across the landing. No one in sight. Sleeping even as their final sleep was nigh.

The sound of his footsteps on stone reminded him of Will creeping along this corridor. Furiously he shook his head. Too late, he told himself, to think about the boy. The only thing that remained for him was to go out and meet his end. Alone. As he had always been. As he always should have been.

No one about as he walked through the palace grounds. He went east, making his way towards the floodplain of the White Nile over which, if he had been the Mahdi, he would have ordered the attack.

There was risk involved in such a strategy. The land was still so waterlogged that a man might sink to his neck. But if the Mahdi waited until the last drops had drained away, he faced the greater risk of an encounter with Wolseley's men.

Wolseley was close but not close enough. This knowledge brought with it a terrible sadness for this city, which the general loved and hated in almost equal measure. For its inhabitants and their frustrating combination of dependence and stubbornness. For the boy, whose trust he had betrayed, and for the impending loss, imperfect as it had been, of his life on earth.

For a moment, a hopeful thought drove away his sadness. Perhaps the floodplain was still too waterlogged. Perhaps Khartoum could still be saved. How wonderful that would be. Not for his own sake — he was ready to meet his God — but for the people of Khartoum.

342

A quick series of dull thuds, like the galloping of giant horses, drilled through his hope and stopped him in his tracks. Such a familiar sound — it was gunfire — but coming from an unfamiliar place, the southern ramparts, where he never had anticipated attack. A pulse began to tick in his neck. Doubt invading. If he had been wrong about the place of attack, was it possible that he had been wrong in everything else? He stood in expectation of the double crack of responding rifles. It did not come. The gunfire had ceased as abruptly as it had begun. He breathed easier. The spasm in his neck died away.

In the houses that surrounded him not a single light was lit. They were all so accustomed to gunfire, and the drums, that they no longer woke for them.

He pushed himself back into motion, walking forward until he was in sight of the floodplain of the White Nile. It was a thick pool of blackness in the dark, and completely still. Completely quiet. Once again hope inflated his lungs as he was simultaneously aware of the despair that filled his heart. He had been so sure that this was the moment of attack. For this he had rid himself of Will.

Now that his eyes were more accustomed to the darkness he saw a wave that seemed to pass over the floodplain. Gently it came and, oddly, there was not enough water for a wave. His eyes must have been changed by Khartoum, as his mind had been: surely he was seeing things that were not there. He stood and stared, trying to make the vision go away. It did not. Instead it was transformed. Now he seemed to be watching grains of sand flowing over silt. They came closer and grew bigger — and then he saw them for what they really were: human granules in the Mahdi's crusade.

Men had laid themselves across the mud, a long line of them stretching across. Others, dark shadows in the night, crawled across their backs. Head to toe and toe to head, in wave after successive wave they swarmed and on to solid land. In horror and awe he watched this tidal wave of wraiths that, rising up as they reached firm ground, solidified into men. A collective monster emerging not from the sky but mud-splattered from the bowels of the earth. A deadly storm come to rock the city and destroy it.

He stepped back into the lee of a house and watched as, half crouching, they fanned out, columns of them streaming through the narrow streets so quietly they might have been the wind.

They were the wind. The elements of a collective storm about to break on the unlucky city. Their dark faces full of anticipation, the whites of their eyes reddened by the rising sun. Dawn was on its way and, riding on it, death, as forward they flowed into the four corners of the city. They were sweating in anticipation, he could smell their odour. As it was. As he had always known it would be.

A single drumbeat. Just one. A mistake, he thought, but no. A thundering of drums, a chorus, signalled the breaking of the storm that shook the living from their beds.

The clap of wood as shutters opened, the people waking to their doom. Cries: men calling for arms and women wailing. The moment they had been dreading was upon them and they knew not what to do.

He drew his sword. He would take as many with him as he could. A roaring of intent seemed to fill his ears.

They were shouting now. He could see that they were. Their mouths were open. He could see the deadened stumps of teeth and hard motion of the sinews in their necks. But the sound that dominated his ears was not their shouting but the raging of his inner storm as he thrust himself forward into the centre of the mêlée.

He had become the storm, a white whirling Dervish that, as it moved, plunged in its sword and pulled it out, cutting and carving through human flesh. Blood stained his white suit, hard metal slicing at tissue so soft it had the power to suck in his blade so that he must pull and pull to bring it out, expecting at any moment to be struck. Still they continued to fall and still he remained untouched, until at last he stopped, a man standing among a pile of bodies and no one left to fight, for the rest of that group had moved on, wild men, hair flying. Now his ears were filled with the victorious cries of those who had endured *haboobs* and fevers and famine, and who had reached the moment they had been hoping for, praying for, waiting for and, with all the accumulated ferocity of their privation, were going wrathfully to inhabit it.

He glanced up at the harsh sky. His blue eyes tried to pierce the heavens, to catch a glimpse of Christ surrounded by His flaming myriads as hosannas resounded. The sky gave back its deadly glare, blinding him. He dropped his gaze to the earth.

All he could see now were black outlines against the bleeding tinge of red. No hosannas here. Only the cries of the invaders as they put Khartoum to the sword. In front of him a man staked before the scream-distorted face of his wife who ran, one child in her arms and another on his feet at her side, from their pursuer. The general ran, too, plunging his sword into the pursuer's back so hard that he could not pull it out. In the time it took him to twist and push away the body, he was forced to watch the woman trip on the mud, among the gore and corpses of her neighbours, her youngest flung out to be run through by an invader's casual sword and held up, a baby skewered to the sky, her other child kicked aside while she was dragged away by other men.

So much death, and still there would be more.

In the months of his long incarceration, he had often heard them praising their Mahdi. "All merciful," they had called, "show us the way." He saw a sword twisted in a stomach. He saw innards tumble. He saw trunks spilled of their belongings, hidden wheat made glutinous by blood, hair torn from babies used to batter doors that would not yield. The Mahdi had shown them the way, and the gate of mercy was shut and locked, and the key was lost. And those who were not killed would be enslaved, chained in misery, until the end of time.

So many . . . Which among them could he save?

This way and that he turned.

Now the enemy no longer seemed to notice him. Like phantoms they rushed on past. They streamed out of houses, stolen gold chains hanging heavy round their blood-streaked chests, fine raiment, hastily donned, trailing through the bloodied mud, and what they left behind was fire and smoke. A city ablaze with cries that choked and, even choking, grew still louder.

Out he thrust his sword and still they fell before him. He was the wraith. The phantom. Haunting his own death, which God had long ordained. "Oh, my God," he called, "take me to Thy place."

How many had he killed? Too many to count and still he bore no scratch. His sword and the hand he had used to pull it out were red with the blood of men as they had been many times before. The blood was coursing through him as well, from them to him and back again. "God is Great," they called and he replied, "God is Great," but hearing his voice calling their words, he stopped.

He was sickened. The dead, his dead, mixing with theirs. He had no stomach for it. Not any more. The battle was lost. All he had to do was die.

It was coming, this he knew, but not here. Not in the streets where the people who had trusted him must suffer and fall. In his palace. There, alone, as he had always been, he must meet his end.

He walked among them to his last home on earth and they did not seem to see him go. He shut the gates and barred the doors — they would have to fight for every inch of him. Up the stairs he went. The ones that Will had always hated.

He stopped. Sword in hand, he turned. He waited.

Axes splintering through wood. Their cries were the onrush of impending death indistinguishable from the dying. He could hear them and he was glad. Not his fate to walk the streets, his feet sandalled, as a Dervish. He was going to meet his God.

"I will not be taken alive!" This he shouted as the first appeared and, struck by the sight of him, stopped. Then the pressure of others, flooding in behind, propelled them up the stairs.

Once, by his courage and his confidence, the general single-handedly had stayed a slaughter. Now as he stood, motionless, on the stairs that had so frightened Will, he knew he could not outshout them all. They would soon be upon him. He would die as he had lived. All that had ever mattered. First God and then his nation: he had stood by both. His sword drawn beside his bloodied self.

"Come," he shouted. "Come."

What he said, or the very fact of his calling out, stopped them in their tracks. There he was, at the summit of the gracious flight, and they not many steps away. Outside a massacre was raging. Inside a peaceful tableau. A bloodied man, and the faceless enemy who had come to kill him, and still not a muscle, not even an anticipatory swallow, stirred. His life extended, stretching far into a future he could not imagine.

Before: a shot.

348

He heard it as a distant thunderclap. He felt it as a blast of warm wind. He crumpled and, as the life ran out of him, he found to his surprise that he was thinking not of his God but of his precious boy.

CHAPTER
THIRTY-FOUR

"Let me go."

Dawn showed itself in the milky light that had begun to filter through gaps in the closed curtains.

They had been praying for many hours. Mary could feel the hard floor stabbing her knees. She tried to concentrate. "Fear thou not for I am with thee." Her voice rose in the chorus of the other women's voices, her collarbones seeming to spread and flatten and her throat to enlarge as she opened her mouth wider to let out the words: "Be not dismayed . . ." Opening herself to feeling. Giving herself to prayer. "For I am thy God; I will strengthen thee; yea, I will help thee; yea . . ." A glorious chant that warmed the air.

And still that litany, "Let me go," was breaking in. Three words, "Let me go, let me go", constantly reiterated.

All around in the circle of which Mary was but one pearl were other kneeling women. Their eyes were closed, their palms together, as their voices lifted high. And at their centre: Rebecca Jarrett. She was on her feet as she had been for hours, calling, "Let me go." Her fair hair twisted limply as, in her agitation, she turned this way and that. "Let me go."

All Rebecca need do was to step through the praying circle. None of them would have held her back. Yet she made no move to go but kept up her refrain: "Let me go. Let me go. Let me go."

Knowing she should not, Mary opened her eyes.

"Let me go." Rebecca's appeal was directed not at God or the other women but at Mary. Now her gaze gripped Mary tight. "Come on," she said. "Come on, let us go," her "us" a sibilant sigh upon the wind so that, among these women, only Mary would have heard and understood it.

"Come on." Louder now.

The praying circle took up the cry and changed it: "Come, O Lord, and show to our sister Rebecca the path of righteousness. Speak to her so that she may join us in worshipping Thee."

They had raised their voices and yet, trapped as she was by Rebecca's fierce gaze, Mary could hardly hear them.

There was only her and Rebecca.

She could not bring herself to look away. She was joined to Rebecca by the thread they had come to sever. Words threatened. She shut her mouth against them, just she tried to shut her mind against her thoughts. They came, anyway, not as sentences but as sound and vision.

First the beating of wings. The air churning dark. A shadow approaching. As it came closer Mary saw it as a huge, menacing spectre. Like a headless bird, but bigger and blacker than any bird could be. She felt its motion as the pounding of danger, and her vision was filled by the flapping span that swooped over Rebecca, casting her into darkness and simultaneously darkening her hair. The two women now twinned by their shared longings.

"Show her Thy goodness," the kneeling women prayed, as Rebecca flicked something off her cheek that Mary also seemed to feel. It was silky, and not unpleasant, fluttering against her skin. Caressing. Whispering its promises of peace. The end of doubt.

It was laudanum's familiar, and it was calling her. She ached to follow it. How easy it would be.

It would not even be her doing. It would be Rebecca's fault, for the bargain they had made, they had made together. If Rebecca stumbled, Mary, too, would fall.

All she had to do was hold her arms wide, offer herself up to it and it would pluck her from this virtuous circle and take her to her place of calm. That was all she need do. Give up. Let herself go. She and Rebecca could flee this room.

Just one nod.

The bird was part of her, beating loudly, willing her to act.

She tried to summon memories of John but, as if he had been for ever erased, only faceless images came to her. She remembered Betty, the girl's hurt at her constant changes of mood, but that thought only made her want to hurt Betty more.

She thought then of the singer outside the public house, the beauty of his voice and the serenity of his

352

expression. His shriek of panic when the rat had landed.

And then another image. She had not called this one to mind but it came anyway: a memory of the sadness and longing in Rebecca's expression as cruel laughter had possessed the crowd.

She could not let Rebecca go. Not for virtue's sake, and not for Rebecca's. For her own.

She shook her head. "No," she said softly. And again, louder: "No. I will not let you go." She spoke so loudly that she seemed to knock the air out of Rebecca.

The women became her chorus. "We will not let you go."

"I will not," Mary said.

Rebecca fell to her knees. Beseechingly, she looked at Mary.

"No." Mary shook her head.

Tears were streaming down Rebecca's face and she clasped her hands at her heart.

"Hallelujah!" the circle proclaimed. "Our sister is returned to us." Their voices lifted, "Our Father, which art in heaven," Rebecca's as well. All of the women intoned the familiar words and, in their midst, Mary — save that the sound that possessed her ears was not their prayer or hers, but her head's pounding, magnified to the thunder of a vengeful drum.

CHAPTER
THIRTY-FIVE

The sound of the beating drum seemed to fill Will's world. That, the darkness and the aching of his every bone. It was as if the drum was pounding him. With great effort he prised his eyelids apart.

Where was he? He had no idea.

"Frankie?" There was no answer, and when he tried to stretch out a hand to feel his dog, pain ripped through him so forcefully it made him retch. Vomit spewed out, filling his nostrils with its sickly, cloying sweetness, colouring the darkness. The stench fed itself and he vomited again, the little food he had consumed, lumps of bilious green. It smelt even more vile than it had before. He tried to crawl away from it but the space he was in was too confined. He used the edge of something to pull himself half up. The ceiling was very low and a tentative stooped step turned into a hard lurch that threw him against a door.

He was buffeted by motion, rocked and swayed to the sound of that drum. He could not get it out of his head.

Was it possible, he thought, that the enemy had broken into Khartoum and, having captured him, had thrown him into a moving cage?

The door against which he had propped himself must be locked. With a great effort he tried to straighten. He teetered backwards, arms flailing to stop himself falling. A pause: ten beats of the drum as he looked around the wood-lined space. No Frankie. He straightened and reached out a hand. It was flecked with green. He wiped it on his trousers and then, quickly, as if to deceive it, he pulled the knob. The door opened. Easily.

He staggered out into a space even darker than the one he had been in, and smaller. As his eyes adjusted he saw he was facing a ladder. For a moment he seemed to see the palace stairs rearing before him, and to hear a sound separate from the drum. It was a man's staggered breath and it came to him riding on the smell of sandalwood. The general's smell.

It dawned on him then that he was on the general's last steamer, the *Zebehr*. The general must have carried him there. Despite the pounding of his head, he smiled. It was just as he had thought: the cunning old man had kept the steamer for this very purpose and, despite his denials, had used it.

"General!" he shouted.

He hauled himself up the ladder. The iron door was stiff: he had to butt his shoulder against it to burst it open. And then he was outside.

He was blinded by the light. He shut his eyes and saw his inner lids stained with red. When, gingerly, he opened them he saw that the colour was not interior to him. It was the rough red glow of a sinister dawn. And something else he saw: a line of men, their backs to him, staring through holes in the boat's steel plating.

They were soldiers, most of whom he knew. He limped over to tap one on the shoulder. The man turned.

"The general?"

The soldier pointed one finger at a city that was in flames, black smoke rising to wash away the redness of the dawn.

Khartoum had been breached and lost. Will dropped his head into his hands. The general had saved Will but not himself.

Something wet against Will's calf. He looked down.

"Frankie!" He threw himself onto his dog. "You're alive." He buried himself in the dog's fur as the spiky tail buffeted his chest madly and Frankie's tongue raked Will's face, his breath so putrid that Will gasped. Clutching him, he got up.

The city, in its death agony, was smaller, the sound of the drums and the cries fainter. Soon the steamer would round the curve of the river. Then the city, and all who had stayed in her, would be gone.

When Will squeezed his eyes against the tears that were threatening to run, he seemed to see the general, not in the recent past but when they had first met. He saw the general washing the dirt and lice off him, just as he had tried to wash out Will's sin and bring him close to God. As if Will, and not the general, was the sinner. As if Will had on his hands the blood of the city, which was still being spilled.

356

The thought rode in on a red rage that possessed him, bursting out in a cry of "You bastard," which he could not stop himself repeating, even louder: "You bastard."

He was consumed by hatred for the mad old man.

For bringing him to this terrible place.

For planning Will's end without as much as a by-your-leave.

For planning his own, and not telling.

As if Will was a marionette that could be pulled this way and that and, at the last, thrown carelessly away.

As if Will was nothing.

"You bastard." It came out in a whisper as the tears he could no longer stop ran down his cheeks. "You bastard." An endearment.

The soldiers had all turned and, to a man, were looking his way.

"You cry?" one said. "For Gordon Pasha?" He gave a dismissive shrug.

And from another: "What is it you English say? Good riddance to bad rubbish."

Will was on the move. Fists punching and legs kicking, he launched himself at the soldiers, his intention to wreak maximum havoc before they felled him.

CHAPTER
THIRTY-SIX

The heavy recoil of John's rifle thumped into his already painful shoulder. No time to think of that. He ejected the cartridge and reloaded, a part of him noting that his speed was improving while another part was concentrated on taking aim and firing as, all the while, bullets banged and bounced against the protective cladding of their boat. In a line with him and also firing rapidly were kneeling soldiers, all dressed, as was John, in the red of the British Army. His uniform, borrowed from one of the Sussex, was too tight, and also, now that the sun had risen, far too hot. No time to dwell on that either: ever since they had passed the meeting of the Blue and White Niles at Halfaya the enemy fire, now coming from both banks, had intensified.

A shout above the din: "They're too well dug in."

"If we keep it up, it'll stop them taking better aim at us." This from another, coolly, as cartridges clattered on to the deck, the crack of shotguns turning to echoes that ricocheted against the bank before dying away, soon to be replaced by another jagged volley.

Something passed close to John's head. There had been enough of them so far for him to know that a shell had breasted the steamer and now, mercifully, overtook it to smash into the river, throwing up spray, which, if not for the fact that the enemy's aim seemed to be improving, would have come as a relief. Behind them, in the second steamer, the navy's long nine, operated by the native troops, blasted. Its bright, blazed discharge was followed by such a quantity of smoke that boats and occupants melded into the thick grey of a fog that only the whine of bullets and the distant thud of the nine-pounder seemed capable of penetrating. And then, as the smoke cleared, John caught a glimpse of their commander who, resplendent in his braided red, was standing on the gun turret, staring through field glasses in the direction of Khartoum.

"He's hoping Gordon will send out a steamer as a diversion." This from the soldier next to John.

"If he has any steamers left."

In the sudden silence created by the cessation of the nine-pounder, this comment carried along the line while the same thought — *If, that is, Gordon is still alive* — occurred to every man but was said aloud by none.

"There's Tuti." Someone pointed at a spit of land that lay in the river. Their skipper signalled to the steamer behind to keep going upriver, while he steered his vessel towards the island.

"Looks like a crowd," someone shouted, and John saw a knot of people at the landing-stage.

"Gordon's reinforcements?"

"What news of Gordon, fellows?" Their commander who had come down from his turret now leaned over the gunwale to shout again, "What news of Gordon?"

The answer, soon delivered, came not as words but as a barrage of bullets that sent the commander ducking for shelter. Tuti had been taken.

Their boat swerved away. Fast, but not fast enough. A loud blast. A shell thudded on to the deck.

A sudden silence.

Although it had not holed the steamer, the shell was big enough to blow them all to kingdom come. Their only escape was to jump overboard into a river so peppered by gunfire its waters whipped and rolled, waves churning and creating a whirlpool in anticipation of sucking down human flesh. In that moment, John looked at his companions. Perhaps the answer to the question would lie in their expressions. Was drowning preferable to being blown up?

He saw the other soldiers, motionless, gazing calmly enough at the shell. In their faces, and their swallowing, he read the truth: they were all going to die.

One hope: that now his time had come, he would face it like a soldier. As Tom had. His hope, it seemed, was granted. In place of panic he felt a furrowing of regret so deep it seemed to suck his entrails and his feelings into a soft dark whirlpool of their own. Regret that he had made a promise to a dying friend that, even as he had made it, he had known he could not keep; that he had responded to a sadistic colonel by volunteering for this boat; that, in doing so, he had broken an even more important promise to his wife.

He was to be given no chance to incorporate what he had learned into his life.

He breathed in, calmly enough, although the out-breath came as a jagged sob. If this is not to be my end, he silently promised a God in whom he wasn't sure he believed, I'll be a better man. Still the shell did not explode. A delayed fuse? He seemed to see, inside its hard case, the fizzing and crackling, the building of energy for an explosion that would sever limbs from trunks, and minds from bodies. His last moment on earth.

If only this moment would last for ever, he thought, and, simultaneously: If only it was over.

"It's a dud." These words, passed though the boat, were followed by a rousing cheer before the men turned away from the shell and once more began to fire, John too, although he found he was shaking so hard that in trying to insert a fresh cartridge he dropped it. He reached for another. The same thing happened. A third as well.

He felt a hand grip his. It was the soldier next to him who, taking John's gun, reloaded it without comment, handed it back, then turned his attention to his own weapon. John fired, teeth gritted to steady the arm that must now eject the cartridge and reload.

"Khartoum," the shout went up. The city hove into sight.

The air seemed to darken as, through his narrow gun sight, John saw flames licking across the top of a grand building on the waterfront. There was a landing stage in front of it, on which there were moving lines that, as they came closer, turned into men above whom floated a forest of flags. The air was now abuzz with bullets so that to raise a head above the cladding would have been to invite certain death.

In one moment they were heading for Khartoum, but not in the next. A churning of water and of steam as their boat veered round, almost colliding with the other steamer, which also began to turn. Then both were racing upriver as fast they could go.

"What's happening?"

"We're retreating."

"Gordon?"

"No flag. If Gordon was there, the flag would be flying."

"It's over."

"Poor bastard."

"Let's hope he's not been captured."

CHAPTER
THIRTY-SEVEN

The sun had long been out. Now it caught the hard edge of the long, curved blade. Such a brilliant, blinding blaze of light as the sword swung down, hacking through skin, muscle, sinew and bone until, at last, the head was severed from the neck. Down it rolled. No blood this time: General Gordon was long dead.

Three Black soldiers; one named Shatta carried in his hands a bloody cloth in which something was wrapped up, and behind him followed a crowd of people weeping. The slaves had now approached my tent and stood before me with insulting gestures: Shatta undid the cloth and showed me the head of General Gordon! The blood rushed to my head, and my heart seemed to stop beating; but with a tremendous effort of self-control I gazed silently at this ghastly spectacle. His blue eyes were half-opened: the mouth was perfectly natural: the hair of his head and his short whiskers were almost quite white. "Is not this the head of your uncle, the unbeliever?" said Shatta, holding the head up before me. "What of it?" I said quietly. "A brave soldier, who fell at his post. Happy is he to have fallen: his sufferings are over."
Rudolf Slatin: *Fire and Sword in the Sudan*

CHAPTER
THIRTY-EIGHT

The two steamers roiled through water that churned and boiled with the force of the enemy bombardment, which, it seemed, would never end — until they rounded the bend in the river and, abruptly, it did.

Heads dropped on to knees. Soldiers sat silent in contemplation of the knowledge that they had travelled all this way and arrived too late. The only sound was the chug of the engine, and the rush of water against the prow . . . until there was a rising of what John first assumed was the wind. But the air was still. He opened his eyes to look across the deck. The sound was coming from the Sudanese. They were sobbing, former members of Gordon's guard who, having escaped the siege, had volunteered for this mission so they could return to rescue their loved ones. Now they knew that their parents were dead, their wives become concubines, their children enslaved, and they left alive for ever to imagine this.

How fortunate John was.

A lookout's cry: "Boat, ahoy."

Grabbing their guns the soldiers, John among them, sprang back to their positions. Their rifles were loaded, their fingers moved to triggers when "Hold steady" came the shout. "She's flying the Egyptian standard."

The men raised themselves to look across to where a steamer was tied by a peaceful bank. The flag she flew was the one they had hoped to see in Khartoum.

Up on the gun turret, the commander called, "Which steamer is that?"

He was asking the Sudanese, none of whom moved a muscle. "Get up," he called, pointing to one.

The man did not seem to register that he had been spoken to. Or if he had, he showed no signs of obeying the order. His face was streaked with tears.

"Get up." A nod from their commander brought two of his own soldiers to their feet. A second nod took them to the side of the weeping man, then to lift him to his feet and push him up the ladder.

"Look." The commander held the glass to the man's eye. "Is that one of Gordon's?"

The man's head lolled.

"Is it?" The soldier grabbed hold of his hair and yanked back the man's head. "Is it?"

The man nodded. "The *Zebehr*," he muttered, or that was what it sounded like.

"Let him go."

When the soldiers did, the man slid down the ladder and sank to his knees. Had he fainted? John went over to feel his pulse.

The man's eyes were open but unfocused, his pulse racing and his lips moving.

"What's that?" John bent closer.

"Blood will bring forth blood." A bubble of foam slipped through his lips.

From a nearby bucket, John ladled fresh water.

The man turned away his face. When John followed with the ladle, the man began violently to shake. "Blood will bring forth blood," he cried. "Blood will bring forth blood."

There was nothing that John could do for a man so crazed by grief. He straightened.

The commander was still peering through his glass. For a long time he looked. At last he lowered it to address John: "Join me, Major."

Beside the commander, John found himself in possession of the glass.

"What do you see?"

He could see the greening of the riverbank, against which grey water lapped. He shifted the glass until he was looking at a steamer that, close up, was very much like their own. From this high vantage point he could see on to the deck where there were men in various stages of repose. Behind them, on the bank, some of their number were using axes to chop up a water wheel.

"They must need more fuel."

"Not there." The commander shoved the glass to the right. "Look to the stern."

Now John saw something else. "A body."

"Perhaps. But I thought I saw it move."

Holding the glass steady, John twisted it until the body of a boy came into clearer focus. He stared at it. "No movement that I can see."

"Looks like a white boy, doesn't it?"

John saw that the commander might be right: what he had taken for a light-skinned Arab might be a sunburned European. "It's possible. Or it could be an albino? They have them."

"They seem to know what they're about," the commander said. "A resourceful bunch, these blacks. They know the lie of the land. They'll find a way to join us if they want to. If not, there's no point in forcing them. And I'm concerned about the draught. It might be too shallow."

What had this to do with John?

"But if the boy's one of ours ... Should we go over?"

John looked again. The boy had moved, and now he moved again, raising his head and looking for something. Someone.

That was how Stewart and Power had met their end: they had been lured on to the bank. If the boy was white ... But what difference would that make? If the boy could be saved, then, no matter the colour of his skin, was it not John's duty to try to save him? But that was what had got Tom killed.

"Should we dare it?"

Lowering the glass, John took in the sight of the weary soldiers who had risked their own lives to save a man and a city they did not know. Then he looked at the Sudanese contingent, sunk in pain. He raised the glass to his eye and now he was watching the lapping of the water against the iron body of Gordon's steamer. He moved the glass to the boy who might be white and was hugging something to his breast. A mangy dog.

Beyond them was the luxuriant green of the bank that would soon fade into the dust that lay like a shroud over this awful country.

He lowered the glass. "The boy's an albino and his movements are strong. He doesn't need saving."

CHAPTER
THIRTY-NINE

Mary folded in the last of her dresses and clicked shut the case. She stood for a moment, looking around the room that had, for ten days, been hers.

She had vented so much silent passion in here that she thought she might see a sign of it. It was as neat, bare and empty of feeling as it had been when she had first arrived. And after she was gone, she thought, no sign of her would remain.

A trundle of wheels and the clap of hoofs against cobblestones. She picked up her case and made her way downstairs.

They would be in the sitting room — not all of them: this would not be a grand farewell. They did not believe in grand gestures and, besides, they thought she would be back. They hadn't asked her so she hadn't had to lie.

They were good women, she thought, and kind — much kinder than she was. They were incurious too. They hadn't even thought to enquire why she had stayed after her mission — the saving of Rebecca — had been accomplished. Perhaps they thought she was lonely without John, which had been reason enough for them to give her succour.

John was on his way back. It was an easier journey downriver, but with the news of Gordon's horrible death on their minds, theirs must be a melancholy return. Particularly, she thought, for somebody like John, who had so wanted to be on the winning team.

She opened the door to the sitting room.

"I shall leave now," she said. There were three women in a circle. When they heard her come in they looked up and smiled. No Rebecca. Which, Mary thought, was just as well. "There is no need to show me out."

Outside the driver took her case. She would have climbed, just as quickly, into his cab but for the sound of pattering against glass. This signal, she knew, was for her. Perhaps she could pretend she hadn't heard it.

It came again, and louder. She did not have the heart to pretend. She turned.

Rebecca had lifted the lace curtain, and was looking out. She was scrubbed clean, her fair hair tied back. She looked rested, Mary thought, and softened. Noting this, she felt, and not for the first time, a sense of loss.

From behind the pane, Rebecca said something that Mary did not catch. She said it again, exaggerating the movement of her lips. This time her "Thank you" was unmistakable, particularly when it came again. "Thank you."

Rebecca lifted a hand and placed it flat against the window.

Mary knew she should step up and match Rebecca's hand with her own. She did not move. She found that she could not. She just looked at that ungloved hand

and that wan face and knew she would rather keep to herself the memory of a wild, undaunted woman she had wanted to befriend. And now?

She did not know this woman and was not sure she wanted to. Better, she thought, to take away the memory of the other and the illusion of a friendship that might have been. She turned away, climbed into the cab and pulled the door to.

PART SIX

CHAPTER
FORTY

Each day, more light crept into the house and the first pale buds of spring were taking shape on the tree outside the window. The onset of spring would make life easier to bear.

She lowered her head to concentrate on her embroidery. She wove her needle to and fro, fashioning an intricate flower that didn't much please her but helped to pass the time. The silence was broken only by the steady tick of the clock and the clink of crockery from the kitchen until, at last, the sound of trundling wheels broke the monotony.

She looked out of the window. A hansom had stopped by the gate. The canary was singing: it, too, was pleased by the imminent change of season. She saw the driver turn to open the cab's door. When a man stepped out her first thought was that he was John. Can't be, she thought.

The drawing-room door burst open. "It's him." Betty's voice was shrill. "It's the master. He's back."

She let the needle drop but kept to her seat. Once more her eyes were drawn outside. She saw John take his case. He was smiling. He looked different, she thought, bigger somehow. She was on her feet.

At the front door she stopped. She watched John turn slowly to the house. His skin was tanned, but deep, dark shadows ran under his eyes. At the sight of her, his smile seemed to freeze.

There he was, the sunlight playing on hair much blonder than it had ever been. Her husband.

In that moment, her heart racing, she heard a familiar sound, a hard beating, and she seemed to see the onrush of dark wings. She closed her eyes, squeezed them tightly shut. Then she opened them up again. No bird of doom: just John.

Down the short path she ran, tearing open the gate so that she might fling herself into his now open arms.

Cruel suspense has given place to sad certainty.

The terrible formula which summed up our policy in the Soudan has been as terribly fulfilled. The garrisons have been speared, and over the whole of the Soudan the Mahdi has now passed his bloody sponge.

Khartoum has been evacuated by massacre, and with Khartoum General Gordon has perished.

But even in the midst of our grief . . . we are thrilled with a proud joy as we reflect upon the splendour of that stainless life now crowned with the aureole of martyrdom.

There is not one of his friends who for a moment regrets that General Gordon was sent to the Soudan to suffer and to die in the defence of Khartoum.

. . . even in the midst of that clay of darkness and gloom . . . a man was raised up who for twelve long months displayed in the sight of the whole world the heroic virtues which our gainsayers believed were all but extinct . . .

General Gordon has demonstrated before all men the might that lies in the arm of a single Englishman who has faith in his country and his God.

W. T. STEAD

Pall Mall Gazette, 11 Feb., 1885

CHAPTER
FORTY-ONE

The boy who came down the gangplank was, apart from a pronounced limp, unremarkable.

His clothes were tattered and his skin grimy, but that was not unusual for a cabin boy. His dog, tied to him by a piece of string, was the kind of mongrel you could find wandering free on any English city street.

A confident boy, if somewhat undernourished. Leaving the shadow of the ship that had carried him into port, he seemed to know where he was going. His dog was less sure. Every now and then it would give a plaintive yip. Then the boy would stop and crouch beside it to stroke the wiry head. Should anyone have gone close enough they would have heard the boy's gentle "It's all right, Frankie. It's all right. We're home."

No one was listening and no one followed them around the corner, or saw the boy lean heavily against a wall. He was breathing hard as if the effort of leaving the ship and arriving on land had cost him dear. His dog also seemed very tired: no sooner did they stop than he sat down. But perhaps the dog was accustomed to such frequent stops. Certainly he did not look up as the boy checked underneath his jumper for the precious scrap of paper he stored next to his skin. And, yes, he felt it there.

No need to take it out. He had read and reread it so many times that he had learned it by heart. *Cruel suspense has given place to sad certainty*, he would begin, and then he would continue to the end.

A stranger might doubt that such a tousled boy would have either the breeding or the wit to read the article, never mind to understand it. Yet the same stranger would have recognized, in the lucidity with which the boy pronounced the words, that he did understand.

Out of his pocket the boy withdrew a brown-stained handkerchief.

The brown was long-dried blood.

Although the boy's eyes had filled with tears, he was smiling.

He tugged at the string — unnecessarily for, as if he had sensed the boy's intention, the dog had already risen.

"Come on, Frankie," the boy said, although he himself did not come on.

He held up the handkerchief but did not dab his eyes with it. He looked at it, then touched it to his lips. He might even have kissed it before he put back into his pocket, his talisman of a man he had known.

A mad old man he would never see again.

ACKNOWLEDGEMENTS

In 1885, the British Army's first ever Camel Corps, sent to rescue General Charles Gordon from Khartoum, arrived too late.

That much is true, as is the part the journalist W. T. Stead played in sending Gordon to Khartoum. I have, however, run a multitude of fictions, date and event changes through this novel, reshaping and reinventing history to suit my story.

I am nevertheless grateful for the many factual accounts that helped feed my book. These include: B. M. Allen's *Gordon and the Sudan*; Michael Asher's *Khartoum*; Babikr Bedri's *Memoir*; Victoria Berridge and Griffith Edwards' *Opium and the People*; Piers Brendon's *Thomas Cook*; Gary H. Bass's *Freedom's Battle*; General Henry Brackenbury's *The River Column*; Daniel Allen Buller's *The First Jihad*; Josephine Butler's *Rebecca Jarrett*; Colonel Sir W. F. Butler's *Campaign of the Cataracts*; Count Gleischen's *With the Camel Corps*; Charles Gordon's *Khartoum Diaries* (ed. Lord Elton) and *Letters to his Sister*; William Hicks' *The Road to Shaykan* (ed. M. W. Daly); Ian Knight's *Marching to the Drums*; Alex MacDonald's

Too Late for Gordon and Khartoum; *The (Military) Surgeon's Pocket Books 1880 and 1885*; Fergus Nicoll's *The Mahdi of Sudan*; Anthony Nutting's *Gordon: Martyr and Misfit*; Frank Power's *Letters from Khartoum*; Milton Prior's *Campaigns of a War Correspondent*; Rudolf C. Slatin's *Fire and Sword in the Sudan*; Andrew Smith's *Victorian Demons*; Estelle Stead's *My Father*; W. T. Stead's articles on Gordon in the *Pall Mall Gazette*; Charles Chevenix Trench's *Charley Gordon*; Judith R. Walkowitz's *City of Dreadful Delight*; Sir Charles Wilson's *Korti to Khartoum*; Lord Wolseley's *In Relief of Gordon* (ed. Adrian Preston); and A. J. Youngson's *The Scientific Revolution in Victorian Medicine*. It goes without saying that any mistakes and deliberate adjustments are mine.

Thanks to Barbara Harlow for inspiration, to Nels Johnson and Fergus Nicoll for sharing their expertise, to Tryphon Calidakis, David Codling, Carolyn Hayman, George Pagoulatos, Tilal Salih and Faisal Sultan for their assistance in my research trip to Sudan, to Jane Shaw, for helping me sort out the meaning of Gordon's beliefs, to David Loyn for talking to me about going to war, and to Michael Crumplin, Gearóid Ó'Cuinn and Lesley Morrison for answering my medical enquiries. Thanks also to the Arts Council and Authors' Foundation for funding my trip to Sudan.

I am extremely grateful to my first outside readers, Cora Kaplan, Fergus Nicoll and Timberlake Wertenbaker, for their pithy and useful comments, and to Hazel Orme and Vivien Redman.

Clare Alexander, Lennie Goodings and Sally Riley have been generosity itself, meeting with me before the book was begun to talk with me about my characters as if they already existed, and following through until the end. Thanks to them for their support, sharp observations and their many suggestions.

And, finally, Cassie Metcalf-Slovo and Robyn Slovo were there throughout the planning and writing of this book, using their charm and brilliance to help and encourage me. Thank you.

Blow on a Dead Man's Embers

Mari Strachan

With her husband shattered by war, does one young woman have the strength to bring him back to life?

In the aftermath of the Great War, Non Davies wakes one morning to find her husband crouching under the kitchen table in a cold sweat and with fear in his eyes, shouldering an imaginary rifle. Non decides she must discover what has changed her Davey so completely. A mysterious letter addressed to Davey gives her the clue she needs and takes her to the city of London in search of an answer. When she returns home Non realises that the dark secrets of Davey's behaviour are working their way ever closer to the surface — secrets that will shatter the fragile happiness of their community if they ever become known.

ISBN 978-0-7531-8946-7 (hb)
ISBN 978-0-7531-8947-4 (pb)

Ghost Light

Joseph O'Connor

Dublin 1907. An actress still in her teens begins an affair with a damaged older man, the leading playwright at the theatre where she works. Rebellious and flirtatious, Molly Allgood dreams of stardom in America. She has dozens of admirers, but in the backstage of her life, there is a secret. Her lover, John Synge, is a troubled, reticent genius, a poet of fiery language and tempestuous passions. Yet his life is hampered by Edwardian conventions and by the austere and God-fearing mother with whom he lives.

Many years later, an old woman makes her way across London on a morning after it has been struck by a hurricane. She wanders past bombsites, wrecked terraces and wintry parks, a snowdrift of memories and lost desires seems to swirl. She has twice been married: once widowed, once divorced, and her dazzling career has faded.

ISBN 978-0-7531-8850-7 (hb)
ISBN 978-0-7531-8851-4 (pb)